The Muse

By Suzie Carr

Also by Suzie Carr:

The Fiche Room
Tangerine Twist
Two Feet off The Ground
Inner Secrets
A New Leash on Life
Staying True
Snowflakes
The Journey Somewhere
Sandcastles

Keep up on Suzie's latest news and projects:
www.curveswelcome.com

Follow Suzie on Twitter:
@girl_novelist

Cover Photography courtesy of T.A. Royce

This book is dedicated to anyone who has ever suffered at the hands of a bully.

Love and light to you,

Suzie

Taking action is more powerful than standing back and hiding.

We serve the world best when we shine our light on others.

Chapter One

I stopped within an inch of indulging in my first kiss when I was fourteen years old. Since escaping that mishap, I've been convinced of one thing – in my lifetime, I would never experience that basic coming-of-age milestone.

I would bet my life that I, Jane Knoll, was the only twenty-nine-year-old person in my office who had yet to tingle at the touch of someone's lips against her own.

According to all modern-day social norms, I was pathetic and lonely. However, I had way too much going on to be forced into believing for one second that I was lonely and pathetic. Just because I lost my BFFs back in the eighth grade when they drew their daggers against me didn't mean I would never smile or laugh again. I've managed just fine without the need of a right-handed, left-handed, and back-handed lover or friend to guide me.

Most people only dreamed of their destinies, whereas I controlled mine by taking action on it. Like just the other day, I wanted strawberry ice cream. So, I bought it. I didn't have to justify to anyone why I ventured out to the twenty-four hour convenience store five blocks away. Nope. I just climbed out of my pajama bottoms, put on a pair of jeans and a bra, and drove to meet up with my destiny for the night – spoonful after spoonful of strawberry heaven.

I've always been grateful for those wide expanses of freedom that defined my life.

I was hardly pathetic or lonely. At least I wasn't the type of girl who would be so pathetic as to neglect watering her plants on Saturdays, or especially not the type who didn't understand the principles of proper Feng Shui and alignment of good space. I made time for those things without having to regard how it would impact anyone else's time and space. When I wanted to place a giant water fountain near my front door, I did so with reckless abandon, pulling no stops on its lavish display. Surely if my mother had ever pulled such a stunt, my father would've crucified her hard work and time by forcing her to take it down, repackage it, and send it back.

I was free, and for that I was grateful.

I was also grateful for my job as a marketing headline writer and proofreader at one of the country's leading sporting goods manufacturers. I just loved my cushy cubicle with its tall beige checkered walls and view of the beautiful spider plant in my neighbor, Doreen's cubicle. She resembled my grandma with her floral dresses, wide hips, and shimmering silver hair that was most certainly set on rollers every Saturday at the corner beauty shop.

She always spoiled me. No one else got to sink her teeth into corn muffins every Wednesday and blueberry bagels with cream cheese every Friday like I did. She respected my space and only interrupted me when she dropped off those delicious treats or wanted to share big news that might shake our days. A few weeks ago, as she passed me my corn muffin, she told me that a new branch had opened up in New York City and some of the new staff members were coming to our Mid-Atlantic office for introductions.

On the last introduction day, my team leader tasked me to brew the coffee and ensure the creamer jugs were filled. She honored Doreen with the task of creating labels for each attendee. We were a couple of important people at Martin

Sporting Goods. How would the enterprise ever remain intact without us if one day we up and decided we'd rather dig holes in a garden and plant tomatoes?

I wondered that all the time when I wasn't fretting over my hair, my makeup, my clothing, or for that matter, when I wasn't worrying over how we'd manage to keep the Earth rotating in its planetary alignment or how we'd ensure that the clouds rained down enough water to keep us drought free for the remainder of the planet's lifespan.

Yup, you guessed it. I happened to be a tad bit sarcastic, and justifiably so. Years of bullying did that to a person.

Hey, at least the cynicism kept me company. If it weren't for its constant presence, I probably would've drunk poison or leaped off the side of the pretentious office building's roof by now.

I enjoyed my daily work. Cynicism didn't stand alone as my friend. Nope. Piles of excitement blanketed my daily grind. I was so thrilled that I spent thirty-thousand dollars on a master's degree in English, and that I enjoyed the full advantage of that big splurge by spending my days swimming in a sea of marketing jargon that touted the world's best-fitted golf shirts and swimming trunks. I was that lucky English major who got to spend her day in a private cubicle searching for misspelled words and parenthetical phrases placed in the wrong parts of sentences. Oh, yes, you guessed it again. I was the lucky one who lived out her dreams correcting others' mistakes. My lips are tugging upwards into a smile with that confession. I was the epitome of happiness sitting in my cubicle, snacking on corn muffins much too stale for human consumption, and drinking coffee that tasted more like dirty water than delicious java beans.

I would like to tell you truthfully what I'd really love to do one day. I'd love to stand up on my desk and tell all the glory stealers to kiss my ass.

Speaking of wanting to tell someone to kiss my ass, Katie, a graphic designer in marketing, just left my boss, Sanjeev, in his office. If anyone deserved to be stuck in a cubicle making less money in a year than what I owed back in student loans, sitting in a chair less ergonomic than a concrete slab, it would be her. Thank goodness she did.

She slapped on a sugary smile each day and fed me small helpings of her sarcasm. She hated me for things outside of my control. I couldn't help it if her husband was a dirt bag pervert, and that Sanjeev would rather suffer a fall down a flight of stairs than deal with her.

In a messed up way, I enjoyed sharing sarcastic smiles with her. We volleyed our fake niceties back and forth like a couple of well-trained experts. She played hard. I did too. My years of bully hell taught me well.

That morning, she walked right past me without regard, strutting by in her high heels and goody-two-shoes attitude.

Sanjeev walked out of his office and headed straight toward me. He straightened his blue corporate tie, smiled into a few cubicles as he passed them, and stopped right outside of mine.

The rest went down as such:

"Hey, Jane," he said with a pleasant smile. "I hope you don't mind, but could I ask for your help with proofing some pieces before our new colleagues get here? I want them perfect." He handed me a black folder with the company's gold embossed logo on it. "Katie mentioned you're in between projects."

"Oh, did she?" I pointed my eyes down at the pile of work she had placed on my desk that very morning with the big note, due by noon.

"I don't mean to bother you. Is it too much?" He always spoke with reserved respect. I adored his Indian accent. He added a 'w' into places it didn't belong.

8

That little speech oddity powered me with confidence around him and created a safe haven for those times when he stared at me a little too long.

"Of course not, Sanjeev." I smiled at him, and he flushed. "I'll take care of it for you."

He whispered a thank you, tapped the doorframe to my cubicle, and strolled away with his hands knotted at his lower back.

Doreen popped over to my cubicle a few seconds later. Her hair was cropped tighter than usual and her lips were a shade too pink for the fluorescent lights. "He's got such a crush on you. It's ridiculous."

"You're insane." I spun my chair away from her and waved her off like I did every time she said that. He only flushed around me because of the time I forgot to button my shirt completely and, to both of our horrors, I caught him staring into the deep cleavage that my ill-fitted bra created.

"He's not going to be single forever."

I swiveled back around to face her. "I've got zero interest in hooking up with Sanjeev." I said that like a pro, like a girl who hooked up all the time. I also had zero interest in men, but like everything else about me, I kept that safe.

Nostalgia danced across her face. "If only I were thirty years younger, I'd be all over that."

I'd love to step inside her worldview for a day just to experience life without the overcast shadows of doubt left behind from years of listening to mean girls tell me how much they didn't like me, and watch as they destroyed my life and the lives of those I cared for the most.

# #

A week later, the new staff from the New York City office arrived.

I dashed off to the bathroom before having to succumb to long speeches and endless applause. I was washing my hands when in walked a tall, dark haired woman wearing a smart, fitted dress and a smile. She reminded me of someone who would've grown up in middle-to-upper class America, living in a mini-mansion in a bedroom swaddled in everything pretty and pink. I imagined she was always followed by a trail of pretty girls who spent their time laughing at girls like me, girls who shied away from anyone who could've damaged their already damaged lives.

She passed by and stopped right before entering a stall.

"I feel really silly asking this," she said in a low, raspy voice, "but can you tell there's something kind of strange about my outfit?" She rested her hand on her curvy hip, posing like a runway model.

I stopped lathering soap in my hands, biting down hard on the derisive words that, had I been a braver woman, would've knocked her down a few notches from her pretty little perch. I knew her type too well – entitled to stares and dropped jaws. Rather than attempt it, I scanned her taupe dress, her bare calves, and her sandaled feet, like a fearful bird pecking crumbs in the wake of hasty tourists. I turned back to the sink and the safety of the running water and shrugged. "Looks fine," I mumbled.

"So, you didn't notice my mistake?"

I looked back up at her reflection in the mirror, skirting around her penetrating eyes, her dark, wavy hair resting at her breasts, and her exotic features. I shook my head.

In my peripheral, I saw her nod with gracious appeal. She turned and entered the stall. "Okay then. All is good."

I continued washing my hands while checking out her slender ankles and the way her sandals cradled her feet so delicately. Her crimson toenails sparkled, and the strings of her sandals flirted with her soft, smooth, creamy skin. I grazed from one pretty sandal to the other. That's when I noticed her mishap. She wore one dark blue sandal and one black one.

An imperfect beauty.

My heart twirled as I shut off the water. I tore off the paper towel and hid my giggle until I passed well out of earshot of the woman wearing two different colored shoes. The joy of such a discovery saddled me in giddiness.

Eva Handel was her name. I guessed her to be part Chinese, part white. When she entered the meeting room minutes later, my breath hitched. She moved through the air as gentle as wind swept through a field of wild flowers—delicate, yielding, and breezy.

When she took to the podium, she sprinkled us in smiles and good wishes for a successful second quarter. Her eyes sparkled under the golden overheads, and they waltzed from one person to the next, connecting us in her sweet lullaby. Her golden cheeks glistened, her dark hair cascaded like pretty ivy around her shoulders, and her inflection pitched in just the right places. Her sandals stood out to me like a well-wrapped gift, offering me a most impeccable view of a most flawless mishap.

She spoke with eloquence and grace, undeterred by her mismatched sandals and the three-hundred-plus people who sat staring at her. She joked about her bumpy motorcycle ride down the New Jersey Turnpike from the city and about how excited she was that her bike came complete with a small hatch so she could pack her running shoes and her sandals. Even from the back row of the room I caught the gleam of humor in her eye as she balanced her secret like a well-trained model balanced a book on her head. She danced around her secret, playing with it and placing it out in front for all to see. A magician with an invisible wand. A hot biker chick with a knack for humor.

Eva Handel could carry a crowd with ease. Where luck failed, she used wit to pull her through. She said how excited she was to be part of our team and eager to learn from each of us how she could take live events to a whole new level. She discussed future plans to initiate a series of public service announcements geared at piquing the interest of the youth into setting exercise into their daily habits. She opened her arms wider and talked with her hands as she climbed the rudders of joy. She loved camerawork and couldn't wait to get started on those short clips.

When she finished her speech, she sat back down on the stage next to a bald guy wearing a bright orange shirt and blue tie. She smiled and joked around with that guy who gazed into her eyes and swayed into her. The two chummed-up in private musings, leaving the rest of us to guess what playful secrets they were sharing. For the remainder of the speeches, I couldn't help but stare at her from the safety of my back row seat. I enjoyed the soft way her lips curled up into a smile whenever someone referenced her and the subtle sexiness of her ankles as she crossed them over each other time and again, a movement so unobvious to onlookers yet so intense to me. At one point, I looked up from her mismatched sandals and up to her eyes. She caught me and offered me a knowing smile. I flushed and sank lower in my seat, surprised by the flutters and my racing heart. I circled my gaze around the room with my head in a halo of joy, wondering if anyone else noticed that the most beautiful girl in the room just smiled at me.

Yes, she smiled at me.

Chapter Two

I had signed up for Twitter a year ago, after being forced into it. Sanjeev required everyone in the marketing department to take part in a free webinar, *Five Easy Steps to Building an Online Presence*, being hosted by his alma mater—College Park. I had sat through the first fifteen minutes of that webinar rolling my eyes at the information, information that I knew darn well I'd never use. Why would I want to socialize with a bunch of strangers from across the world when I could walk out my front door and be trampled on by any one of the eight-plus million people who lived in the greater DC and Baltimore region?

I was too sarcastic for my own good. I knew that.

Sarcasm comforted me, though.

So anyway, while everyone else listened in to hear all about Twitter's bells and whistles, I played Solitaire. When the tone of the instructor's voice changed to that of a person set to close up the lecture, I tuned back in to ensure I didn't miss her instructions on how to access the presentation slides. I had no doubt that Sanjeev would insist on some sort of follow-through action step. Even in his most reserved state, he was a manager who exuded passion about education. He loved learning new things, and his enthusiasm toward personal and professional development overpowered his soft tone, averted eyes, and flushed face.

Twenty minutes after that webinar ended, Sanjeev rounded us up like cattle at feeding time and requested that we each create a Twitter handle that mirrored our personalities. Then, he instructed us to follow each other and test it out. For thirty agonizing minutes, I combed through the downloaded PowerPoint slides, racked my brain for a unique Twitter name, and finally created my online persona, @jktwitter. I opted to use the generic "egghead" image Twitter provided for my profile picture. Katie, with her one-thousand and eleven followers already, had followed me first.

I didn't reciprocate the follow.

I followed Doreen right away, and then a few others. I read their feeds for about one month, entertained with the conversations between people. Tom, a graphic designer, told Carly, a print production associate, that her smile was lovely. Yes, he used the world lovely. She responded with a wink and "ditto." A few short weeks later, they snuck off to lunch alone. Soon, I found them snuggling up in a hug at the copy machine, walking hand-in-hand around the duck pond, and sharing many more winks and kisses on Twitter for all of us to see.

During that first month, I would try to sneak into a conversation and add my opinion, but each time, I'd go well over the one-hundred and forty character limit. I'd try erasing a period or a comma, but I couldn't bring myself to send out grammatically incorrect tweets. On those lucky occasions when I could fit my thoughts within the character limits, I'd erase it anyway. My comments were usually derisive and challenging, and the last thing I wanted to do was toss myself out to marketing and the rest of the world like shark bait.

One time Glenn, the associate director, tossed a good tweet out there that demanded an intelligent response. He asked what we'd do if we were president of America for a day. People came up with the usual boring answers like feed all the hungry, no taxes for a day, blah, blah, blah. I wanted to say I'd fire all the current staff and hire a competent one. That would be the truth. The current White

House staff wasn't letting the president do his job. Fire their asses, I'd say. But, @jktwitter kept silent, sat back, and observed her colleagues socializing. From behind my computer screen, I lived vicariously through their emoticons, whimsical phrases, and banter with perfect strangers about weather, sports, politics, causes, and celebrity mishaps. I didn't need such affirmations and ego-massaging to keep me intact. I quickly grew bored with that e-voyeurism and resumed my exciting life as a proofreader and marketing headline writer in a cubicle.

I survived through one winter and one season of *House* without logging into my Twitter account.

Then, three days after our introduction meeting to the New York City staff, Twitter managed to pique my interest. I had been proofing the latest sporting goods catalogue, sipping on some lemon-flavored iced tea, and licking a cherry Tootsie pop when Doreen popped over to my cubicle.

"I'm following Eva Handel on Twitter—you know that funny one with the motorcycle?"

I shrugged and shook my head, putting up a compelling act. "Which one was she? I don't remember."

Doreen smiled. "She was the only other pretty girl in the room besides you."

I smiled back at her and chuckled. Doreen spoiled me with compliments all the time. That's what mother figures did. They baked you muffins, fed you fattening bagels, and smothered you in niceties to try and build up your self-esteem. She offered them to me so often that, after a while, thanking her seemed a futile thing to do.

Dodging the compliment, I charged ahead. "I didn't notice. You know me. I don't pay attention to that kind of stuff."

"Well, you might want to pay attention to it this time because you'll never believe what she said on Twitter."

Had she mentioned me? Mentioned our smile? Mentioned her mismatched shoes?

I flushed. My temperature spiked. My skin prickled and, in a flash, a blanket of goose bumps covered my arms. I twisted around the chaos and whispered, "What did she say?"

"She tweeted that she loves everything about the mid-Atlantic—especially the wonderful hospitality of her new colleagues—but she despises Old Bay seasoning." Doreen stretched her eyes in horror like Eva had insulted her personally, and she expected me to defend her.

I happened to love Old Bay seasoning, and, as a good Marylander, held it in the highest regard. Old Bay represented Maryland perhaps more than the Ravens, more than the Orioles, and more than Inner Harbor. We doused our burgers, our fish, our clam cakes, even our salads with the stuff. She may as well have insulted our intelligence, our culture, and our belief systems. I latched onto that stimulant, gripping it like it was a machete that I could use to clear the pathway to the likes of people like Eva. Instant access.

"I might just have a reason to get back on Twitter, my friend."

Doreen nodded with a hint of pride weaved into her wide smile. "Good. Go get her."

# #

For the rest of the afternoon, I sat in my cubicle proofing. At one point, I read the same line of text over and over again until my eyes blurred. I turned the page and focused in on a block of sidebar text. I read it. I read it again. I read it a third time and still I didn't know any more about the stroller with one wheel in front than I did the first time my eyes scanned the information. The only thing I did recognize after a tenth final attempt was that I wanted to tweet to Eva.

Even though my deadline for proofing the fall catalog loomed in front of me, I took to the Internet and opened up Twitter. Curiosity sneaked its way in and wouldn't release its grip. I logged on about ten times that afternoon, typing in my tweet comeback to her, and each time going well over the character limit. Each time I backspaced my comment, my eyes wandered to her picture. Warm flutters tickled through me as I settled in on her sly smile; her dark, rich hair falling past her golden shoulders; and the light twinkling on her lips. I snapped away from her picture each time, sidestepping the danger of my ego-driven mind. I'd last a few seconds before focusing back on her again. Her eyes, cascaded in mystery and intrigue, peeked up over an oversized purple mug, teasing visitors to her Twitter page. My tummy rolled. I stared at her and imagined that secretive smile spreading across her face again.

I clicked into her images and scrolled through screens of her in different shots. One she was jogging. Her legs curved and sculpted like I'd always wished mine could be. Another she was hugging a Boxer puppy and looked about ready to burst with love. I loved Boxers and remained firm that, one day when I bought a house with a fenced yard, I would get one. In another shot she was swinging on a tire hanging from a tree. Her hair fanned behind her, spraying the air.

I used to swing on a tire, too. We had so much in common.

I landed on another shot, that one a seductive pose. She was leaning back against a wall with one foot bent against it and the other supporting her. A sexy, sneaky smile danced on her lips. Her eyes bore into mine, as if she knew I'd be sneaking around her photos one day. Just as I leaned in a bit closer, Doreen sprang up behind me. Flustered, I spun in my chair.

"Do you have last week's hard copy proof of the *Escape Outdoors* ad we were running?" I shuffled my feet around for balance. My face grew red hot. Her large figure overtook my senses, overpowered my breathing, and stole all air from my cubicle. I was a little girl caught playing with matches, flushing deep shades of red, and covering up my naughty snooping secret with a rapid tap to the computer screen's power button.

My emergency response system fired off all sorts of pulses, which raced along my arms and to my chest, exploding like firecrackers on my delicate skin. "Hmm." I circled around pretending to rummage through my file cabinet, knowing full well I never put the proof in there. I needed an escape. "I'm not feeling well." I bolted past her. Her curious eyes branded me in embarrassment all the way to the bathroom.

Burying myself under work protected me from those types of crazy situations. I wasn't used to leaping into fire pits, taking to the open road, or diving into pools of hot lava. I never ignored a looming deadline. I shoved that deadline way into the back seat that day. My mind wrapped around one thing, and that one thing had nothing to do with whether every letter 'i' was dotted and every letter 't' was crossed in a sporting goods catalog.

Eva Handel intrigued me. Playing with such intrigue tickled me in all the right places. I was addicted, and it wasn't even lunch time yet.

I stood in the bathroom and splashed water on my face, shook my head, and tucked some loose strands behind my ears. Composed and back in control, I went back to my desk and pressed the on button to my monitor. Without looking back into her eyes, I clicked the little x to close out Twitter and its compromising effect on my sense of control. When Doreen asked me what happened, I simply shrugged off her question and told her I was fine. I was always fine.

Absolutely freaking fine.

# #

My neighbor Larry understood me. I understood him, too. When he first moved in across the hall from me, I freaked out because he knocked on my door wearing nothing but black boxer shorts with yellow smiley faces and a look of panic. He danced on his toes and wiggled around like a worm, screaming about a spider in his bathroom sink. I led the march to his bathroom, weaving us through a tidy maze of moving boxes and stopping only once to take in his beautiful upright Baldwin piano. He pointed me to the farthest door at the end of his condo's hallway. His scrawny chest bellowed in and out, and his fingers, stuffed halfway in his mouth, trembled. I never saw a man look more like a scared little girl than I did in that moment. His fear comforted me right away, breaking down my usual defenses before they even had a chance to stack up.

Larry was gay and just finally started to date a decent guy. He had been seeking a boyfriend since that day I met him; that day I removed the rabid wolf spider from his bathroom sink. In his defense, the spider was big and hairy. I understood his need to cry once I picked it up with my bare fingers and placed it in a plastic cup. I stood bravely against anything nonhuman that could threaten my salvation. Stick an Anaconda in front of me and ask me to wrap it around my neck and take it out for a walk, and I'd be just as comfy as if I were lounging in a bathtub of soapy bubbles listening to Baroque. Yet, put me in a party environment where cracking jokes and idling on current events were supposed to pass as fun, and I clammed up tighter than a hermit crab basking in the glory of salt water.

I trusted insects, reptiles, and amphibians because I understood why they acted the way they did. They didn't set out to be mean. They didn't set out to bully others just for the fun of it. When they attacked, they did so because that survival mechanism weaved into their DNA. They killed for food. Their survival depended on their ability to be the fitter, the stronger, and the alphas. Human beings, we didn't need to do that. Yet, we swung around like a bunch of wild monkeys shelling out insults and punches like useless banana peels. Instead of killing each other, we hurt each other and that hurt lingered on, sometimes, like in my case, forever. That hurt sneaked up on me at odd times, like at a buffet when someone pushed me to grab a slab of bacon, or like when my birthday rolled around and I blew out candles alone in a dark room because I remembered the pain of humiliation from when no one showed at my slumber parties. I'd rather be alone than deal with rejection. Facing such ordeals alone was just easier.

Did it suck? I would imagine for someone who was social and outgoing, it would. For someone like me, someone more comforted by solitude, not in the least bit. Being alone was a freaking party; one big, laughing opportunity after another. I got to celebrate holidays eating as much pie and cookies as I wanted and never had to be judged by onlookers wearing skinny dresses and monitoring their water, fruit, and veggie intakes. You would never find carrot sticks and celery overflowing with cream cheese at my solo parties. And salad at a Thanksgiving Day table? Ha! Please, I would never eat rabbit food. But, sweet potatoes floating in a sea of brown sugar and melted butter? Now we're talking.

Another great benefit of being alone was I never had to share the remote control with someone. If I wanted to lounge in my baggy sweatpants in front of the tube and watch a *House* television marathon, then move over to-do list.

Single life didn't suck.

Single life *fucking* sucked.

20

I lived my life hidden behind my condo door, behind my endless piles of crap work, and behind my pile of rejection letters from editors of magazines. Living life from behind a comfort prop, be that a slice of pizza, a laptop, or a double locked condo door, sucked. It cored me open like a volcano and spewed all sorts of life-erasing lava around so no one could get near me. Well, no one except for Doreen and Larry.

Thank goodness for those two, otherwise I might've been committed to a rubber room where guards served me happy pills round the clock just to keep me from stabbing myself with the leg of a folding chair.

Before Larry met his newest love interest, Tim, a man I had yet to meet, he obsessed over finding a boyfriend. We'd have web search parties. We loaded up profiles on every gay dating site known to mankind. He would get some hits, but none ever met his standards. He wanted a hunky, tall, rich man who enjoyed dogs, kids, and sailing. Oh, and the man needed to love Riesling wine and own a company. He was not into men who desired to climb any corporate ladders. They needed to tout an entrepreneurial spirit, because that spelled adventure and free thinking. According to Larry, that dream guy needed to be on his same path. He'd say that with a straight face as if he owned and managed a life of his own where he could come and go as he pleased. The only trek Larry took out of his comfort zone was volunteering at an LGBT youth center. Larry, by all other accounts, was what I could only refer to as a security and safety junkie. He worked for the government for five years, was fully vested in his retirement account, enjoyed his fringe benefits package which included, but was not limited to, twenty-two vacation days a year, twelve sick days, ten holidays, and of course a flexible spending account.

Yup, you guessed it; Larry was just as screwed up as I was. I couldn't love him more for that. If he was straight, and I was even a smidgeon attracted to him to the point I wouldn't throw up if he tried to hold my hand, then we'd be a perfect couple.

Larry was the only person on the planet who knew my story. Well, part of my story. He could only handle so much drama. Yes, a gay man, who screamed at the sight of sugar ants crawling up his windowsill, wanted to avoid drama. Let's just say his brain could only cradle a certain amount of backstory before he exploded into a torrent of tears. I couldn't stand to see a grown man cry. Especially a gay man who tended to slip into overdramatic weeping at the confession of a bully attack.

Big deal, I was bullied and tormented as a kid. Bigger problems plagued the world than a teenager, in her most vulnerable years, being bullied by her supposed best friends at the time. The global economy was going to shit. The air quality was ridiculous. Gas prices had soared out of control. Children were starving in the streets. So what, I had to brave a dozen girls and their mean attacks for several years during my most formative stage and my parents and sister had to uproot to avoid the retaliation? Oh and that little sister was still battling a drug addiction brought on by moving away from all stability and being tossed into a feeding frenzy of popular girls doing drugs.

If you hadn't guessed by now, I caused not only myself loads of trouble, but also everyone who trailed alongside me, too. I was danger. I should've worn a sign attached to the center of my chest that read 'toxic.' If, as members of society, we had to create a tag line for ourselves, mine would definitely be, 'I fuck up lives.'

I only allowed myself to go into the deep, dark recesses of my mind every once in a great while. Usually I dove into them around the same time when the leaves started to crisp and fall off the trees in piles deep enough to jump into and get lost. Something about the ripened smell of Macintosh apples and brisk mornings pulled me back to those days when I'd press my thumb onto the tip of a bottle of Jean Nate perfume, armed to defend myself as I walked past the tangle of girls drenching me in insults. They'd line up like a chained link fence, supported in strength by their numbers, and laugh as one would trip me with an outstretched foot, or pelt me with rocks as I ran into the building's only unlocked entrance. They'd call me names, chanting rumors about my being a lesbian.

At twenty-nine-years-old, I still cringed when I traveled back through the memory of my former best friend, Barbara, and how she grabbed my personal journal and bolted down the school hall laughing at me for what I'd written about her. I was a dumb teenager, high on hormones or whatever. I wrote some silly stuff about her eyes sparkling and wanting to kiss her petal soft lips and a bunch of other sexually explicit stuff that I should never have written down. I had stupidly left my locker open as I talked with a couple of other girls, and Barbara decided to snoop around. Well, she locked in on the bright blue spiral notebook tattered and littered with flower and butterfly stickers and hearts that said things like – 'I love someone' and 'I think someone's cute.' Barbara, being my best friend and all, took that to mean she could read its contents. I was too busy chatting with the others about Brian Luding's new haircut and didn't notice her reading it. One moment I was bubbling over in giggles with the girls about how adorable Brian was when he swung a baseball bat, and the next, I was ripping the spiral notebook out of my shocked best friend's hands. Not fifteen minutes later, my life spiraled out of control along with her laughter and her lack of concern for my future happiness.

They marked me as disgusting, a mere pile of crap to avoid at all costs for the remainder of my time at the middle school. Rock pelting, foot tripping, profane graffiti on my locker, squirt guns, and the occasional black eye and bruised cheeks followed.

When I entered high school, and our neighbor ran to my parents and told them he had just saved me from suffocating under a pile of boys who were attempting to gang rape me into being straight, my father did the thing any respectable father would do. He called a real estate agent and placed the first home he had ever owned, his pride and joy, on the market. Within one day, a young couple with a dog and two toddlers purchased it. The U-Haul pulled up and all of our aunts, uncles and cousins piled all of our shit into it and moved us four towns over where surely my bullying days would end.

Thankfully they did. No one bothered me. I turned to reading instead of seeking out new friends. Books became my new best friends. They would never hurt me like people could.

My sister required more than a book to entertain her. She needed to belong, to be part of the in-crowd, and to live life out loud. So, she turned to drugs. She got reeled in by the popular druggie crowd. She smoked pot every night and dropped out in her senior year. She never came right out and said she hated me for uprooting her, for taking her away from the safety of a cheerleader squad, and for dropping her in the middle of what could only be described as teenager hazing hell. But I knew, when she scurried off to work as a bagger at the grocery store, she resented that I caused that rift in her future dream of becoming a doctor. Many would argue she carved out and followed her own path. I would argue back that

24

with desperate times, came desperate methods. She didn't know how to be unpopular. So, pot, and then other more potent stuff, massaged that cruel, new world into something doable, livable, and eventually unmanageable.

My parents still held firmly to their position that they don't hate me for ruining their lives by forcing us to pack up all of our belongings and run away from the abuses of many. I still don't believe them.

I often wondered if my bullies thought about me and wrestled with conflict over what they did to me back then. The intelligent adult in me understood their actions were marred in fear. The inner young lady who never got to dress up for prom, go on a date, or experience a first kiss, still shook and ground her teeth at the loss of it all. Now, as an adult, my life sped by, and time, my big enemy, stomped down on me, robbing me of experiences.

I dreamed about a day when I would arrive at their houses and spray paint their pretty faces and clothes, toss mud at them, flatten their tires, and of course, punch each one of them square in the eye and laugh as I watched their eye turn black as mine did so many times. The ultimate would be to sneak up behind each one of them and cut off their hair just like they did to me every three months or so in class. I'd love to see how they'd deal with raggedy edges.

Actually, the ultimate revenge would be to emerge as a successful writer and show up holding my head high, my name now famous—my badge of honor, my gun, my spray painter, my scissors—and surprise the prettiness right out of each and every one of them. I, Jane Knoll, despite being bullied and attacked and treated worse than a rat in a New York City alleyway, would be somebody they'd want to know now.

I mentally carved out my dream. Of course after receiving enough hurtful rejection letters for magazine articles to wallpaper a house, that dream took a back seat. I didn't totally abandon the idea. I just put it to rest for a while until I could figure out a way not to break into a fit of tears every time I got rejected. Without a dream, what would be left? Sweet potatoes drowning in brown sugar and melted butter? Television show marathons for the rest of my life? More visions of Larry imploding from my sad, teenage stories?

I needed the dream to wake back up. That dream would restore me to the girl I used to be. It had to.

#

When I returned home to my empty condo that afternoon, I headed to my laptop and landed back on Eva's Twitter account. I read through her tweets and got sucked in by her wit. She played with followers, stringing them along with short musings, clueless that the girl from the bathroom stall who knew about her mismatched shoes reveled in snooping in on her.

So, I did what any other bumbling, hormonal idiot would do and tiptoed through her profile, through her mentions, through her Twitter feed, through her followers list, through her following list, and through her random images. Then, I sank into a warm and gooey crush I couldn't squash. I needed to learn more about her.

I stared long and hard into her deep, dark eyes and welcomed in the flutters. She sucked me into her soul with those eyes. I sat helpless and vulnerable on my stool, a victim to the beginning stages of a crush that would tempt me, dance on my heart, and prey on my romantic weaknesses in the middle of the night.

I could be anyone to her from the safety of my computer. I could turn myself into a gorgeous babe with a flirty side that twirled her heart and sent her off into the land of flutters and tingles, too. That sent me reeling.

This could be fun.

A switch clicked in me. A challenge erupted. A jolt of what could be electrified me.

I would reinvent myself and tease her about hating Old Bay seasoning. Goodbye @jktwitter. Hello new self.

Who did I want to be? Rich? Fit? A published writer? A traveler? What a fun article that could turn into for a high profile magazine—an experiment in social networking where shy girls got a chance to have some fun from behind the protective barrier of a computer screen and whether that enhanced their pathetic lives.

If anyone's life was worth testing, it was mine. All in the name of experimental research.

Sitting on my stool, still uncomfortable in my skirt that was a dress size too small, I set out to create my brand new Twitter account; one that marketing wouldn't recognize; one that I could bait Eva Handel with about her hating Old Bay seasoning.

I stared at the blank fields that asked for a username and password. What could I call myself? Something cool. I needed something edgy. Something that sounded sexy. Something that would pique Eva's attention. Something daring. Something bold.

Ten minutes later, after rifling through my thesaurus for different takes on sexy, bold, edgy and cool, I decided on @CarefreeJanie.

Someone stop me. I was so original and creative I astounded myself at times.

I needed a picture.

An egghead wouldn't do.

I clicked through some of my photo albums. I was such a dork. My hair always looked like I needed a highlight, even though I'd never had a highlight in my life. My eyebrows were far too light. I was twenty pounds too heavy.

I needed sexy, alluring, desirable.

I took advantage of the magic of the internet and searched Google images. *Why not use the tool if it handed itself to me?* If I were on a deserted island and needed to construct a raft, and wreckage of my downed plane floated past me, you bet I'd improvise and mold that wreckage into something useful. Plane wreckage, images, eh same thing—both tools in a worthy pursuit.

I scanned. Perhaps I could go with something artsy, like a book. Or something sensual, like a curvy leaf. I scanned stock photography and plugged in the words sensual, cool, edgy, sexy, daring and bold. The erotic choices stunned me. Clearly, I'd been living under a rock.

In the soft glow of my living room, I scrolled through the breasts, the thonged butts, and the voluptuous curves that ran rampant across my screen. I scanned page after page of nudity and insanity before landing on an adorable animated picture of a pretty girl partially hidden behind a Victorian fan.

In my bio, I played myself up. I was a lover of words, of risks, of playful debates. I, Victorian-fan-waving @CarefreeJanie, was someone fresh, someone fearless, and someone interesting.

Once complete, I tweeted to Eva Handel, "How can you possibly hate Old Bay seasoning?"

I waited for twenty minutes in front of my computer, staring at it, waiting for something to happen. When nothing did, I closed my laptop, stood up on an exhale and pushed back, away from Twitter, away from the obsession of wondering what she'd say back, and away from the ridiculous notion that she'd even care that someone named @CarefreeJanie wanted to know why she hated Old Bay seasoning.

I washed my dinner dishes slowly, caressing the handle of my scrub brush as I slid it in and out of my coffee tumbler, watching as suds piled up the sides of it and overflowed in a frothy mess down the white ceramic of my kitchen sink. I'd always enjoyed the simple pleasures of performing acts like that. They calmed me, centered me, and expanded my presence in my small kitchen nook, placing me in the path of something grander than I was in the life I led outside those walls.

My lemon colored walls, with their daisy flowers sprinkled around the border, had always cradled me in peace, blocking out the gray world that existed outside where people yelled, honked horns, and chucked each other the bird. In my small kitchen, I was safe and free to enjoy the simplicity of running water, of fresh-smelling bubbles, and of green ivy leaves waving at me from the window sill.

Oh yes, my life was one big joy fest being obsessed over domesticated novelties and now possible tweets from Eva Handel.

Carr—The Muse

Chapter Three

The following night was laundry night. Every Wednesday I gathered my dirty clothes and lugged them down the condo steps and out to Larry's car. I hated doing laundry on Wednesday nights because it got in the way of my favorite show, *American Idol*.

Larry could only do laundry night on Wednesdays because he over-committed himself every other night. When I told him no way, that I'd be doing my laundry on Saturdays like the rest of the people do in the town of Elkridge, he got down on one of his scrawny knees and begged me not to leave him alone to face the cockroaches.

Of all people's legs to land on, a cockroach had to land right smack on Larry's leg one time out of a thousand that he'd visited the laundromat.

The ordeal went down as so: Larry sat in one of the hard, plastic orange chairs, reading Jeannette Wall's memoir, The Glass Castle, when something crawled on him. He looked down at his leg and a big, fat cockroach, with antennae at least an inch long twitching and fluttering about, crawled on him. He jumped up, flung his book and ran out of the laundromat screaming. When he arrived banging at my front door, he looked as if someone had chased him for miles through the town. He panted like an overheated dog, sweating and convulsing, trying to catch his breath. "I need your help," he said, grabbing my shoulders and shaking me. "You need to come with me."

Without blinking, I reached for my keys. I forgot about the boiling water on the stovetop, about the garlic bread in the oven, about the marinara sauce simmering, and followed him. If I was one thing, I was Larry's saving grace in situations that I could handle and he couldn't. He'd never put me in front of an obnoxious crowd or ask me to fight on his behalf. He only ran to me for help if a bug threatened him. I followed him down the exterior steps to our parking lot and straight to his waxed, cherry red Lexus.

"Where is it?" I asked him, reaching for the car keys, ready to tackle the bug with bare hands.

"At ABC Wash Center." He handed me the keys. "I'm sure it's long gone by now, the ugly bugger." He shivered, wiggling with such force, his teeth rattled. "I need you to pull my clothes out of the dryer. I left them there."

Not until I arrived at the laundromat ten minutes later did I realize I had forgotten my dinner cooking on the burner.

A year later, Larry still refused to step foot in that place without my trusty bug-swatting self by his side. Ask him to stand in front of a crowd of people and talk about the first thing that came to mind, no problem. Ask him to call the cable company and complain about poor reception, not an issue. Ask him to accompany me to a work party so I didn't stand like a complete ass by myself, and he strolled in like he owned the company, chatting it up with the company executives about golf games and fine cigars. Ask him to walk by an ant on the sidewalk and he squealed like a girl wearing a tutu, catapulting all of his one-hundred-seventy pounds into my arms.

I loved him anyway. My sweet friend Larry.

He arrived at my front door carrying his netted laundry bag over his shoulder like a satchel of presents. I closed up my laptop, disappointed Eva hadn't replied to my playful tweet. I still smiled for Larry's sake.

He needed me. For that I needed to remain grateful. If Larry didn't exist in the world, no one would care if I lived, breathed, laughed, or cried. Larry needed me. That carried a greater purpose than a tweet I had only just sent twenty-four hours prior to a girl way out of my league and even out of CarefreeJanie's league.

We spent our two-hour laundering session talking about Larry's LGBT youth center. A group of philanthropists opened the LGBT center in an old church, and over a year's time it had grown into a safe haven hang out for at-risk kids. The center included an expansive library of books and movies, a basketball court, an art center, and a meeting hall. Apparently, one of the kids played guitar and offered Larry lessons at the center. Poor Larry tried many new things and never quite mastered any of them. "He's teaching me 'Stairway to Heaven.' He says everyone can play it." I nodded to that and swallowed my sarcastic remark.

"So, tell me more about this new man in your life." I folded the sleeve of my shirt over the other without taking my eye from my friend.

"Tim looks like a younger version of Pierce Bronson." Larry caught his breath and gathered enough control to continue. "When I tell you his eyes melted right through me the first time I met him, I'm not lying." He blew out an exhale. He looked about ready to cave into a moment. He plucked up matching socks and folded them together, tossing them into his netted bag.

"So, is he the real deal or another heartbreak we'll need to mend?"

Larry cranked his head toward me so quickly that he could've broken his neck right off of his shoulders. "No raining on my parade here. This guy is perfect for me."

I wondered how many more times I would have to endure another 'perfect lover' comment. "I've got two names for you. Randy Hines from your office party and Mike Cotters from the choral group."

"No judging." He pointed his finger at me. "That was our deal, remember?"

I stopped all folding and faced him. I took his hands in mine. "You look really happy, and that makes me really happy. So good for you." I released his hands like I would confetti, and he smiled like a kid who just earned a lifetime supply of strawberry ice cream.

"Of course, there is this one thing about him."

I rolled my eyes not surprised. "Spill it."

"It's nothing." He waved off my disdain. "Just forget I said that."

I reached out for his arm. "Oh no you don't. Tell me."

He squinted at me. "No."

"No?"

"It's no big deal. End of discussion."

Insulted, I released him. "Fine. Then, you will not get to hear my latest news."

He squinted more. "Fine."

"Fine."

I finished piling my clothes into my bag and then led us back out to his car.

On our drive back to our condos, I couldn't help myself. I asked Larry if he hung out on Twitter.

"Of course. Everyone does."

"I was thinking of joining," I said, tossing a peppermint candy into my mouth.

"Thinking of joining?" He stretched his face. "You speak of this as if you've mulled over the pain-staking decision for weeks now." He opened his palm up to me. "Got one of those candies for me?"

I unwrapped one and dropped it in his palm. He tossed it between his lips and continued. "Listen, you're not deciding to join the military or a one-way space trip. It's just Twitter."

"I know." I wanted his buy-in and support as I had fun with it. No one else would get that Twitter would most likely be my big ticket to a social life, even if it was a fake one. "Aren't you even curious why I want to be on Twitter? Me? Jane Knoll? Ms. Hater of Whiners and Bullshit?"

He took his eyes off the road and contemplated that in a long stare at me. "It's pretty obvious to me. So, please don't make me say it." He looked back at the road, swerving to get back in his lane. "Twitter's going to be good for you."

He got me. I stared at the row of trees lining our community, comforted by their constancy. They never failed one another. They stood proudly together as a unit, beautifying the view for everyone attuned enough to take notice. That jolted me, spinning me into a state of joy. At least for that moment, all was right in the world. "You're right. Twitter might be just what I need right now."

"Baby steps for the socially ill at heart."

I punched his arm. "I didn't punch your face because I know you're joking around with me."

He leaned his face in toward me. "You might want to punch it because this gay boy isn't joking. You are in need of a total social overhaul."

I flicked his cheek, and we settled into the rest of the drive through our adorable condo community on mute.

A few minutes later, when we returned from the laundromat, I avoided my computer, despite my self-promise that I'd be able to open it when I returned—the prize for being a loyal friend to Larry and being patient with my new obsession.

I didn't open it because I didn't want to taste the grit of disappointment. I wanted to imagine that a tweet from her sat ready for my eyes.

Hope sprinkled around me—hope that I refused to squash. So, I poured myself a glass of milk, sat down with my newest Kindle book, *Life in the Balance*, and dove into it. I embraced the moment.

The longer I relaxed, the more happiness bubbled around me. I reveled in the possibility that, later on, I'd get a peaceful night's sleep, the likes I hadn't known for quite some time. In my dreams, Eva could be sipping a glass of wine contemplating the return of her reply to me. The hope for something fun, new, and intoxicating protected me from seeking comfort from my computer. I would wait until morning to be disappointed if she hadn't responded. For that moment, I would cherish the anticipation of 140 characters arriving in my dried-up world like a refreshing spring rain, sailing directly to me over invisible, complicated internet connections.

#

Not five minutes later, I popped back up and headed for the laptop.

The lure of her reply called out to me. I flipped up the screen and began typing Twitter into my browser. Before I got to the second 't', I stopped myself.

I was acting like an idiot.

I would wait three days. I would not cave. Punishment for caving would be no whipped cream on my strawberry ice cream for a month.

I closed my laptop and went back to my bed. I rolled around tucking a pillow under my backside, then between my legs, and finally under my knees. Nothing seemed to cure my restless behavior. I folded my hands behind my head and stared up at my ceiling fan. It whirred like a hummingbird, and even that peaceful distraction didn't stop the tease of what Eva's tweet might say back to me. I lay there, a zombie to anything not Eva, allowing potential charms to pile up in my mind. Possibility after possibility stacked on top of each other, tumbling down and spilling into all the hollow recesses of my mind.

By two a.m., my back hurt. I got up, went straight to the medicine cabinet, poured a helping of nighttime anti-inflammatories into my mouth and swallowed them bone dry. Rest would soon come.

When my alarm blared at seven a.m., I hit the snooze button. When it rang again, I whacked it with my pillow. By the fifth time, I ordered myself out of bed and into the shower. I prepped for the rough day ahead with two generous scalp scrubbings using my tingly, minty shampoo followed by a long pause under the stream of water hot enough to scald my skin.

Forty-five minutes later, as I drifted into my cubicle, my mouth watered for one of Doreen's blueberry muffins. Why couldn't it be blueberry muffin day?

In the first day of my three-day commitment to stay controlled, I succeeded by volunteering to adhere mailing labels to five thousand letters going out to new subscribers of our loyalty rewards program. I sat in the mailroom at a metal folding table with a stack of mailing labels and boxes of envelopes and smiled to myself. I enjoyed the empowerment of self-control.

That night, I went to the movies solo to see a new Jennifer Aniston flick. I stood in line to get my usual movie treat—a large bucket of popcorn, buttered, and a jumbo Coke. I eyed the popcorn guy as he drizzled butter on his customer's popcorn. The longer I stood there, the more conscious I was of the oversized shirt I wore to conceal the fact that I could no longer fasten my top button. I hated the way I looked. I looked down at my loose shirt and cringed as if I'd only just opened my eyes and saw its pink-and-white vertical stripes for the first time.

I backed away from the line and watched the movie hungry, stirred by another incredible dose of empowerment.

By day two, I could've faced a sea of buttered popcorn and not have been tempted.

I swam in self-control paradise.

The internet didn't even tempt me. Well, at least not for the first thirty minutes of my workday. At right about the point that I typically logged on to check for an email from my mother, I started questioning things, like what if Eva had responded and waited for me to reply? I would never *not* respond to someone who walked by and said hi. I would never ignore someone's smile without reciprocating. I would never in a million years wave off someone's effort to dig deeply and understand the complexities of hating Old Bay seasoning if asked. I was not a bitch. Neither was CarefreeJanie going to be.

I logged on, braving all for the sacrifice of whipped cream, and clicked right over to my mentions. I would be the bigger person in that situation and answer the lovely girl if she had mentioned me. I hated being ignored and I refused to start playing that bitch who did it to others as some sort of payback for being wronged throughout her entire life.

So, there I went to my mentions tab. Wouldn't you know it? I didn't have one lousy mention from anyone, especially from Eva Handel. My heart sank. I tossed my head down on my desk and groaned. Not only was Eva just like every other unattainable person in life, but now I couldn't even mourn that fact over a bowl of strawberry ice cream smothered in whipped cream.

By my afternoon break, anger seeped through my bloodstream. How dare she ignore my tweet? I didn't get it. Maybe Jane Knoll would be afraid to confront her, but CarefreeJanie was no wimp. No. I created her to be equal to the likes of someone who could carry a room full of people despite wearing mismatched shoes. I created a super woman who was not only a hottie, but someone smart, witty, and someone who didn't take anyone's crap.

I put on my best CarefreeJanie hat and retweeted my tweet to her. If that didn't blanket her with some guilt, what would? CarefreeJanie didn't need selfish tweeps in her social circle. She would only accept the interactive and friendly types, and maybe the occasional debater to show off her challenging side. That's right, CarefreeJanie was not only beautiful and worthy of interaction, but she would also become someone whom others would not want to miss. She'd be listed on Twitter. Listed under such categories as 'tweeps not to miss,' 'twitters of influence,' and I would never leave off from that list 'successful writers.'

A smile stretched across my face. My head buzzed. My heart galloped. I loved being CarefreeJanie so much more than plain Jane.

I dove head first into the fun with my retweet.

Larry would be so proud of me.

#

Within two minutes, I rechecked Twitter. I hovered over the mention button for several seconds and finally clicked it, squeezing my eyes shut and inhaling deeply. Then, shaking off my fear of not seeing her tweet, I braved all and opened my eyes to a squint. There before me, rested a tweet from Eva Handel.

My heart ballooned.

"Does it help that I adore Baltimore's beloved colors, orange and purple?" she asked. Her picture flirted with me, beckoning me to answer right away.

A smile too big for my face blossomed. I bit down on my lower lip, easing up on its pull across my face. That didn't help. I read her tweet five times before looking away to find Sanjeev standing behind me with a clipboard in his hand. I jumped forward in my seat.

"Sorry," he whispered. "You looked deep in thought and I didn't want to interrupt."

I arranged my head in such a way that it covered my screen. "No problem. *What's up?*" What's up?

"Katie mentioned that you were interested in speaking at the next quarterly meeting. I just wanted to come by and thank you for that."

"Did she?" *Did she also tell you that she can't spell the word 'definitely' or 'separate' and that I have to correct her each time? Hmm?* Ms. Graphic Designer of the Year messed with the wrong girl. She knew I'd rather die than make a fool of myself.

He draped his arm over the clipboard. "I'll send you the topic points to cover for the marketing division in a few days. I'll try to make it fun."

Fun? Fun was watching Adam Sandler in "The Water Boy." Fun was watching Larry try to pick up a straight guy. Fun was not humiliating myself.

"Fun. Yes. Great. Uh. I should get back to work." I managed a weak smile.

He nodded. "Right, then." He turned and walked away, bouncing in his long stride.

Two seconds later, Doreen rounded my cubicle wall. "That bitch."

"I know, right?" I mirrored her dropped jaw. "I'll figure out some way to get back at her." I winked at her and spun back around to face Eva's tweet again. Her

40

cute words played on my eyes. I adored how they sat next to my @CarefreeJanie Twitter handle.

I clicked the reply button and wrote, "That takes away a small bit of the sting. But I need more. What else can you offer?"

I sent it off and a giddy rush swam through my veins. I just flirted with a beautiful girl.

Not a blink later, Twitter informed me that Eva Handel was now following me.

My breath hitched.

I leaped up from my chair and hurried off down the aisle, not knowing what else to do with the flurry of excitement bubbling over in me. I passed the executive offices where men and women stressed over their laptops about things they deemed important but really, in the grand scheme of what just happened, paled in comparison.

I weaved around a group of gossiping women who always stopped talking whenever I reached their no fly zone. They pointed their heavily mascaraed eyes at me, shifted in their high heels, and swiped lip gloss from the corners of their lips with the tip of their fake nails. As usual, they stopped whispering when I weaved, and I didn't bother to apologize that time. I just kept striding ahead powered by a dizzy gale. I headed straight for the back door where I'd be free to release some of the crazy joy on the unsuspecting flowers, trees, birds, and green grass of the office park. A man riding a lawn mower stopped and waited for me to walk past him. I waved back at him that time.

I walked with a new spring in my step. The warm air swaddled me. The green grass, as deep and thick as carpet, swayed with the gentle breeze. Birds chirped. Cicadas hummed. Puffy clouds floated against a gentle blue sky. The sun shimmered like crystals on the tiny ripples in the duck pond. I inhaled the sweet honeysuckle scent and savored the moment. The world flowered into a livelier place. For once, I didn't want to stick my head in the duck pond for the rest of eternity.

##

When I arrived back at my desk, Doreen lunged at me. "Katie came by asking where you were." She rolled her eyes.

"What did she want?"

"To torment you for sure."

I loved Doreen. I loved that Katie annoyed her just as much as she annoyed me.

Katie and I toyed with each other, always trying to one-up the other. Call it my post-bully revenge. She tossed out the first punch, and I followed suit because I knew she could handle it. She hated that Sanjeev appreciated my knack for improving his writing. Doreen, of course, would argue his appreciation for me had little to do with words and more to do with his crush on me. He invited me to luncheons and to work on special projects because I, unlike everyone else at Martin's, didn't yack on and on. One day, Doreen would come to understand that good looking, highly-educated men from India did not come to the United States to date shy, reclusive women like me who lugged around years of baggage too ugly to open. Until she understood that, I just let her ramble on about crushes, potential marriage proposals, and romantic getaways on the company dollar.

##

Turned out Katie had swung by my desk to give me a friendly heads-up on a major project coming down the pipeline. Friendly, my ass. Anyway, apparently, the new events manager, as Katie still referred to her, needed a high-profile presentation that she could submit to the executive leadership team so they could better understand her services and the benefits she brought to the table.

"I'm happy to help," I said, meaning it for the first time ever.

She clicked her tongue. "Yeah, I bet you are."

My body fired off its alarm. "What is that supposed to mean?"

"You're redder than a tomato." She poked me with her sneaky eyes.

"Just send over the stuff when you get it, and I'll work on it." I turned my back on her, pissed that she won that hand.

Katie and I worked together more often than I'd like. We sparred, and that, more often than not, resulted in brilliant outcomes. In our attempts to outshine each other, we ironically illuminated the entire company.

Katie loved her job. It defined her. She probably dreamed about it all night long. She was always showing up at my cubicle with her 'ideas' to turn one of my paragraphs into something more readable. As a graphic designer, she constantly changed my headlines around to suit her own designing needs, then took full credit for that by failing to tell me. I'd discover the new headline weeks later when browsing an online ad or reading a newspaper.

She also claimed to be a computer whiz. She studied computer programming in college and decided to become a graphic designer instead because "her heart sang" whenever she indulged in creating a flyer or eye-catching advertisement. She talked about that to anyone who would listen. I could be pouring a cup of coffee, taking a pee, washing my lunch dishes, or thumbing through the file cabinets in the aisle and have to hear her tell that tale to newbies.

Even though she loved designing, she bragged about her computer hacking courses and how she never failed to break into a system and get that perfect grade for the class. I didn't buy it. How could someone so genius about computer hacking not find work in some cybersecurity job that paid double what she earned as a graphic designer?

Blah. Blah. Blah. I couldn't stand her. She couldn't stand me.

Of course, we didn't always hate each other.

She actually really liked me when she first started. She would ask to tag along on lunch strolls, and I'd look at her like she had ten heads. No one ever wanted to stroll with me for lunch. She came along a few times and drove me nuts with her constant need to talk. So, I excused myself from that ridiculous duty by lying about a sprained ankle I suffered from tripping down my condo staircase.

She even sent me a get well card with my favorite dog on the cover, a white boxer.

Well, that came down from my cubicle immediately following the day of one of our company happy hours. I invited Larry to tag along because I hated to walk into a room and not have someone to turn to and talk to. I did that once, and every eye in the room branded me when I stood like a fool fiddling with my pocketbook strap and shifting from one foot to the other one too many times.

So, Katie showed up with her husband, a tall, dark haired man who dressed better than most red carpet stars. He wore an earring in his ear, a gorgeous watch on his wrist, and smelled rich and woodsy. Well, place Larry in the same room as someone of that caliber and his eyes would be flashing, nose would be sniffing, and feet would be walking to get closer. And, did they ever. Larry stuck to the guy like mosquitos on a halogen light. Katie and I had been chatting it up by the tortilla chips and laughing over something Sanjeev had said in one of our weekly meetings when she looked over at her husband and gasped.

Larry had been gazing into her husband's eyes like a goofball and sliding his thumb down his cheek. Her husband didn't seem to mind. A wide grin sat on his face and he tilted his head as he cued into Larry's charm. I left Katie with a handful of tortillas and pounced up to Larry. That's when all the shit hit the fan.

I told Larry to go over to Katie and keep her company while I asked her husband a few questions. The guy checked me out from head to toe. He told me I was beautiful, then insisted on buying me a drink. To keep Larry at bay, I walked over to the bar with him. I looked back on Larry and Katie, and she stared at me, ignoring Larry.

Her husband placed a hand on the small of my back and ushered me along to a private corner of the bar where he flagged down a bartender who looked to be no more than eighteen with spikey hair, a nose ring, and a waist smaller than most ten-year-olds. He shot us a smile. "What can I get for you two lovebirds?"

I gulped. Her husband caught me as I pushed back against the bar to flee. He rolled me up into his arms and I fell against his chest. He whispered into my ear. "Relax, beautiful. I've got you." Then, he kissed my cheek, resting his lips on my skin. Too shocked to move, I stood plastered against his command.

Katie charged toward us. "He's my husband. You do realize that, right?"

I jumped out of her husband's stronghold.

An amused smile sat on his face as if he enjoyed hurting his wife like that.

"It's not what it looks like," I said, clamoring for her understanding, one girl to another.

"Girls like you can't be trusted." She just shook her head, crossed her arms, and viewed me as the most disgusting girl to ever walk the face of the Earth.

"Girls like me?"

"You prance around this world like you're a gift to men, flinging your hair over your shoulders and batting your long eyelashes. You do the same thing with Sanjeev."

"What?" The defenses rose. The claws sprung. The little hairs on the back of my neck stood tall ready to launch a full scale attack should one be necessary. "I'm not interested in your husband or Sanjeev." I said that with perhaps a tad bit too much sarcasm. *Or any other man for that matter. I'm a lesbian trapped behind lips that have never kissed. I'm a ragdoll who has been pelted, kicked, punched, and taunted. I do not prance or bat my eyelashes unless someone is chasing me with one foot ready to kick me or an eyelash is scratching my cornea.* The arguments circled my brain, twisting up into knots too bulky to undo. Perhaps I should've kept my mouth shut, but what flew out next sealed my fate for a future at Martin Sporting Goods that would test my resilience. "Besides, I think hubby prefers Larry over me."

She lunged forward, and that's when I bolted. Larry and I ran from that building as if it were about to explode.

Two years had passed since then. The animosity swelled out of control. We hid it well from Sanjeev and our colleagues. But, put us alone in a room and the daggers flew, the capes rose, and the toying unfurled with reckless abandon.

# #

After eating lunch outside with Doreen amongst pretty butterflies and rays of sunshine, I returned to my cubicle and clicked onto Twitter, excited to see Eva's response. To my delight, a new tweet sat for me. My heart zoomed.

"Oh, sorry, I'm afraid orange and purple are all I've got to offer you," she wrote.

I stared frozen and stung at her closed-ended comment. It left no room for further banter. She cut me off just as quickly as she turned me on. It hurt more than a rock to the head.

Hope of a beautiful afternoon faded in a storm of dread as tears gathered up inside, threatening to overpower me. Just once, I wanted someone of value to pay attention to me.

I hated my life.

A new pity party welled up inside.

Not here. Not now.

I just wanted to be home, alone in my living room sobbing to a sad song.

I gathered my paperwork into a manageable pile, shoved it all into my book bag, and snuck out. The bitter salt of my tears burned the back of my throat as I forced them back until I cleared the building. By the time I climbed into my car, the flow erupted into a torrential downpour the likes of which I hadn't dealt with since my cat, Oliver, died two years before.

I sat in my car and pounded the steering wheel with my fists. I hated myself for being so sensitive, so easily unglued and manipulated by other people's actions and words.

I experienced that level of sting only once before when I was twelve and told my friend Barbara her eyes were pretty. We were washing my dad's Ford Mustang in my front driveway. She wore my favorite pair of blue jean cut-off shorts with a white tank top. The sun blazed above us. Freckles dotted her pale skin, and she looked up at me at one point, cupping her hand over her eyes for shade and asked me to pass the bucket of soap. Her blue eyes sparkled like gems, and I just blurted out the compliment. She arched her eye at me and backed away like I'd just told her I carried the small pox disease and could infect her in an instant with just a breath. I stumbled back on my words, not sure why I would've said them in the first place, and told her what I really meant to say was that my mother thought she had pretty eyes. She shook her head and told me she needed to get home. She left me standing there with half a sudsy car to still hose down. I could've run after her to clear the weirdness, but I just stood there with a leaky hose dangling from my numb arms and watched her jog down the sidewalk back to her house.

Two days later, we met up again at school. She paraded through the hallway with me like nothing had ever happened. She even slung one of her toned arms around my shoulder and laughed with me about how Rhonda Williams wobbled down the hall like a penguin with two left feet. I laughed like that was the funniest thing in the world, ignoring that inner beating in my brain that told me to shut the hell up.

I spent the rest of the school year laughing with her and her friends at Rhonda and other kids who weren't perfect. I wanted to fit in. I wanted Barbara to like me as much as I liked her. My ticket on her train was laughter. My gang of friends laughed, so I laughed and watched in horror as the kids we laughed at turned red and blotchy or worse cried because of us. If I didn't join in and laugh at nerds with glasses too big for their faces and pants too short to hide their ankles, or kids who were chubby and snorted when they laughed, or who were unfortunate enough to have a head full of frizzy hair or faces brimming with zits, then I feared Barbara would turn and look at me with that same look of disgust she did that day in the driveway.

She was my world, and I needed to prove my place, despite wanting to throw up every time my words or actions caused someone to cry.

I was one laugh away from being bullied myself. I didn't have the gift of money like the rest of those girls did. I slid into that circle through the sheer luck that Barbara and I were born to mothers sharing a hospital room who later became PTA friends. If it weren't for our mothers forcing us to play together on long, hot summer days at Spring Lake and our fathers eventually working together at the news station, I would be that girl walking halfway around the other side of the school to avoid Barbara and all of her pretty friends. Because my mother was fond of playing Rummy and drinking afternoon martinis, I escaped the cruel side of life. My best friend, Barbara, protected me from it. For a little while anyway.

Barbara and I, along with ten or so other girls, walked around the school with our heads held higher than the rest. Well, I didn't carry mine as high, just enough to show I half-belonged. I walked with trepidation next to the girls with clout, confidence, and power.

I used to promise myself when I'd laugh along with them at some poor unfortunate classmate, that one day I'd make up for the hurt I caused by doing good deeds for strangers. I called it my redemption process. That smoothed over the cruel callouses of guilt I suffered from doling out a lingering snicker that got all the other girls going even louder. I had a knack for getting the engines hot on the cruelty, and the rest of the girls would just sneak right in and take over the attack. So, after I honed in on some unsuspecting kid with stringy hair or a set of scrawny legs, and buttered up the path to his attack with some good old-fashioned insults, I'd slide backwards and plan more of my redemption process over again.

My redemption process sucked, but massaged the guilt at the time. I planned out a whole future for myself where I'd mow strangers' front lawns, help the elderly with their groceries, volunteer to walk neighborhood dogs while their masters worked long hours, and definitely serve the less fortunate by spooning soup into their empty bowls at shelters. Yeah, I planned on being a martyr when I grew up and finally stopped bullying kids who didn't come from upper middle class homes, who didn't enjoy birthday bashes at a catered banquet hall, and who didn't wear designer clothes and enjoy the best haircuts from the top salons and spas.

Not until after Barbara ran around the school spreading rumors that I was gay did I start to rethink that promise. Shortly after that humiliating day, I flushed my promises down the drain because what I endured punished me far more than any redemptive act I planned to take. The moment I got hit with my first rock, I realized good deeds would never make up for what I'd done to others. By the third time of being tripped in the hallway and falling flat on my stomach in a belly flop, I decided I deserved that treatment and it would serve as punishment.

I deserved a cruel life after all the pain I must've caused other kids. I'd never forget the agony on a girl's face the day I told her she couldn't sit with us popular girls at the lunch table. Her name was Rhonda. She gathered her tray, sat alone, and peeked up at me while shoveling a sandwich in between her chubby mouth. Tears spilled down her cheeks.

I devastated lives, and when the tables turned, I had prayed the torture would take the sting away. Wishful thinking. Pain took on a whole new level when you realized you'd caused yourself that pain and deserved every blow.

I wondered, as I sat clinging to my steering wheel in the parking lot, whether all of those kids I bullied had grown up to be like me, someone who lived life in the dark shadows always clinging to a false hope that maybe one day they'd smile and really mean it.

Chapter Four

On Wednesday night, Larry and I met over laundry. I was folding a towel, searching inside its folds for peace, when he asked me why I was so quiet.

I shrugged off his question. "I'm fine."

He eyed me.

I waved him off. "Fold your shirt."

He took my hint and didn't say another peep until later when he dropped my bag of laundry on my living room floor. "I have cheesecake."

Many stories unfolded between us over cheesecake. The creamy, sugary slices of heaven cocooned us into a safe harbor where anything could be revealed and not a single judgment passed. Larry always had a cheesecake on hand for those spontaneous moments when one of us needed to unleash. If, on the odd occasion, he didn't have actual cheesecake, he always stored cheesecake flavored yogurts for emergencies.

I first learned about how Larry's uncle sexually abused him when he was eight-years-old over a slice of strawberry. I confessed to stealing one hundred dollars from my parents' savings jar to buy a new pair of jeans when I was a freshman in high school over a slice of blueberry. A talk over a slice of New York style helped him come to terms with the fact that his older brother might never answer his calls again because he feared Larry's homosexuality. Most pivotal was when cheesecake paved the way for me confessing to Larry that I didn't have one iota of desire for men. Even still, however, cheesecake never did drag the most embarrassing of truths out of me, the one that tortured me in the middle of the night, the one that swept sand over my dreams, and the one that shoved me back down the dark tunnel every time something good started to poke its happy rays through the surface.

I feared the cheesecake that night. Its sweet innocence could reach up and into those guarded regions, curl up its magical swirls, and lead an army of ants to its death. What power did I have against it? I didn't trust the cheesecake's power to protect me against my ugly past that night. Though, a flicker of truth highlighted the fact that until I confessed the hideous part of my past to my best friend, I'd remain jailed to it. Still, I resisted. "I'm not in the mood for cheesecake," I said.

He lowered his bottom lip and opened his arms up wide. "Come here," he said. "Let me get a hug."

I walked into his arms and sank into his embrace. He smelled like a spring day. He patted my back and cradled me to his chest.

"I'm feeling bad."

"I know." He continued to pat my back. "Tell me all about it."

I clung to him, comforted by his long arms and big spirit. "I'm tired of myself."

He rocked me.

Since tweeting to Eva, I had wasted countless hours escaping into a dream world where I captured her attention and the two of us twirled around in Twitterland bliss bantering back and forth like a couple of fresh, young lovers. I imagined her soft lips landing on mine, her warm eyes gazing lovingly at me, and her soft hands caressing my skin. Those daydreams stirred me and left me panting.

"You need cheesecake, darling," he whispered.

My tears exploded on impact. I bucked against his chest like I'd just witnessed the end of a life. The pain seeped out, poking, pinching, and scratching its way through my tiny pores. "Yes, I need cheesecake." I finally surrendered.

We left my bag of folded clothes in the middle of my living room floor and walked across the landing to his condo. Within five minutes, we sat cross-legged on his black Italian leather sofa and fed on red velvet cheesecake. I dug my fork into it. "I'm scared, Larry."

He stopped mid-chew and squinted at me. "Of what, darling?"

I swallowed a bite, waiting for its magic to take over and help me voice the thing I promised myself for years that I'd never say out loud. "Of living the rest of my life alone."

He dropped his fork on his plate, wiped his mouth with a napkin, and sat up taller, "Finally."

"Finally?"

"Yes, finally we can have this conversation." He readjusted, folding his legs under him and steadying in for a deep talk. His eyes twinkled. His lips curled into a devilish smile. "I want to hear all about this girl who's breaking your heart right now."

"I never mentioned a specific person."

"You never wear mascara, and for the past few days, you're wearing it."

I nodded. I needed another mouthful. I swallowed and stabbed the cheesecake with the fork waiting for it to help me explain. "She doesn't even know I exist. Well, not really anyway."

He scooped up a helping and fed it to me. "Tell me her name."

I lingered on the bite, rolling the sugar around my tongue, mystified by its power to level out solid ground as I rolled out my confession. A smile fought its way to the surface. "Eva. Her name's Eva. She just started at our New York City branch. And she's why I joined Twitter."

He giggled and scooted up closer. "She's all you can think about, right?"

"So pathetic, isn't it?"

"Very." He wiped my mouth with a napkin. "However, it happens to the best of us. So tell me the real issue here."

"Well, let me set the story for you. With my bio and my fake picture, I explained my exciting life. You see, I'm gorgeous, a professional writer, a world traveler, and as if that's not enough, I can also run marathons in under two-and-a-half hours."

He piled another forkful in his mouth. "You've created one hell of an alter ego, darling." He twisted his mouth. "A world traveler? Really?"

"I could be." I smacked his upper arm.

"A trip to the Smoky Mountains doesn't count as world traveling, and neither does Skyping me when I traveled to Australia."

I punched him again. That time even harder.

He winced. "I digressed. I apologize." He rubbed his arm. "My point is, you could be all of that if you just stop being so hard on yourself."

"So, I'm not gorgeous? That's what you're saying?"

"That's your takeaway?" He sat back.

"Well?"

He sat up again and laced his fingers through the end of my ponytail. "If you'd style your hair in more than that ponytail, you would be." He batted the frizzy end of it in between his fingers. "Seriously, get this trimmed."

He dropped my frizz in lieu of another forkful of creamy cheesecake. He smacked his lips, swiping them with his tongue and wiping every last morsel of the decadence from them. His lips had kissed many. That fact only reminded me of how pathetic I was and that I would certainly spend the rest of my days failing at the one thing that came so easy to most every person on the planet. Geez, my cousin kissed her first set of lips at five when she and her friend, Mike, hid under a bush in a game of hide-and-seek. "When did you have your first kiss?"

"I was twelve. At George Washington Grove State Park in campground site number twenty-two. He was nineteen. His name was George and he invited me to his site to drink beer. I took three sips and then he moved in and started making out with me on his picnic table. His tongue was slimy and took up my entire mouth. He had just smoked a cigarette, too. He tasted like an ashtray. I wanted to throw up. His kiss grossed me out. I'd never tasted anything as disgusting. In fact, I swore off kissing for eternity after leaving his site." He arched his eye. "Well, that lasted a day." He giggled and scooted in closer. "The very next morning, my secret boy crush walked by me as I lathered soap onto my chest in the community shower. He smiled. I smiled back. He cocked his head to a changing stall. I followed. The rest was history, darling. Lot of first times happened that weekend for me." He winked.

I dug deep, pausing before I launched into my confession. "I've never been kissed."

He dropped his plate on the coffee table, sat back and exhaled like I'd just told him I grew up as a member of an alien species who had flown in from a planet far beyond the Milky Way Galaxy. His hands flew up to his face, cupping his mouth. "I need a moment to marinate this."

After he marinated, Larry arrived at a half-baked idea to christen me into the land of the kissing. "Kiss me."

"Over my dead ass."

"Okay, then." He shrugged.

I punched his arm. "Yes, okay then."

We both agreed kissing each other would cause permanent irreparable damage to our friendship, because from that point on neither one of us would be able to look each other in the eye with a straight face again. Larry's lips had never landed on a woman's. As he shoveled his last piece of cheesecake into his mouth, he confessed that the thought of kissing a woman caused his stomach to hurl.

I couldn't have been more relieved that I'd saved him from performing such a sacrifice.

# #

The next day at work, I logged into Twitter and read through my timeline of the twenty people I followed. Eva had tweeted five times in the past ten minutes, mainly replying back to people who mentioned her in a tweet. Even her tweets dripped of her sweet and sultry personality. Her words, colorful and fun, danced across Twitter like poetry. Eleven hundred and twenty-five people followed her. I joined that rank. She followed back five hundred eighty people. She had a lot to sift through to get to my tweets.

I clicked onto my mention tab and read through two mentions thanking me for following them. My eyes scrolled past those and onto my third mention, a mention from my dear Eva Handel. My heart bucked.

"So, don't you know when a girl is just playing with you? I was hoping for a few volleys with you (wink). Do I get at least one?"

She winked at me.

Eva Handel winked at me. Well, okay, she winked at CarefreeJanie.

I lost my breath. I tapped my chest, making sure I was still breathing, still seeing the wink, and still Jane Knoll, the girl who knew nothing about how to play with a girl as lovely as Eva.

I knew nothing about volleying banter. Girls like me never learned to banter. We learned to hide. We learned to walk around the world to avoid the sting of people not wanting to banter with us. I needed to learn, and learn fast.

So, I did what every resourceful twenty-nine-year-old girl who had never been kissed would probably do in my situation. I took to the Internet and pleaded with any of the powers that existed to guide me to my answer. I searched for articles on how to flirt, how to play coy, how to attract using words, and I came up with endless results. The only problem, not one of them told me what to say. They recommended silly things like cueing in on the eye contact, tilting my head, and swaying my hips forward. What a bunch of useless crap. What about instructions for those of us who preferred a keyboard over red lipstick and a sultry smile?

I dove in deeper to research mode, and meanwhile, precious time ticked away. Comedians couldn't walk away just before dishing their best punch lines and return minutes later to tell it. Timing primed everything brilliant. Respond too soon, look like a desperate fool. Respond too late, risk her forgetting why she played with me in the first place.

I called Larry. "What would you say?"

He sighed. "It's not supposed to be this hard. This kind of stuff should just flow naturally. You're not drafting the Declaration of Independence here or a set of wedding vows. You're simply telling her you're either into her or not."

"You've got nothing. That's why you're saying that."

"I've got nothing. I do all my flirting in person."

I hung up and stared at her tweet again. I stared at my fan-waving alter ego. "What would you do, huh?" I imagined her winking back, egging Eva on with a simple tug of mystique. She didn't need words. Her fun sprang from within. CarefreeJanie was a playful lady who waved that fan of hers and created magic dust. She played with the air, commanding it to swirl in just the right circles, to pass through clouds without a hitch, and to dance provocatively in the spaces where the visible merged silently with the invisible and created a field of sexy, uninhibited bliss.

CarefreeJanie didn't fret over incidentals like which word choice would better suit her lips. No, she decidedly curled her lips up into a sweet, sexy smile and typed back something meaningful, something stirring, and something that would rattle Eva Handel's world. I typed back a wink to match hers. I examined it for flaws, comparing it to her previous tweet about playing, volleying and winking.

My wink looked friendly, but not flirty, and certainly not engaging enough to spur Eva into continuing on with the dance. I needed a cliff hanger, a 'please enter' symbol, a 'come here and let me banter with you some more' lead. I added a question mark and had to admit, it looked like the cutest thing in the world at that moment.

I sent off my winking question mark with an air of confidence.

I sat for several lingering minutes with my eyes closed, enjoying the sweet thrill of the dance swaying in me, the magical ride, and the pulsating spread of something wild, lustful, and animalistic.

Oh that wink.

My head twirled. I floated up and away from that dreadful cubicle with its remnants of Katie, away from the miserable anguish over my failed love life, and far away from the guilt-riddled grime built up from years of fretting over stupid things I did way back when I was a young idiot of a kid.

In that moment, I was free. I floated up to where lucky people hung out, to that place I often looked to with envy, to that place I had always longed to visit. I finally arrived at it. It shined even sunnier than I expected. The colors were brighter. The air was lighter, cleaner, and fresher. I loved that paradise. I wanted to live in that paradise. I wanted more. God, please, let me have more. I just needed a tweet or two a day to pressurize the air and keep me flying up where eagles dipped their wings in the air and soared on the mild breezes of Mother Nature's art.

After several long minutes of nothing, the fear slowly started to poke its pointy prick into my bubble, lowering me back to where I just sort of flounced mid-air, waiting for the inevitable bubble to burst and for Eva to not understand my questioning wink.

Then, the tiny slit of pastels and warm liquid converged on the horizon of my prayer. My screen moved, and in danced another tweet. "Aw, thank you, doll. How did you know I adore winks?"

Doll. That rolled off my tongue so easily when I whispered it. A carnival lit up inside and sent some serious flutters pirouetting through me. Walking that tightrope, I balanced on its delicate edges with toes pointed, insteps arched, and arms extended. I welcomed in the thrill. As naturally as I would put one foot in front of the other to balance over a ravine, I typed back, "You adore winks, but not Old Bay seasoning?"

In the time it took to part my lips to take in a breath, she responded. "Winks trump Old Bay."

"Do they trump purple and orange?"

"I have to go with winks."

She was flirting with me. I couldn't stop the spread of my smile. "Is there anything about Maryland you do like?"

"Well, you're kind of fun," she wrote.

My inner thighs twitched. I could've indulged in that warmth for months and not tire of it. It fueled me on, causing me to banter like I grew a set of flirty wings that twirled me around like a princess. "I can trump that."

"Please try."

I pulsated. "Well, you're kind of cute." I sent it off in a blink, flirting like a pro from behind the protective zone of my computer.

"DM," she wrote back.

DM? What was DM? We had been volleying the ball perfectly, and I went and snapped it too hard and shot it out of bounds. I called out to Doreen. "What does DM on Twitter mean?"

"Direct message," she said.

Of course! A smile popped onto my face. I clicked on my message tab. One sat waiting for me from her. "You are making me blush," she wrote.

I caused Eva Handel to blush. I wanted to jump around in circles. My fingers danced wildly across the keyboard, into a daring set of flips in the greatest contemporary routine ever fashioned by someone like me. "You must look even

60

more beautiful when you're blushing." *Where was I getting all of this? Ah, how I love you, CarefreeJanie!*

"You certainly intrigue me CarefreeJanie."

My body pulsed. I swallowed, and not without great effort. Overloaded, my system shut down. I could only send a wink back in return and then cave into myself to steady the rush. I melted into a pile of liquid, and it took everything I had to solidify again when Sanjeev knocked on my cubicle wall asking if I had completed an article he'd asked me to proofread.

My eyes blurred over my files. "It's here somewhere." I flipped over folders, binders, and even knocked down my hazelnut coffee in search for my mind. "I'll find it and get it to you right away." I couldn't catch my breath.

He bent down to help me pick up the mess I created. At that point, Katie walked up to us, stopped for a moment to offer me a fake pout, and then kept on walking. Sanjeev stood up with a pile of wet files. "I'll get some paper towels." He dropped the soggy papers down on my desk and hurried off to the kitchen. Meanwhile, I spun back around to find another message from her.

"I've got to run off to a meeting. This has been fun. Don't be a stranger, okay? (wink)"

I exhaled and dropped back in my seat, not caring about the coffee that dripped onto my cream pants.

Chapter Five

At Martin Sporting Goods, the chief executive officer had decided on his second day on the job to institute something fun. Not a fan of private offices, he set up shop in a double cubicle and turned his office into a collaboration room where all staff could go in at their free will and get creative. He removed all stuffy office furniture and replaced it with funky table tops without chairs, a coffee bar that came complete with flavored creamers and artificial sweeteners, and a fridge stocked with fruit drinks, sodas and sparkling waters.

On his third day, he called us all into the collaboration room and told us we all needed to show up the next day with our two favorite CD collections, complete with CD covers that we were willing to forfeit over to him for our creative benefit. So, the next day, I handed him a Bruce Springsteen and John Denver CD knowing full well Katie hated both of them. I knew that because every time Doreen played one of them on her iTunes, Katie would pop up in her cubicle and ask her to turn it down.

That morning, I walked into the collaboration room to get some coffee and, just as I tipped the coffee pot to my cup, in walked Katie. As if the universe mirrored my sentiment against her presence, John Denver's "Rocky Mountain High" played over the speakers.

She stopped short of opening the fridge and scanned my shirt. "Orange? Really? That's an interesting choice. It so suits your magnetic, bold, and social personality." She arched an eye and flaunted a smile as she opened the fridge and pulled out the vanilla flavored creamer. "Oh wait. This has nothing to do with originality, does it? You're just following the Orioles crowd."

I continued pouring the coffee and should've just ignored her, but the sarcastic side of my personality pushed my magnetic, bold, and social one aside. "Maybe I just like orange. It's fun."

"It's one of my least favorite colors."

"Not surprising." I placed the coffee pot back on the burner.

"Ah, good jab." She reached for the coffee pot.

I stole the creamer from the counter. "I emailed you some ad copy. Before you go changing the headline on me, I should tell you that Sanjeev already approved it."

She narrowed her lips to the point they disappeared into her mouth. Her eyes zeroed in on me. "Why would you show it to him?"

"Because I really liked it." I stirred my creamy coffee and brought the cup up to my lips for a sip. The warmth steamed my glasses. I pushed past her to get a napkin.

She cradled her coffee mug and laughed. "You're so naïve, which is good for you. Reality can hurt." She turned and walked away, tapping her heels into the ground as if hammering roofing nails with them.

I hated that her headlines outshined mine.

Two days later, Sanjeev called a meeting. He blew me away when he announced to the division that my work on a recent public service announcement won national attention and the segment would be showcased on the CBS news sometime later in the month. I focused the advertorial on bullying and how teachers in elementary schools could better serve the needs of less popular kids by stepping up and protecting them from ridicule. The advertorial outlined some easy to implement actions. Katie had designed the ad, wrote the headline, of course, and changed the entire piece to suit her style. Apparently, when she read my words, she couldn't follow my pattern of thinking, so she changed 'a few things' around. Admittedly, the finished advertorial shined brighter when Katie added the glimmer and meat to it.

"Jane worked tirelessly on this assignment, researching and conducting interviews with school officials, teachers and even students." I had lied to him about that. I actually researched all of it online, and Katie pointed out that weakness. She conducted her own interviews. "Join me in giving Jane a big round of applause."

The entire office applauded, and I blushed. All eyes turned to me. Sanjeev's voice rose above the applause. "Jane, please come up here. We have a little something to give you for all your generous work and talent."

Doreen nudged me forward, and I trudged past the hundred or so employees. The room tunneled before me. A fog buried me. My heart raced. Even the tips of my ears burned.

Sanjeev greeted me with a soft handshake and pulled me into an awkward hug. He smelled like he'd taken a bath in aftershave.

He handed me the shiny, black, etched glass plaque that read 'Outstanding Community Hero Award, presented to Jane Knoll in recognition of her dedication to anti-bullying, safety, and wellness of children.'

I stared at it. Most people in that position might feel the threat of tears or the inclination to bow or say some words of wisdom. Not me. No, I broke out into hysterical giggles. My nerves shot through me and nothing I could do could stop the percolating of laughter that brewed deep within. Even with all eyes pointed at me, I couldn't stop. I laughed harder, trying to stifle the edge of hysterics.

I bolted, cradling my undeserved plaque like a baby.

I ran so fast I twisted my ankle halfway through the crowd. It throbbed, but I didn't cave into the pain until I passed the aisles of cubicles, ran past the bathrooms where I first met Eva, dashed through the back doors to the outdoor trails, and fell to the ground. I winced, watching as my ankle swelled to the size of a Gala apple.

Katie stormed through the double glass doors and sprinted toward me with her face glowering, her lips pursed tightly, and her stride long and purposeful like a track star in a dead heat. She landed at my feet with her hands fisted at her hips. "You are such a selfish person. How dare you take all the credit for that? How could you?"

The sting of her words hurt more than the pain of my throbbing ankle. "I'm sorry. I was embarrassed. Did you see how red my face turned? I couldn't think straight. Everyone blurred. You saw me. I lost it up there."

"You're selfish. We sling crap at each other, but not at times like this. I worked hard on this project. It was important to me. This could've set me up for more assignments just like it." Her chin quivered. Her eyes watered. Her cheeks sunk low.

I felt sorry for her.

Her contempt brought me right back to the last time I saw Rhonda, sitting on the steps to the middle school, staring at me with pained eyes from the lashings I'd dealt her.

"I'm really sorry. I didn't mean to claim it all for myself. I'll be happy to go in and say something."

"Don't you dare," she said with a chill to her voice that sent shivers through me. "You'll just wreak havoc on my career if you do that. Sanjeev would never believe you. You've got him under some kind of spell. You can do no wrong in his eyes. He'll think I put you up to it to stake claim on something that isn't mine." She walked away, shaking her head and sighing. Then, she turned back around. "Next time when you email something like this to him, just as a courtesy, please add my name to the byline of it, too."

"Of course," I said, too numb to rise. I sat back and watched her walk away from me as a loser claiming another person's work as her own.

I was nothing but a dreamer. Katie was the doer.

# #

When I arrived home later that afternoon, I went straight to my office. I read through my wall of rejection letters. The last one, dated over a year ago, stood out to me. It had stopped me from attempting to write another short story. The editor wrote, "This is your fifth submission, and I'd be remiss if I didn't respond accordingly. I just can't connect to the characters in this short story. I'm sorry to burst the bubble, but you're just not very good at writing short stories. Your writing is grammatically fine. What it lacks is emotion. I don't want to spend an hour with these people you created. They bore me. Sorry to be frank. Writing is just not your strong suit, I'm afraid. I'd rather you not waste any more of my or my staff's time."

I locked myself inside my condo for eight days after reading that letter. I ate nothing but rice and beans and rose up out of my bed only to go to the bathroom, to heat up said rice and beans, and to drink water. Larry pulled me out of that funk by calling me to his rescue to remove a cicada from his front door. His frantic yelping and the bright sunshine brought me back to life. When I returned to my condo, I took a shower, pulled on a pair of jeans and a sweatshirt, and buried my fictional writing dreams.

I wrote my first short story in high school when my teacher assigned it to us. I wrote a story about a turtle named Newton who ran away from home and got lost in the woods. My inspiration came from a disturbing situation that happened to my cousin years ago. His pet turtle ran away from home. A man found him later that day cracked and on the side of the road. The story scored big brownie points for me. My teacher sat me down after class one day and urged me to keep writing. She told me my writing was worthy of being published and that I should submit stories to magazines that published them.

She tickled a part of my soul that day. After that, I had spent all my free time writing stories, trying to reclaim the magic of that one short story that stirred my teacher's soul enough for her to tell me I was worthy of something other than being ridiculed. Every editor since had failed to see the same magic as she.

Larry read my old stories and would 'ooh' and 'ah' over them until nausea set in. That's what friends did. They told each other things to build up instead of break down. For instance, I would never tell Larry that he had a better chance of having his skinny ass drafted by the National Football League than he did in being known for his singing. He loved to sing. He sang endlessly and really believed he sounded that good. How could a friend burst that bubble of joy? What would be the point? Singing brought joy to his heart, just as writing had, at one point, done that for me. Now if he ever told me he planned to audition for *American Idol* or something else that could be a potential disaster to his ego, then, I might have to sit him down and have a serious chat with him. Because, that's what friends did for each other.

I'd sat him down on many occasions crying about a rejection letter and begging him to tell me the truth about what he really thought of my writing. Larry, being the good friend, would hug me and tell me it was brilliant.

I would believe that when someone other than my gay, happy friend said that.

I stood staring at the letters, squinting to read some that were scribbled by hand, telling me to keep trying, keep submitting, and keep the words flowing. While some letters were just plain hurtful and cold, others offered hope that one day, when the timing was right, and all the elements aligned properly, I would start writing again.

I stared at the framed sign Larry had given to me two Christmases ago. Its words had comforted me each time I had tacked up a new rejection letter nearby it. *Your finest days are still out in front of you.*

"Maybe," I said. After all, Eva Handel was following me on Twitter now. I made her blush. Best of all, I intrigued her.

If I could accomplish that, surely I could write a decent story and have it published.

Like Katie, I could be a doer, too.

Carr—The Muse

Chapter Six

As a girl who never kissed anyone, I had spent many moments in front of a mirror acting out possible scenarios where I stood before a beautiful girl and flirted. I'd acted out the better part of my life. I pretended to be a great orator, a fun entertainer, a witty friend, a sexy date, oh and of course, an accomplished writer hired to spread my knowledge to the masses.

That morning as I got ready for my quarterly meeting, the one where I supposedly volunteered to speak on the marketing team's behalf, I broke into one such scenario. The entire company would be present for that meeting. Eva would be watching me give the marketing updates via video conference.

My heart rolled.

I dressed my best. I wore a tight pair of dark blue jeans, high heels, and a fitted red button down shirt; clothes I bought at Larry's insistence a year prior after he begged me to go with him to a charity event. He had planned to introduce me to a spectacular girl who worked with him. I caved at the last minute, blaming my absence on a migraine. The outfit came in handy now. I felt sexy, as Larry insisted I would.

I painted my lips with plum lip gloss and applied a double coating of mascara. I pulled my hair back into a low ponytail and decided to allow some fringe around my face. I talked to my reflection, smiling, nodding at just the right inflection points, and moving in closer when I imagined her flirting back with me.

71

I brushed some wisps of hair away from my face with a quick flip of my wrist. Repositioned, I stood tall, hands on my wide hips, and nodded. I imagined a sexy hotel lobby setting with leather back chairs accompanied with a low round table with two glasses of red wine ready for our thirsty lips. She'd be sitting with one leg crossed delicately over the other, her sandals dangling from her pretty toes, and her hair swept over one shoulder like a stole, smooth and silky. Our eyes would meet as I crossed the threshold of no turning back. I'd walk right up to her and introduce myself as CarefreeJanie. She'd slide out of her seat and meet my height, gaze into my eyes, and offer me a warm, tender smile, the kind that set her eyes sparkling and her lips curling upwards in a delightful curve.

We'd sit in adjacent chairs, our feet mere inches from each other, flirting ever so subtly as they swayed to the light soft rock music filtering through the otherwise silent bar. The warmth of the golden accent light would play with the caramel highlights in her hair, bringing out the golden flecks in her dark eyes. We'd spend the night bantering, moving in closer and eventually tickling the softness on each other's bare forearms with our occasional touch to drive a point even deeper. At one point, I'd take her by the hand and twirl her around, dancing my way around her heart with the sweep of Sinatra, the grace of Ginger Rogers, and the allure of Marilyn Monroe.

I loved to dream.

On a creative roll, I imagined a scene where we'd sneak off down a quiet hotel hallway. I'd trace a lone finger down her cheek while staring into her hungry eyes and land on a soft, dewy kiss, complete with lots of petting, caressing, and moaning. I'd be safe in her arms. She'd look at me with admiration and gratitude. A twinkle of guile would sneak from her eyes and hold me in sweet hostage.

She'd bring out my inner glow, and I'd shine my light all over her pretty olive skin, bathing her in warmth. She'd smell just like a spring meadow after rain and feel as soft as satin in my arms. She'd hold my hand up to her heart, and I'd lose my breath in her tantric beats.

My tummy clenched in a delightful tuck.

I stared long and hard at my reflection in the mirror. My eyes twinkled. My skin pinked. My chest danced in a fast four beat rhythm under the pull of my red shirt. The flyaways crawled their way back to my cheeks and teased them, lifting me up and out of the shy geeky girl inside.

In that scenario, Eva would never notice the annoying freckles on my face or the way my upper lip slanted to the left when I smiled. She'd focus only on those parts of me worth a second glance, like my blue eyes, my clear complexion, and my creative mind.

I leaned in closer to the mirror to sneak a better look at my thin lips and my teeth that, up until that moment, were just fine, productive, practical parts of me. I should've whitened them at one of those booths at the mall where the clerk stuck that white thing between the lips and placed that bright blue light above to work its magic.

Did everyone turn into an obsessive, compulsive freak when flirting with someone interesting? Did their hearts pump extra hard and their pussies twitch with such frantic intensity? Was I the only fool too afraid to step into reality and give it a real try?

How I wanted to be that person in real life, staring at Eva with power, mystery, and intrigue. I wanted to dance on her heart and send her twirling.

I looked like a clown with all the makeup caked on my face and dressed up like I was ready to hit the Roxy for a dance fest on my own podium above a sea of crazed, drunken idiots below. I tore a piece of paper towel off the roll and began wiping that ridiculous girl away.

I wiped so hard, my skin burned. I smeared cold cream on my face to help quicken the process of removing the disappointment from my life. I'd never be that girl anyplace other than in front of my bathroom mirror.

I hated makeup. I didn't dress in provocative low-cut shirts unbuttoned down to my boobs. High heels sucked and hurt my feet. And the tight jeans cut into me.

I was fabulous just as designed, as plain Jane. Who wouldn't love to be me, the faded flower on the gray wall?

I continued to rub my skin and question why I couldn't have been born normal. Why couldn't I walk around in a pair of high heels without twisting an ankle? Why did makeup make me look like a scary clown?

What did I expect? After what I did to that poor girl so many years ago, I deserved to look like a clown. I deserved to be easy prey. I deserved to stand alone in my condo and act out fantasies instead of live them.

Really, with that justification, all the girls that bullied me should also be rotting in their apartments like me instead of living extraordinary lives. They probably married rich men and had three kids a piece who they dressed up in prissy clothes and drove to summer camp in their Mercedes. They probably all got together each weekend for summer block parties on their grandiose decks overlooking the waterfront. They probably had perfect asses, toned thighs, and waistlines that didn't need to be unbuttoned to allow for breathing room. No doubt though, in the far reaches of the night, they, too, succumbed to nightmares of fangs and claws digging at them, torturing them into remembering the pain they caused another human being.

The longer I stared at my stupid reflection, the more ridiculous I looked. I scrubbed my face down to a raw state, moisturized it, and tossed the used paper towels in the garbage. Then, I tore off the clothes, ignored my pale reflection as I walked past it, and put on my typical Friday dress down day outfit – a pair of loose fitted jeans with a long t-shirt underneath a short-sleeved Old Navy one. Just for kicks, I left my hair dangling messy in the ponytail.

I stole one last glance at myself and shrugged. "It's not like she'll know I'm CarefreeJanie."

Before walking out of my condo, I hit the spacebar on my laptop and it brightened to life. I logged into Twitter and trickled through my feed, through my mentions, and then finally through my direct messages. My heart flipped when I saw her pretty picture next to a new message. Her smile reached out and tugged at my heartstrings.

"My boss changed plans on me today. I was supposed to video conference in on a meeting with the main branch, but he thinks I should be there instead." Her message continued. "So, now I'm heading to Maryland to be there in person. I'm going to attempt another try at Old Bay. I'll let you know what I think."

My hands flew up to my parched face in full panic mode. I dropped my head into my lap, waiting for the rest of me to catch up with my heart.

# #

I drove in silence, comforted only by the lulls between my engine hums. I pulled into a convenience store to get a pack of gum. I parked and watched a group of teenaged boys and girls prance around each other, laughing and carrying on like awkward, silly kids. The boys wore long hair that fanned in front of their eyes and the girls dressed in black with weaved pink and blue feathers through their choppy hair. A tattoo of an angel with wings draped along one of the girl's shoulder blades. She flirted with the cuter of the boys, tossing her hips around like they were powered by their own utility substation. That girl certainly didn't have a shy vibe hindering her.

How did one go about getting over being shy? How did people just randomly go up to another and strike up a conversation like they'd been talking their whole lives together? What did people say? How did saying hello lead to in-depth discussions on politics or scientific discoveries? Or more importantly, how in the world did saying hello lead to holding hands, making out, and snuggling up in front of a fireplace listening to soft jazz, drinking vodka tonics, and massaging each other's sexual libidos?

How did one go from walking in the front door of a bar to walking down the aisle? Why did others get hit on, but not me? What about me said stay away? I wasn't downright ugly. I wasn't beautiful, either. I stood in that in-between space teetering between common and pretty. I was presentable.

So, why did people pass me by like they passed by a field of growing grass?

# #

We always gathered at an offsite location for our quarterly meetings. That day, we met at Dave and Buster's at the Arundel Mills Mall. My tummy knotted up as I passed through the door and up to the hostess station where Katie stood with a clipboard.

She rattled me. Since receiving the community hero award a few weeks prior, Sanjeev invited me to be a part of the discovery team for the sneaker line instead of her. She worked for weeks on buttering him up for that position, preparing detailed presentations on ways they could strategically position the sneakers in international markets. He walked right past her cubicle and straight to mine, asking me to join him and the other twenty in the focus group for a breakfast meeting. I sucked. I never spoke. I sat like a statue and listened to the other focus group members debate and offer their colorful opinions. Katie would've been much better suited for the role.

In the days that followed my induction into that focus group, she raked me over with sneaky glances and extra critical feedback on my copywriting. She also insulted my intelligence by pointing out my mistakes in front of the marketing department at our morning meetings.

She had taken it all too far. I offered to come clean, but she wouldn't let go of the guilt grip. That angered me.

Katie stood tall at the hostess station, pumping up her smile. "Excited for your speech?"

"I should be asking you that question," I said, mirroring her smug smile.

Her smile widened. "You better believe I am."

"Don't worry. I won't disappoint." I walked away from her and toward the smell of eggs, cinnamon buns, and flavored coffee. I entered the big gaming room, and the buzz and lights of chaos hit me hard. I hated video games. I hated loud noises. I hated the look of frenzied people yelling at machines for proving them unworthy. I scanned the room looking for Eva. Underdressed, I wanted to kick myself for being so careless in my choice. What if no one else wore jeans? What if those flyaways on my face looked ridiculous? What if I lost my voice to her? The fears poked me like a bully and stole all of CarefreeJanie's magical wit.

Doreen landed by my side wearing a loud purple and orange paisley dress. "Hey," she said in her happy beat. "Are you ready?"

"Doreen," I whispered. "I don't want to be here."

She looked me square in the eye. "You're wearing lip gloss. You're not going anywhere." She placed her hand on the small of my back and pushed me toward the back of the establishment, to that tall, slender figure standing like a princess in waiting by the side of the buffet table. Eva looked up at me, then back down. My breath stopped short halfway up my throat.

"That food smells heavenly, doesn't it?" Doreen asked. "Let's get some."

I wanted to run back to the car. She'd cause a scene if I attempted. I struggled to maintain direction as she pushed me closer to where Eva stood. I massaged my glossed lips together, worrying I had overdone them. "Doreen," I said, pulling at her dress like a five-year-old. "I need to go to the bathroom."

She looked down at me. "You don't look so good." She cradled my shoulder with her hand.

I looked back over at Eva. She had scooped eggs onto a small plate for Emily, the eccentric girl in customer service who wore her hair in pigtails most days. They laughed together over something. Eva's whole face blossomed. Her cheeks rose up like sweet plums. Emily tapped her upper arm, lingered on Eva's toned bicep for a moment too long, and then walked away. Eva continued to smile after her. Jealousy ripped through me – jealousy over a life I'd never experience.

I could never make Eva Handel laugh and smile like that. "I need to go now." I shoved off back to the entrance, and back to where Katie stood like a martyr. I rushed past her. "Everything okay?" she asked, her words drowning in exaggerated sweetness.

I waved her off and ran past her to the bathroom.

# #

I managed to weave enough activity into my weekend to keep me from poking into Twitter. I went grocery shopping, washed my sheets, cleaned out my garbage disposal, walked my neighbor's dog, hosed down the wooden steps of the condo, and went to visit my grandmother in the nursing home, where I got roped into playing several songs on the piano. The patients were easy to please and didn't cause me too much discomfort. They wouldn't laugh at me or kick my shins as they passed me by on route to get their meds or have their adult diapers changed. They certainly wouldn't set my parents' backyard shed on fire for kicks or spray paint obscenities about me on the front door. No, that kind of shit only happened to me when I did stupid things like proclaim how badly I wanted to screw my best friend Barbara over and over again under the canopy of stars in my parents' backyard hammock.

By the time I hit the bed on Sunday night, I obsessed less on the whole meeting ordeal and focused more on how much fun I had that day at the nursing home. A few people smiled because of me that day, and that jolted me with some much needed joy. Before dosing off, I sealed in a mental note that I would have to do that more often. My heart lightened as a result.

I dreamed about Eva's chocolate brown hair that night. It wrapped around my fingers so easily as I twirled it and stared into her deep, delicious eyes. I woke up caressing my pillow, oddly turned on. I rose out of bed and staggered off to the kitchen for some coffee. The computer teased me from the counter.

I didn't want to see her reply message because I knew, in my most intelligent way, that regardless if she flirted back with me or not, I could never face her. So, what would be the point? Why torture myself?

I poured myself a cup of coffee and sipped it thoughtfully, gazing over at the laptop waiting for a good enough reason not to sit in front of it and just see if she had responded to my last flirt. "Oh, the hell with it." I rounded the counter, plopped down on the stool, and logged in for the ride.

Her message dangled in front of me like a prism, all sparkly and glistening. "I tried Old Bay again. I'm still not a fan."

I couldn't help myself. I typed back right away. "I must make you a fan."

A moment later, she responded. "I'm a fan. Just not of Old Bay."

"A fan of what?"

"Of you. Of your words. Of the way your words entice me."

I hugged myself. "Thank you. It's what I do. I write."

"Like a published writer?" she asked.

Hadn't she read my lavish bio? "Yup. I've had some stuff read by others." I didn't totally lie on that one.

"I'm in awe of writers. I wish I had that talent."

"It's not talent, just hard work. Anyone can write if she puts her mind to it." I spoke like a real pro, as if I owned a bookshelf stuffed with my novels, and as if I earned a living writing by a dim light in my condo sipping sangria and smoking cigarettes as I pounded the keys on an overworked keyboard.

"What do you write?"

Paintbrush in hand, I could create a fun imaginary world full of color and mystique. Who needed to write a novel when one could play out the scenario real time with a real love interest at her fingertips? Perhaps that could be a working novel. A girl falls in love with another girl via Twitter. They live happily ever after in the Twitterverse, tossing each other romantic tweets and creating their life as they pressed the enter key.

I flicked some color on my imaginary canvas. Perhaps I wrote mystery novels. Of course, that could prove much too difficult if she started asking questions. I flicked my illusionary brush with a deeper color. Perhaps I wrote horror stories. Did I want her to think of me as a deep, dark girl who took pleasure in scaring the shit out of people? I wanted to stir her mind with intriguing thoughts. I stroked my canvas with pretty tones. "I write romantic stories."

"Romantic, as in girl-meets-boy, or romantic as in girl-meets-girl (wink)?"

Oh that wink stirred wonderful things in me, causing my legs to tremble and my nipples to tingle. "Girl-meets-girl of course. That is what you prefer, I hope (wink)?"

A force outside of my control typed those flirts; a force that grew a garden of flirts that bloomed organically and on cue with when I needed them to blossom so that at any time, I could pluck one up and shower her with its brilliance.

"I want to read one of your stories. What's your name so I can look one up?"

An electric shock zapped me back to my dull condo with its practical lighting and monotone walls. *Great job. Open your big mouth.* I side-stepped her question on my name. "They're just short stories in anthology books. I'll send you something."

"I'll be waiting."

I searched my garden of flirts for something smooth. "Sure. Listen, I've got to run. Here's to us both enjoying a beautiful day."

I logged off, and the panic drove like shards through me. I deemed nothing I wrote worthy enough for her beautiful eyes. I'd need to rework something. I ignored that I only had thirty minutes to get showered, eat, and drive to work. Instead, I ventured into my office and straight to my file cabinet where I saved printouts of everything I ever wrote, including that first and only piece my teacher had praised.

About thirty minutes into my journey to Jane Knoll short story hell, I realized that all of those letters covering my wall were accurate. My writing sucked and needed some major lift if I ever wanted to see my name in a byline someday. After reading the third sucky story, I called Sanjeev and told him I wasn't feeling well. I'd be taking a sick day. I needed at the very least eight solid hours to write something that could potentially tickle that girl's life. I blamed my sick day on the sour stomach from the quarterly meeting.

Doreen called me not more than five minutes later. "Katie gave your speech."

"Did she mess up?"

"Get this. She acted like the saving grace of marketing. When Sanjeev announced he needed a volunteer because you had gotten sick, she stepped right up and acted like she had just forfeited her seat on one of the lifeboats of a sinking ship."

"Of course she did."

"Sanjeev winked at her." She said that like I would be heartbroken. "She joined him and the new events manager for lunch after that. She came back afterwards and told me that Sanjeev invited her to be on the advisory board committee."

"Good for her."

"Don't be jealous."

I rolled my eyes. "I'm not jealous."

"She's got nothing on your talents."

If only she knew how untrue that was. "Thanks, my friend. Listen, I've got to run. I'm still not feeling great."

Thirty minutes later, still sitting on my couch contemplating my story, I decided I'd procrastinated enough. I cleaned my bathtub, folded my clothes, and hoped an answer would just sweep into my brain and take it on a pleasant journey through the lives of two people falling in love.

By noon, and with my hands resembling the finer side of a pumice stone from scouring the tiles in my bathroom, I began pacing my condo in search of an idea. I folded my hands behind my back and willed a plotline to come pouring down on me. I passed by my magazine rack several times, then finally dropped down on my knees in front of them and started scanning them for ideas.

I picked up *Reader's Digest* and breezed through the table of contents. A girl named Betty Lou Summers wrote a short piece called "My Little Secret" about a housekeeper's diary. I couldn't imagine how many times Ms. Betty Lou Summers must have jumped around her living room when she first saw her story published in *Reader's Digest*. I would have broken a leg for sure.

I picked up *Mademoiselle* and scanned the articles about fashion, dating, kissing, picnicking, friendships, and panicked some more. What did I know about any of those topics, and how would I ever tie them to romance?

What place did I have writing about any of them, especially kissing?

I needed to live those things. I needed to experience them. I needed to understand literally and figuratively what it felt like to hold someone, breathe in someone, and fall in love with someone.

I needed wine.

I lifted the key to Larry's condo off my key hook and hunted for some sweet red wine. In addition to scoring an open bottle, I also took off with a bag of Doritos and a half eaten sleeve of thin mints. I needed inspiration. I prepped to launch into my most important writing. I needed it to shine. I needed it to dig deep. I needed Eva to reply back with more exclamation points than words.

I drank two glasses of the wine and ate half the bag of Doritos and two of the thin mints before I finally took out my kitchen timer, sat down at my laptop, and stared at the blank white screen. Before setting the timer, I needed a jumpstart – a word, a sentence, anything to get the fingers typing for ten solid minutes without critique. I drummed my antsy fingers against the counter and stared at my reflection in the toaster oven. I traced my finger down the side of my face, imagining Eva's featherlike touch. I closed my eyes and breathed deeply, seeking that sweet spot of peace.

I imagined Eva coaxing me with her soft voice, urging me to write something sweet and romantic. Her eyes would follow my fingers as I typed, mesmerized by their ability to follow my mind's lead. She would lean in close, bathing me in her pure light, and erasing all traces of fears and insecurities.

Eva, my muse, would nourish me with rich energy, refreshing all tired pulses, nerves, and cells. Her flirty powers would lift me up and open my mind to serve as a symbiotic partner to the world that existed outside my condo and sheltered, boring life.

I opened my eyes at that point, poured myself another generous helping of wine, and took to my couch. My head spun delightfully and my fingers and toes buzzed. I leaned back against my couch and sipped my wine, imagining Eva curled up beside me, our legs entwined, her hair falling like feathers over her bare shoulder, and a sultry smile resting like a twinkle on her face. I closed my eyes, breathed in the wine, and imagined Eva's soft lips brushing up against mine. In that reverie, she swept in like a graceful ballerina, bathing me in her sweet breath. Her lips—soft, moist, and warm—guided me to a romantic spot where together we twirled on point to a flamenco beat that rose and fell in alternating quick and slow successions. Our tongues swayed suggestively, hypnotizing us into a space flowing with elegance, passion, and perfection. My heart soared to great heights, and leaped in sync with hers as she carried me along her fluidity in her strong and defined arms. Ever light with her touch, my lips melted under the beauty of hers. I craved her and wanted to caress her soft body against my own.

When I opened my eyes, I floated like a feather back down to Earth, breathing heavily, chest bellowing in and out rather quickly, and the most delicious twitch taking up flight in between my legs. I cradled my arms around myself and enjoyed the pulse that radiated through me.

When I could stand without risk of falling and cracking my head open on my coffee table, I walked over to my kitchen counter. Move over Jane. CarefreeJanie controlled the driver's seat now.

I began writing. I wrote over five thousand words without ever even setting the kitchen timer for my allotted ten minutes. I just wrote, ignoring the red marks under misspelled words and the comma splices, and the incorrect verb tenses. I couldn't backtrack. I had too much in me that threatened to drown me if I didn't get the words out onto that screen. I poured myself into that story about a passionate kiss between two women set on a seaside bench, sharing an unquenchable desire, a forbidden moment, and a truth too powerful to deny. I ended on a sultry note and dropped my head to my knees to catch my breath.

How would I live a happy, fulfilled life without ever indulging in the touch of her soft lips on mine?

# #

Larry and I sorted clothes that night in silence, each caught up in our own reveries. He was probably thinking about his date with Tim later that night after we finished up our laundry session.

Larry had first met Tim at the mall. He walked into Outdoor World and headed over to the rock climbing mountain in the center of the store. People were clapping and whistling, and so he picked up his pace to catch a piece of the buzz. He stood behind a dozen or so other people and watched a man, with the best calves he'd ever seen – his words, not mine – mount the side of the fake mountain like a monkey. He swung his arms and catapulted himself up with the ease of a child playing on a jungle gym. When he reached the summit, he waved at all the people below. As Larry recalled, the man looked right into his eyes and winked. Well, Larry, being the big 'in-person' flirt that he was, latched onto that wink and invited the guy to get some Mexican food at Chevy's. Larry said he knew from the moment the guy asked for a Cosmo over a beer that he adored him.

Larry dumped his pile of clothes in the washer. "The best thing about this guy is that he runs his own mortgage company. He's got twenty loan officers working for him." He cocked his head waiting for me to agree that yes, indeed, any man would be lucky to have him, the great catch.

I turned to my washing machine instead and spoke while pouring my detergent in the hole. "When do I get to meet him?"

"You're going to meet him soon. I promise. He's different than the rest I usually date, though."

I fed coins into the machine. "How so?"

He wet his lips and pulled his lower one into his mouth the way he did when something stressed him. "Well, he's in a complicated situation."

"How complicated?" I slid into our usual seats by the window, careful not to touch the arms of the chair because I'd seen too many people stuff their face with food and then run their grimy hands all over the arms. Larry just stared ahead out the window.

He crossed his arms over his chest. "Nothing we can't handle," he said in his high-pitched, I'm-just-fine voice.

I sat still and took in his stress. "If you don't tell me, I can't promise you're going to sleep well in the next few nights." I looked over his crossed legs to the magazines sitting idle on the table next to him. "Can you pass me the Mademoiselle?"

He exhaled through his nose and his nostrils grew large, flaring like a bull. "I can't stand when you do that." He stood up.

I remained calm with my hands folded neatly in my lap. "When I do what?" I loved toying with him like that and seeing him come all unglued.

"Bully me with vague threats."

"Bully? I'm not a bully." I stood up and faced him. "How dare you call me a bully?"

"But you are." He stared down at me.

Everyone stopped their folding, their pouring, and their reading and stared at us. A man reading a newspaper folded the tip of the paper down to get a good look. A mother with her baby stopped staring into her child's eyes and instead took in our sights. The attendant eased into a lazy stance against the counter and watched us instead of her soap opera on the television above her folding station.

He broke the stare, and his chin buckled. "You can be a little mean." He looked back at me. "It hurts sometimes." His chin revved into overdrive on the quivering.

I grabbed for his arm. "What's really going on here?"

He exhaled, not taking his serious eyes from me. "I really like this one, and I want you to be happy for me."

"I was just messing with you." I tousled his hair, and he backed away.

"Easy. I kind of liked the way it fell into place tonight." Finally, he broke into a small smile. Not quite big enough to ease my concern that my best friend almost started to cry right in the middle of ABC Wash Center for reasons still foreign to me.

We sat back down. An awkward echo of unspoken words sat between us like a mountain. I thumbed through a magazine. He joined me, and the two of us sat there in silence. I read a short story about a girl who traveled to two different continents in search of herself. She searched for two months in mosques, in poor towns, and in overcrowded city streets for a sense of wonderment that would entitle her to the fresh sprig of life and the power of being valued. Plagued by the guilt of bad mistakes, she craved to find the truth and forgiveness that would set her free to indulge one day in love and blessings. When she landed back on her own country's soil, she finally discovered that she didn't have to look as far to find her answer. Her answer stood at the baggage carousel with a dozen red roses and a big sign that said "Will You Marry Me?" I tossed the magazine down with an extra hard lashing. "How do these people get this crappy stuff published?"

Larry continued reading his gardening magazine and simply murmured in agreement.

"Let me ask you something," I said to him. I tore the magazine away from his face. "Do you think the fantasy of being with someone is better than actually being with someone?"

"Depends who we're talking about. If you mean that guy Jeff I dated, fantasy won on that one." Jeff kissed like a sloppy mess according to Larry. "Most times, I'm pretty satisfied with reality."

"Do you think it's possible for someone to imagine the taste of say a cherry pie if she never in fact ever ate a piece of cherry pie?"

He stopped reading and pondered that with a tilt of his head and a massage to his now stilled chin. "You'd have to have one heck of an imagination. But sure. I suppose if you concentrated on what a cherry pie might taste like, you could imagine the tartness mixed with the sweetness."

We stared straight ahead contemplating that. Finally, I released my concern on a deep breath. "I wrote a short story that I want to get your opinion on before I let anyone else read it."

A grin stretched across his face revealing deep grooves where his happiness always sat. "It's about time." He dropped his head and perused his magazine again. "You know I'm going to love it." He flipped to a new page. "I love everything you write, darling."

"This one is very different. I need you to read it objectively." I didn't take my eyes from the washing machine in front of us. "This one has some kick to it."

"All of your stuff has kick to it." He sounded like a father complimenting his young child's wild, red head full of unruly, untamable cowlicks.

"I want you to read it before you go out tonight."

He flipped to another page and winced. "I'm picking him up at eight."

I reached into my satchel and pulled it out. "Read it now."

His eyes lingered on the stack of papers that my fingers cradled. "Right now. With you sitting right here?"

I needed his reaction. "Right now."

I sat still pretending to read more of the horrible magazine. I watched Larry from my peripheral vision. My heart leaped when he smiled, soared when he groaned most likely at a conflicting point for the characters, and twirled when he shook his head wildly side-to-side in obvious agreement with my characters.

Twenty minutes later, he sighed and said, "Wow." He stared at the last page with awe.

I sat up tall, allowing my smile to fully embrace the moment. "Wow, as in…?"

When he turned to look at me, I saw the slightest twinkle stemming from his watery eyes, and that caused my eyes to spring much of the same. "Wow as in *far* different."

I fished. "Far different in a good way?"

He cocked his head. "Give me a break. Like you even have to ask that." His forehead creased. "I take it to write this kind of sexiness that things are going well with that girl Eva?"

I blushed for the first time ever in front of Larry. "A girl's got to keep some things secret." I couldn't even look at him.

He shoved at me. "Tell me."

"I've been flirting with her." I finally looked up at him. "A lot. You'd be proud."

His smile said it all.

And, I'm sure mine did, too.

# #

When I returned from the laundromat, I went straight to my computer, logged into Twitter, and sent Eva a direct message alerting her to look out for my short story I had promised her. I did that without taking my pocketbook off my shoulder. Then, without blinking, I emailed her the story.

Not until I sat down with a glass of milk and some chocolate chip cookies, picked up my mail from the past few days, and thumbed through some bills and advertisements did I really stop and contemplate what I had just done. Eva Handel's eyes would soon scan my literary work, my words. She would absorb and bury them deep into her subconscious mind.

In a matter of half an hour, if she had already started to read, she would intimately connect to that part of my brain that fired off lustful chemicals.

That thrilled me.

I stared at my laptop from the couch wondering if Eva's eyes were moving to the beat of my sentences, if her heart fluttered along with their rhythm, and if her inner thighs were squeezing together to intensify quivers that could quite possibly be stemming from my words.

I rose and paced my floor. The confidence of a few minutes prior waned along with my milk and cookies. I stopped in front of the mirror, took a good long hard look at myself and wondered what Eva would think of my red cheeks, my messy blonde ponytail with darker roots, my squinty eyes, and the half-moon wrinkle on my chin. One of my bullies once told me I reminded her of a Vidalia onion. Since then, I'd never eaten one and I refused to pass them by at the grocery store.

I didn't look like a Vidalia onion at the present moment. My skin actually glowed and my eyes sparkled. I fixed my ponytail, blew a few loose strands away from my face, and smiled. My lips were rosier than usual. I'd dare say even kissable. My lips needed the moisture of Eva's. I traced my finger along my bottom lip imagining Eva's finger in its place. I gazed into my eyes and imagined what Eva would see in them. Currently, my pupils were large. They took over the blue of my irises. Would she see a woman yearning to kiss her? Would she see a woman craving to run her fingers down the heart of her cheeks? Would she see a woman who wanted to lose herself in her long, thick dark hair? Or had I become so adept at hiding that woman, that all she'd see was fear in my eyes and a lack of confidence? Would I be able to pull off a strong enough flirty vibe to send her reeling over the edge of self-control?

I exhaled a shaky breath.

I shook my head, walked away from my reflection, and sat at the breakfast bar in front of my computer. Before checking my email to see if she'd read it, I reread my story. I cringed when I found two typos. Surely, she'd see those and see an amateur, liar, dreamer, illusionist, idealist, or worse, failure.

In essence, I had failed. I was twenty-nine-years-old and never been on a date, never held hands with someone, and never even, up until recently, flirted. How dare I attempt to write about a kiss convincing enough to curl the toes and fingers of Eva Handel? I'd imagined many people accomplished that already. What would she ever see in me, the coward who used computers as her shield against the cruel and bitter world? What would Eva ever see in someone like me if she ever met the real me, not CarefreeJanie?

What if she wanted to meet CarefreeJanie?

I couldn't let it happen. I would never be as skillful without my keyboard and computer screen as companions.

CarefreeJanie offered me a chance to taste the sweetness of delivering a compliment. She allowed me to tickle a girl's heart without freaking her out with my social awkwardness. As CarefreeJanie, I could leap like a well-trained dancer and spin her head in wide, wonderful circles. At least in my mind's eye, Eva would experience all of that.

What if she read my story and didn't like it? Would she scan it, looking just for keywords she could later cite when we tweeted again?

If she hated my story, then she would hate my story. Nothing I could do at that moment would be able to affect the way she responded to it. I sat victim to the second hand click on my kitchen wall clock, shaking my legs and staring at my two glaring typos. If she hated it, better to know upfront and create my getaway plan before I got sucked in too deep into her enticing world. Of course, knowing what I knew about her already, if she hated it, she'd never tell me. I guessed by her sweetness that she never critiqued anything more than Old Bay and her own silly mistakes like mismatched shoes. If she read it and hated it, she'd probably send me a direct message saying something like my third grade teacher would've said to me, 'Oh great job, sweetie.'

Living life always in the midst of the shadows of doubt, I could read through the lines. When my mother would write me an email and use an exclamation point, I knew what she really meant was 'nice attempt' instead of 'way to go.' When Doreen would fill her emails with three or more smiley faces, what she really meant was 'I feel sorry for you so here you go my friend, some smiles to get you through your sad life.'

If Eva responded with anything less than five adjectives, I'd know instantly that she didn't like it.

My throat dried up. A sense of dread scratched its way up my spine the longer I sat waiting.

An hour later, I decided that if she hated it, I wouldn't care. I would simply move forward in my life the way I always had, one foot, albeit a clumsy foot, in front of the other in a direction that suited me. If I couldn't be a writer, maybe I'd go back to school for something completely opposite—accounting or chemistry or something that used the other part of my brain. Maybe I'd spent too much time trying to activate the wrong side of my brain? What if Barbara called it right all those years ago when she told me that I should never put pen to paper because all I ever wrote was icky and gross? Was I that idiot who thought she could sing, tried out for *American Idol*, and got placed on the finale for the world to laugh at my naivety in thinking all along that I was the next Mariah Carey?

How would I ever know? How did anyone really know unless she braved all and tossed her work out into the world for strangers to critique? Pen names appealed to me suddenly. They offered writers a way to avoid ridicule and reinvent ourselves, should our first set of books suck. If bad reviews poured in, we could change to a new name and toss another book out into the world, hoping it was strong enough to stand on its own and be worthy of literary praise that won awards, gained the attention of high profile publishers, and created a wide gap from where the writer stood financially one month to the next.

I refused to waste any more time worrying about what Eva thought. The longer I worried, the more annoyed I became. I braced to launch a full scale defensive attack against her, and she was probably dining over a friend's house getting drunk on cheap merlot and hadn't even known I sent her a story to read.

I played a game with myself. If I opened my email and she had not responded, I would never tweet with her again because my heart couldn't take that kind of pressure. I would chalk it up to destiny. If the universe wanted me to continue flirting with a girl I never planned to meet, then she would email me within the next hour. If the universe planned to protect me from being sucked into the intoxicating vortex, then I would know by my empty inbox. I'd let fate decide.

I set my timer for one hour, then drew a bath.

I lounged back against my bath pillow and soaked up the steam. My head swirled, so I closed my eyes and inhaled deep, rejuvenating breaths. I placed my hand to my chest and relaxed with its beat. I pictured Eva sitting behind me, holding me in her arms. Her hands grazed around my waist and her chin cradled in the crook of my neck. She'd tickle my neck with her lips, dragging her tongue against my skin. She'd tickle my belly button with her fingers and caress me tighter when I giggled. She'd forfeit the tickle for my serious escape into her hands where we'd fondle each other's palms as we stared into each other's eyes. She'd say to me in a breathy whisper, "You are so beautiful, my princess. So beautiful."

My tummy rolled.

I cradled a handful of bubbles and blew on them. Then, I spread some bubbles over my arms, chest, and breasts, circling my nipples and watching as they hardened. My breathing quickened, my lower body buzzed. The air lightened. The bubbles smelled stronger. My skin felt softer.

Eva Handel, what have you done to me?

An hour later, I emerged, puckered and wrinkled. I sat in front of my computer, scared for what my eyes would see. I opened my email and braved all.

There before me, shiny, new, and bold was my beautiful present, an unopened email from my unknowing muse, the beautiful Eva Handel.

From: Eva Handel ehandel11@gmail.com

To: CarefreeJanie CarefreeJanie@yahoo.com

Sent: Wednesday, July 25, 2012 8:46 PM

Subject: Re: a little something I promised you, if you have the time…

If I have the time? Are you kidding me? Janie, it is okay if I call you Janie? Janie, my heart is swelling right now. I wouldn't even know what word to type to express what your story just did to me. I am flushed. I am in love with these characters. I want to hang out with these characters. I want them as friends. The kiss moved me like you can't imagine… oh Janie, the kiss. You are brilliant. You are talented. You need to tell me where this was published so I can run out, buy a copy and have you autograph it. Where is this available?

Hop on Twitter. PLEASE!

Your newest fan,

Eva

Before the clock could click through a second, I landed on Twitter.

"You are so sweet," I wrote.

"Oh my gosh, honey, I'm still reeling from reading."

She called me honey. The word chimed like a beautiful song. "You're too kind."

"How do you do it? How do you place words together and make them come alive like you do?"

"See, now you're making me blush."

"I wish I could see you blush," she wrote.

"You realize you'll always have to flatter me this way now, right? There's no cheapening out on adjectives after all this gushing."

"I want more," she wrote.

I soared high. I floated way past the confines of my condo and up to where eagles hung out. "You're super inflating my ego."

"It's well deserved. You're very talented."

We messaged for almost an hour nonstop. She told me all about her favorite pastime—acting—and how she dreamed of a career in front of the camera. She told me about all of the plays she acted in and how she enjoyed performing in dinner theatres in front of full audiences that clapped and cheered. She asked me questions about my writing process, and I made things up as I typed, citing wine as a great muse for stories that required I go deep. She told me about her cat, Jarvis, a Siamese who liked to eat lettuce and hang out on the top of her couch while she read each night. When she spoke about that, I imagined curling up next to her and laughing as Jarvis tapped our heads with his paw.

She had just explained her new job to me, and how excited she was to be a part of something fun and stimulating, when she suddenly tossed out a message that rocked my world.

"I wish I could kiss you," she wrote.

"I would love that."

"Mwah."

My tummy flipped. "I liked that."

We continued flirting and chatting about our writing and acting dreams when she said, "So far everything I've acted in has been kind of silly. I need something powerful and emotional to get me in the door." She continued. "I need something more compelling."

"Who's been writing your stuff?"

"Me. It's not my strength. Hey—want to be my writer?"

"Ha. Sure. I'll just jot a script down on the backside of a napkin next time I'm at Starbucks and send it to you."

"I'm not kidding. I need something deeper and more meaningful to work with. I'm thinking Sundance Film Festival worthy."

"Maybe I'll squeeze some writing in between my other projects and surprise you one of these days."

"If you write one like your story, I definitely have a future."

"That is the sweetest thing anyone's ever said to me." I broke into a big smile. "You made my day." Then for the sheer thrill, I added, "Babe."

"You just made my day by calling me babe. Mwah."

"I'm glad." I stared at her word mwah. Its meaning blew like a gentle breeze across my face. "By the way, maybe it's just because I'm a word girl, but I love the word mwah."

"Do you just like the word mwah? Not necessarily my mwah?"

My head swirled. I loved flirting with that woman. I surprised myself with how I so easily reached up and plucked wit from the air. "Words alone mean nothing to me without passion behind them."

"Can you elaborate? You know, I'm a bit low on understanding deep meanings (wink)."

Her toying tickled me. "I highly doubt that you're low in understanding anything with deep meaning." I continued typing. "Okay, here goes: your mwah carries passion; therefore, I like YOUR mwah."

"Ah, my heart is flipping. Hey, can I get a mwah, too?"

My heart galloped. "Of course. I can't just take and not give. I'm so not the selfish type. So, here you go: mwah and XOXO."

"Are you flirting with me?"

"Who? Me?" I asked, giggling like a fool in my condo. The rush intoxicated me. "Do you like it?"

"It's making it hard to resist you."

"Who said you have to resist me?" Even my fingers pulsed.

"I wish I could meet you in person," she wrote.

I couldn't inhale deeply enough to catch a breath. I needed to exercise some restraint before CarefreeJanie lost complete control and landed me in a heap of trouble. "I must rest this beating heart of mine."

"What is your beating heart saying? Is it telling you to come close to me?"

My underwear had never been so wonderfully wet before. "Hmm, some thoughts are just better left to remain a mystery."

"I like mysteries. You know what else I like?"

"Don't leave me hanging."

"I really like talking with you," she wrote.

I moaned and fell over for a brief second to take it all in. "I'm not going anywhere. I enjoy this, too."

She sent me a wink.

"You know what I really like?" I asked.

"Writing a script for me?"

"Ha. One track mind," I wrote. "I like your mwahs a lot."

"Come close, so I can give you a big mwah."

I closed my eyes and sealed in the warmth of her. "Mwah and a big hug."

We signed off and I remained glued to my stool, squeezing my legs together to enjoy the trembling and mounting pleasure.

I would never be the same again.

Carr—The Muse

Chapter Seven

I've never been a health nut. In fact, describing me as a couch potato wouldn't be too far of a stretch. I much preferred sitting in a sauna and pretending that body fat melted off on its own than mounting a treadmill or pedaling on a stationary bike to nowhere.

Of course, all that would change now I suspected after reading through Eva's online profiles on various social networking sites. Pictures of her covered in mud, climbing up rope mountains, skiing down steep hills, and pounding volleyballs at other people drove me to that conclusion. Eva was athletic. She ran road races, swam open water, cycled up and down hills, crawled through mud, and tackled every sport known to man, even martial arts. What did the woman not do?

I wanted to be fit and healthy suddenly.

I had joined many gyms in my lifetime only to look like a fool walking in the places. Pretty girls with toned muscles pranced around acting like if they weren't working out, they'd all of a sudden gain ten pounds of fat and look, heaven forbid, like me. My romp into a gym always started and ended in much the same fashion. I'd sit in my car for a good half hour planning my circuit. Once all people cleared from the parking lot, I'd dash out and hope no one saw me walking in because surely they'd laugh at me for even trying to compete on the level of those beautiful women and chiseled men. I could just imagine the hushed voices whispering in their heads saying things like 'this girl better not get in my way.'

I carried an extra twenty pounds, and it all gathered around my middle. A convention of fat cells met and partied on, clinging to the hopes that I'd keep sitting around watching television and eating yummy treats that dripped of sugar and salt. I didn't want to be a size two, but I also didn't want to be one of those who pretended to be in love with my above average size.

Whenever I had entered a gym and stared at all that complicated equipment with its shiny metal and dangerous curvy fixtures, my self-conscious whistle always played a cacophony of noise where reason and logic should've chimed in. Upon entering, I typically walked directly to the locker rooms where I'd hide behind the curtain and persuade myself that not everyone stared at me or waited to have a good laugh at my expense. Bullying brought on strange, compulsive behavior like that. It forced people like me to sit in stalls behind curtains, hiding until all people vacated the locker room and I could enter without humiliation. Fear of humiliation shrouded me constantly. If someone stared too long at me, cocked her head too much to the side, or rolled her eyes too quickly in my direction, I braced for an attack.

The longer I mulled over Eva's athletic pictures, the more I decided against going the gym route. I'd start with DVDs and work my way up to gym member. Or maybe just forget the whole stupid idea of working out and Eva Handel and go back to safety mode where my fat tummy and dull hair didn't matter.

Yes, we flirted a bit beyond friendly the other day. That flirting reshaped my world. I would bet my condo that Eva, having already experienced many flirty romps through Twitterland, thought little of it. She'd get over me just as quickly as she discovered me.

I couldn't bear to have her be disappointed in the real me. How long could I keep up the charade of being an athlete myself, running marathons like they were romps through the city park? I couldn't compete with that gorgeous lady, and I certainly didn't want to be the fool in the end assuming she'd actually enjoy life with someone like me, the real plain Jane who worried about things like whether words would stay trapped in the back of my throat when I opened my mouth to speak.

I wouldn't know what to do with her.

The flirts probably didn't even mean anything to her. She was just a nice person who liked to have fun. She could walk up to anyone in real life and flirt. She didn't need a computer screen and keyboard as her crutch. She'd get tired of that quickly, no doubt, and beg to meet me.

I couldn't imagine the scene. I couldn't very well get drunk on sangria every time I wanted to date her. I'd surely climb to a size twenty in no time.

I faced a hopeless fork in the road.

So, I made another one of those promises with myself. If I opened my Twitter and had a message from her, I'd take that as a sign to have a bit more fun with it before putting it to rest. If there was no message from her, I'd cut myself off and walk away from the addiction.

I opened Twitter, and she beckoned me right away with her mysterious force, luring me back into that land of flirts.

We bantered back and forth a little, then, as if fate sat above my keyboard and started messing with me, she asked me if I worked out. Of course I was like, "Oh my gosh, yes, of course. All the time." And I even threw in another 'babe.'

"Fitness is so sexy. I admire when people honor their bodies and treat them like the temples they are."

"Oh, yeah, absolutely." I sucked in my gut, willing it to go away.

"Do you run?"

Oh, yes, sure. From situations like this typically. "I do a little light jogging from time to time. It clears the mind." *Shut up, Jane!*

"I'm coming to Maryland next week. Do you want to join me for a run?"

My heart drummed way too much. "Next week you say?"

"I checked the weather and it's going to be blue skies and sunny every day."

I treaded in water much too deep. "Are you kidding?" I tossed in a frown. "Seriously next week?" I could lie and tell her I was heading out of town for a friend's wedding. She'd want to see pictures for sure. I could say I faced a strict deadline for a work project that would require me to focus the entire time on just that. Then, she'd ask me where I worked. My CarefreeJanie cover would be blown, and all the fun would vanish as quickly as it arrived. Better she continued to believe I earned my living writing short stories about passionate kisses.

"You're not going to be there are you?"

I waited for my garden of insights to grow something I could use. Nothing did. When I found myself in a state of doubt, vague always worked best. "No. I've got a prior commitment."

"Next time, I guess."

Thank God. "What a shame. Maybe I'll surprise you and get up to see you first." I just had to keep the ball rolling.

"Come and I'll take care of you."

I could just see her, bending over me with a blanket, tucking me into her couch, kissing my forehead with her petal soft lips, and brushing a few strands of my hair away. "I bet you will."

"Mmm. I really like you, CarefreeJanie."

My core filled with sweet joy. "Likewise (wink)."

"I hope you have a great rest of the day. I'm off to get my motorcycle serviced."

I had seen her straddled over her shiny blue motorcycle in many of her pictures on Facebook. Of course, I couldn't tell her that. "Oh, you ride a motorcycle?"

"Yup. So much easier than dealing with a car in the city. I'll give you a ride one of these days."

"I'd like that."

"Me too."

#

I ran over to Larry's condo and stole his precious Insanity DVDs. He had praised that Shaun T guy for getting him into respectable shape the past summer. For three months, Larry dedicated himself to spending every morning with Shaun T and the gang, sweating and pumping his muscles full of life and vigor. He glowed. He walked taller. He even managed to turn more heads.

I needed that.

Within fifteen minutes, water bottle filled, sports bra in place, couch moved back, and Larry's yoga mat front and center, I began jogging in place as Shaun T, with his gleaming bald head and rock hard body, instructed me to breathe, dig deeper, and follow his lead. I watched the timer at the bottom of the screen. It hadn't even moved a minute. My heart already raced, my face burned, and the sweat already sprang up on my forehead. I felt great. I broke into jumping jacks, mountain climbers, and ski abs like I'd been doing that workout my whole life. I inhaled, exhaled, and tore through the workout, proud of myself for pushing myself into that frenzy where my heart beat faster than it had in years. Then Shaun

T instructed me to get a swig of water so we could go into stretching now that our muscles were nice and warmed up.

Apparently, I had just endured the warm-up.

Before I knew it, I jumped into full workout mode. About half way into the first set of circuit exercises, I quit. I couldn't take one more squat. I sprawled out on Larry's yoga mat with my arms and legs spread wide, panting and willing breath to once again enter my body and relieve me of the nagging pull on my lungs.

Half an hour later, I climbed to my feet and sat in front of my laptop again. I peeked at the pictures of Eva I had downloaded from her Facebook; the ones of her covered in mud with clothes clinging to her muscles. Yup, I turned from innocent twenty-nine-year-old virgin to creepy stalker overnight.

She was so healthy and vibrant.

I wanted to be just like her.

I wanted for once not to be embarrassed about the way I looked. I wanted to be able to snap a photo of myself and be proud of the image I captured.

I could start slowly. I didn't need to kill myself with Shaun T and the gang.

I would start out with a walk the next day.

Yep, I could take charge of such an exercise life. That woman powered me with something far greater than any junk food could. She made me want to be a better version of myself.

#

In the days that led up to Eva's visit to main headquarters, I talked to Larry about Eva coming to town. He told me I was absolutely nuts not to walk up to her that time, smile, and congratulate her on wearing the same shoes.

When the meeting day arrived, she messaged me. "What a shame you aren't around today for that run. I've never seen the sky so blue."

"You sure know how to tempt a girl, don't you?"

"We could take a ride on my motorcycle after and get lost somewhere on the open road."

I pictured the two of us together on her bike. I'd be cradled up against her, smiling into the wind with my hair blowing all around. I swam around in that scene, lingering in its sweet wake when I boldly typed back, "A girl on a bike. Can you be any hotter?"

"Come for a ride with me today."

"Oh, how I wish." I needed to stop it before she peeled back the corners of CarefreeJanie. "Hey babe, I've got to run. Safe travels."

# #

I dressed extra nicely that day, even though I'd avoid her at all cost. I even blew dried my hair smooth and wore a light coating of foundation to smooth out my freckles. I drove in, and when my building rose on the horizon, my throat clenched. In just a few short minutes I would see my beautiful Twitter crush.

I imagined the scene. She'd be pouring herself a cup of coffee and most likely be wearing a pencil skirt and a fitted button-down dress shirt that hugged her waistline. She'd lean forward to ensure the coffee landed in her petite mug. That would cause her calf muscle to flex, and I would undoubtedly walk right past the collaboration room and back to my cubicle, beet-faced and choking back a giggle. Doreen would have to come out of her cubicle and ask me what happened. I would back down and tell her I just tripped, and Doreen would be kind enough to walk away with all questions squelched and swept away out of sight.

I would try to get close to her again once she slipped into the bathroom. I would enter a good thirty seconds after she did so as not to appear like I was, in fact, stalking her. I'd just go in and pretend to wash some ink off my hands. She'd be in the stall, and I could once again examine her shoes, her shapely ankles, and maybe even her cute, painted toes. My heart fluttered imagining myself only a few dozen feet away from her again. She'd walk out and over to the sink next to me, smile, then her face would blossom into a sneaky grin, knowing I had been the one to catch her the first time in that precarious situation. That would relieve all pressure from me and impose it on her. Of course, she'd take it in stride and continue to smile coyly at me with her head bowed, her eyes shadowed by a hint of embarrassment, and then a twinkle as she glanced up and saw me watching her. Our eyes would lock in an intense moment of recognition that something just sparked between us. I'd break the silence with Larry's suggestion of her well-matched shoes. We'd both have a hearty laugh over that and end with a friendly tap on each other's arms.

Sadly, my fantasies would always remain that way. I would never follow her into the bathroom. I would never watch her as she lathered warm soapy water between her delicate hands. I would never brave a sly smile. I would most certainly never face her and tell her 'oh by the way, I'm CarefreeJanie.'

I enjoyed the mystery. I wouldn't ruin that precious intermission in my boring, reclusive life. For the first time since seeing Rhonda's hollow eyes stare at me through her tears, guilt lifted in the presence of Eva's beauty. I relished in some fun finally. I deserved a chance to flirt with her, fantasize about her, and kiss her, if only in my dreams.

I yanked open the door to the office building on an emphatic yes, absolutely I deserved all of that and so much more. I blew into the foyer with a determination to keep the charade going as long as possible. I would gift myself with it. The universe would gift me with it. Eva would undoubtedly view it as a gift, too, and would not be ready to face what reality dealt her just yet. I couldn't disappoint her that way. We both benefited from it. I would not destroy that for her. Not now. Not yet. Perhaps not ever. She'd never have to find out the real me.

We could totally work as a virtual fling.

Yes. Of course it could.

I strolled in staring down at the brown carpeting, struggling to keep my laptop strap balanced on my shoulder and hiding a goofy grin brought on by musings of suds and sensual kisses in my steamy bathtub fantasies.

I waved to Ron the mailman who perched up in the receptionist booth. "Hey Jane," he yelled out. I cringed, scanning the open foyer for her, suddenly worried she'd hear my name and connect me with CarefreeJanie.

As I rounded the corner to my department, muttering to myself what an idiot I was, I slammed right into her.

I slammed right smack into Eva Handel and her coffee mug.

Her coffee flew straight up in the air, spraying us both and splashing right down the front of her cream, fitted blouse. Coffee also spilled down the front of my taupe capri pants and into my sandals. My laptop fell to the floor, as did the box of donut holes I brought in for Doreen. Balls of dough rolled around Eva Handel's perfectly matched shoes.

To my horror, her mouth hung open in shock. She patted the front of her blouse and looked down on herself as if she'd been shot. Her dark hair, swept to the side in a sexy, low ponytail, even dripped. My hands flew up to my mouth, and I just kept repeating "Oh my gosh, I'm so sorry" over and over again.

She glanced up at me on my fifth repeat, placing her hand on my upper arm and said, "It's okay. It's just coffee. I shouldn't have rounded the corner at such blazing speed."

I melted under her caress. Her hand softened and warmed on my arm. I looked down, unable to control my trembles in the wake of her sexy voice, her penetrating eyes and the smile that rested on her lips, the same lips I fantasized about every other minute of the day. I couldn't even respond to her, I just nodded and closed in on myself.

She slipped her soft hands off my bare arm. "You're that girl from the bathroom!"

I inched my eyes up the full length of her and met her friendly gaze.

"Look," she said pointing to her shoes. "I managed to match today."

In my peripheral view, I saw disaster walking toward us. "Oh my gosh," Katie said, staring at the coffee spill on Eva's shirt, her voice sailing high, so screechy, that all of marketing seeped out of their cubicles to get a peek at what clumsy me did. Even Sanjeev appeared. "Jane, why don't you get her some towels in the kitchen?" Katie said that like I was ten and a complete imbecile.

"Don't be silly," Eva said, stooping down to help me gather my loose papers and laptop. "I'm the one who ran into her." She handed me my notes on my latest project, then stood. "I'll go and get us some towels." She rushed away.

Katie crossed her arms over her chest and giggled.

All eyes fell upon me, poking at me like a piece of kindling, stirring flickers and then flames. The room shrunk. Sanjeev moved in closer asking me if I needed some water and if I wanted to sit down. As if I took one step backwards and reentered my pathetic teenaged life, I blushed deep purple.

I couldn't let Eva see me like that.

I gathered my stuff and ran. I ran so fast I dropped my lunch tote and just kept running all the way to my car, all the while reprimanding myself for tossing out the Old Bay seasoning question in the first place. I could've ignored the way her private smile twirled my heart and just gone about life as usual, watching reruns of *House* and eating Doritos. I would've been dunking donut holes in my hazelnut coffee and laughing with Doreen over something stupid Katie said that morning, instead of fleeing the scene like some wacky woman tripping on bad drugs.

Great going, CarefreeJanie.

Chapter Eight

Later that afternoon, I read a tweet Eva sent out to the masses. "When all else fails, toss your hands up in the air and laugh out loud."

That's exactly what I did. I tossed my hands up in the air and laughed out loud to my messy condo. I was a one-woman comedy show. All my life, I doled out comedic relief to people. They laughed when I sat alone at the long, lonely eight person tables in school. They laughed when they hit me square in the middle of my shoulder blades with a rock. They laughed when I entered a room and stood silent against a wall. They laughed when I wore too much makeup or dressed in an outfit one size too small for my above average sized frame.

If anyone was going to laugh at me, it should've been me. I stood in the middle of my living room amongst a plate from breakfast with a half-eaten banana, my socks from the night before, and Larry's exercise mat that I forgot to return. I pictured the spilled coffee dripping down Eva's shirt and into her bra and I spun around in circles, hands extended up to the ceiling laughing from somewhere deep in my belly.

After a few moments of that nonsense, I stopped spinning and laughing.

I imagined Eva after witnessing my fiasco, walking into the office bathroom. With coffee stains already setting in, she would peek under all doors to make sure no one else was inside, then toss her delicate arms up in the air and lose herself in a beautiful giggle over my clumsy mistake. I stopped short on that thought. I could never reveal my true identity to her now. She'd think I was a stalker, a nutcase, and an insecure flake for not telling her right then and there, while her hand rested on my skin, that I, plain and red-faced Jane, was actually CarefreeJanie.

Never. I could never reveal my real self. With the decision cemented, the pressure released and freed me from future self-talks about how I should definitely just tell her who I really was.

I settled my fate with Eva. I would remain a mystery. I would live out my days in my beautiful fantasies, cherishing and tucking safely into them. In their embrace, harm and judgment couldn't poke at me.

I'd drive Eva wild and crazy with the recurrent question of how she could be so crazy over a girl she'd never even met.

She could never know I was Jane Knoll, proofreader at Martin Sporting Goods and a twenty-nine-year-old kissing virgin. She could never know I was the one who caught her with two mismatched shoes or the one who sprayed coffee all over her expensive blouse and dashed out without a proper apology or at least an offer to pay the dry-cleaning ticket.

What an ass I was. Yeah my identity would remain bottled, sealed, shut off from every source of light to prevent spoiling it.

So, as long as I bottled up that identity, I could play with reckless abandon and live life vicariously through the computer screen. I could be that sexy girl, that mysterious girl, that girl someone like Eva would fantasize about meeting and falling in love with.

First, I retweeted her "laughter" tweet to my twenty-two followers. Yup, twenty-two people followed me. A few posed as eggheads with no faces and no followers aside from me, and a couple claimed to be internet gurus specializing in social media marketing and search engine optimization crapola. Then, there was my beautiful Eva, the girl who wrapped her heart around my writing and adored me for what I might be able to produce for her one day.

I could totally write a script for her. Mark Twain used a pen name. Why couldn't I?

I landed back into my direct messages and sent one out to her. "Hey, girlie. How's your day going?" So innocent and clueless I sounded. I loved being CarefreeJanie.

Within a minute, she messaged me back. "What a day. I had a small coffee fiasco this morning but other than that, I'm doing fine."

I wanted to know more about her take on the fiasco. "What happened?" I sealed my fate. I was CarefreeJanie on the road somewhere and not the one who spilled coffee down her shirt.

"I smacked right into some chick at the office. I splattered coffee all over her pants and my shirt. I felt so bad for her."

I groaned. "Why? Did she get burned or something?"

"No. But, she turned bright red."

"Well, I would've, too. Coming face-to-face with a gorgeous girl like you would certainly turn me a few shades of red."

"I adore when you flirt with me."

My fingers fluttered as I typed back. "Is that all you adore about me?"

"I'm starting to adore a lot about you, honey," she wrote.

I rocked backwards on my heels, floating on the softness of her words. "Mmm."

# #

"She adores me." I twirled around, modeling a summer dress for Larry.

115

He stood with his feet shoulder-width apart, chin propped up with his fist, and waved his other hand. "I don't like it."

I spun around again for him, enjoying the flowing pretty tickle of the soft fabric against my thighs. "What's wrong with it?"

He stood cupping his chin in his hand. "Doesn't do anything for you."

I scoffed and patted my hips, examining them in the mirror.

"It's too puffy and doesn't do anything to show off your nice curves. You look like you're about to crochet a sweater for a granddaughter."

Larry once told me that my hair resembled the last stages of an overused scouring pad. He said that after I had gotten a body perm for volume. We had spent the better part of that night hunched over my kitchen sink pouring neutralizer on it, conditioning it, applying a hair mask, and shampooing it five times to straighten it back out. I ended up having to cut my shoulder-length hair into a short bob that hung at my ears. It took me two years to finally get it back to just below my shoulders. The shiny smooth texture never did return after all that abuse. I stopped using smoothing creams altogether and just dealt with the frizz and wooly texture. That was up until just a few weeks ago, back when I thought I'd be brave enough to walk up to Eva at the quarterly meeting. I'd been spreading smoothing cream into my luscious locks ever since, and I had to admit, the marketing people who wrote that copy on the bottle were accurate. It really did smell like coconuts and add an element of shine. I stared at my puffy skirt and tamed hair and laughed.

"Help me, Larry." I turned to him. "I just want to feel pretty and sexy."

"Then, darling, get your ass out of that mess."

"Find me something else?" I bent forward squeezing my hands together. "Please. You know how much I hate shopping."

He ushered me backwards toward my dressing room. "Get in there before someone catches me with you. That skirt's beyond embarrassing."

I stepped inside and closed the door. "I'll be waiting."

"Sure dear."

I tore off the dress and angled back toward the mirror. I could hardly notice the stretch marks in the light. I turned to check out my ass, and that, too, improved under the soft golden mist of proper lighting. A few more weeks of brisk walking could do wonders. I placed my hands on my curvy hips and posed. With the right outfit, I could disguise my waist.

"Hey," Larry whispered. "I got you something."

I reached up over the door and grabbed a set of lacy, French cut undies with a matching bra. "What the hell is this?" It dangled from my fingers.

"Nothing screams sexy like a pair of red lacy underwear. You cannot say no."

"I will never wear these ridiculous things." I stretched my legs through them and pulled them up. Then, I fastened the bra. When I looked at myself in the mirror, my jaw dropped. I actually looked halfway decent in them. Dare I say, almost sexy?

A few minutes later, fully dressed back in my jeans and Nike t-shirt, I balled the undies and bra up and carried them out of the dressing room like a football. "Come on. Hurry before someone sees me buying these ridiculous things."

He slinked up beside me, grabbed me by the hand, and smiled like he just caught me making out with the prettiest girl in town.

# #

I emailed the short story I wrote for Eva to five of the country's top magazines. Two days after, I received an email message from the editor of

Glamour asking if I'd accept two thousand dollars for the piece and agree to their attached copyright terms.

I flew off my stool and ran circles in my living room. I jumped on my couch and flipped several times. I screamed. I high-fived the air. Then I ran over to Larry's condo and knocked so hard my knuckles shined bright red by the time he answered. Shaving cream still bearded his face. The words spilled out before my brain could keep up, and what came out was "Story... published... two grand... oh my God..."

We jumped up and down in the cement hallway that separated our condos. He squealed higher than I did. "Didn't I tell you? I told you that you could write. And, you didn't believe me." He clung to me, spinning me in wide circles, leaping with me, and celebrating my big victory as a published writer.

I couldn't wait to tell Eva. I would owe her part of the check. If she hadn't pushed, I'd still be plain Jane burying my time in the quicksand of humdrum nights filled with short-term sugar highs from too many Oreos.

# #

I couldn't hide the smile spreading across my face that morning when I arrived late to work. I logged onto my computer and within two seconds Katie appeared, digging her claws into me. I turned, and she handed me a stack of tear sheets from ads we had created. "Can you find the one that is advertising the executive golf bags? Sanjeev is asking me for it, and I've got to get ready for a meeting with him in an hour." A sweet smile played out on her face, the likes that concerned me. What was she up to?

"Sure."

"Late night last night?" she asked.

"Alarm failed me."

"Ah." She tapped my cubicle wall. "You might want to check your email."

I did. I hopped on immediately. Sure enough, she had emailed Sanjeev the production schedule and highlighted three projects of mine that were late. That bitch changed the dates on me, shining the light on her, the glowing star of marketing, the glorious one meeting all her deadlines ahead of schedule.

I popped over to Doreen's cubicle a moment later. "I feel like having some fun today."

"How?"

"Let's steal her keys and watch her panic."

Doreen looked up from her desk. Her pink lipstick shimmered a bit too much. "Just breathe for a few minutes and let it pass."

I wrapped my arm around her shoulder. "Actually, I don't even care about her today. She can't ruin my mood."

"Do tell."

"Well, I bet you never thought you'd be able to say that you're friends with a writer whose work is going to be in *Glamour* in two months."

She pulled away. "You're writing again?"

"Yup."

"I thought you were tired of being bullied by mean editors?"

"I got inspired."

"How?"

"By my muse."

Her eyes stretched wide and a smile danced onto her face. "What's his name?"

Not even fear could squash my joy. "Actually it's 'her' name. And, I don't kiss and tell."

She covered her mouth and squealed. Her blue eyes sparkled under a fresh layer of moisture. I bounced away, feeling lighter and happier than I had in a very long time.

#

Wearing sexy underwear thrilled me. I wore them that day to buy groceries and when I walked down the cereal aisle, my hips swayed more. The lace lifted me up, way up to a crazy, birds'-eye view level where I could soar across the shiny floors with eloquent rises and falls and agile force that even turned one young stock boy's head. He looked up from his boxes of oatmeal and smiled at me. No one ever smiled at me. I didn't know what to do with that smile, so I just sort of giggled and bolted toward my Chex Mix section.

Later when I messaged with Eva about my short story success, I decided to take off the sweatpants and lounge on my couch in just my red undies. I munched on a bowl of my Chex Mix and waited for her to respond to my question about whether or not she would prefer flying on an airplane or riding her motorcycle cross country.

"You've never been on the back of a motorcycle have you?"

I couldn't imagine more of a thrill, clinging to her and flushing my body up against hers. "Never."

"I'll be your first."

I swallowed hard. A fire stoked deep inside. My chest ached. "I'd love that."

We continued talking about silly things like how her cat, Jarvis, liked to smack her radio alarm clock each morning to wake her up and feed him and how I once walked around the Columbia Mall in boxer shorts. I didn't know it until I was halfway around the mall.

She asked about my life growing up as a budding writer, and whether I sat around and mulled over stories while playing with dolls and building tree houses. I embellished just a little and told her all about my wonderful, happy childhood. I talked about growing up in a neighborhood teeming with friendly kids who invited me to their birthday parties and to go bike riding down Sycamore Street, a winding wooded road where the trees acted as canopies for miles.

She asked me many innocent questions, and I enjoyed filling her curious mind with answers that shined of the good times that a normal, well-adjusted person would offer.

"Janie, will I ever get to see a real picture of you?"

My breath rolled around in my chest. "You must already have an image of me in place? You know, like a character in a book?"

"I do. I picture you all the time lately; when I'm sleeping, when I'm walking, when I'm showering."

I bit my lower lip, riding a series of waves so strong they toppled me over. "What do I look like in your mind?"

"You're gorgeous."

"Go on," I wrote.

"Come on, no fair. You get to see me."

"I don't have many pictures of myself."

"Just snap a picture and send it. What are you afraid of?"

I stood up and backed away from the computer like it was a ticking time bomb. I planned out everything in my life according to logic and strategy. If I were walking through a park and someone tried to pull me into a bush, I would whack the creep with the bottom of my hand right upside his nose and knock him out. If I were driving and my brakes stopped working, I would put my car in neutral and sideswipe an object if necessary to prevent massive damage. I stored forty cans of kidney beans and another forty jars of peanut butter in my storage unit in case of emergency. I planned things out to the point of an extremist. Yet, I forgot to plan an answer for something that important? "I'll get one to you."

"I just want to see the beautiful girl I am talking with every day."

My head swirled in delightful circles. No sangria in the world could rival that buzz. "You're more beautiful."

"I really want to kiss you."

I floated. "Please do."

"Mwah."

"Mmm, I felt that one." I traced my lips imagining hers.

"Was it yummy?" she asked.

Luscious, juicy, warm only touched the surface of adjectives to explain the potential yumminess. "You taste like sweet berries, babe."

"I really like when you call me babe."

My entire body quivered. I could only manage a wink.

"Please send me a picture. I'm waiting."

"Okay. I'll get one to you, soon. XO. I've got to run. Have a great rest of your day."

I logged off, hung my head between my legs, and breathed like I had just crossed the finish line of the New York City Marathon.

She could never know that the real CarefreeJanie was really a shy, geeky girl too afraid to admit her true identity. I couldn't possibly send her a real picture.

I stood up on that buzz kill, placed my fists on each end of my hips, and panicked. She'd take one look at my picture and recognize me, the girl who caught her wearing the wrong shoes, the girl she most likely saw run out of the quarterly meeting like the building was on fire, and the girl who could've just come clean and admitted she dropped the coffee all over the front of her boobies. I ruined my chance of ever being trustworthy, of being confident, and of not looking like the dweeb I really was.

I whined out loud to my condo. I didn't want the stress. I couldn't afford stress to enter into the equation. I wanted clear, concise, to-the-point emotions here.

I needed a drink. Wine wouldn't cut it. I needed to take out the big guns. I dashed to my kitchen, reached up to the top of my fridge, and pulled out my unopened bottle of the Absolute vodka I had bought for New Year's Eve in anticipation of Larry and me drinking it up in front of the television. Instead some asshole lover, who turned out to be a drug user, stole him from me that night.

I poured myself some orange juice and Absolute and downed it in less than three gulps. I waited for the buzz to grip me. Slowly, lusty bubbles tickled my brain and relieved some of the panic. I drank another, that time adding just a smidgeon more vodka. Five minutes later, I perched in front of my laptop researching cameras.

Okay, so I didn't play the move very strategically with Eva. Not a big deal. I could still survive that small little storm of stupidity by continuing to play along with her. It didn't have to end there. I could get creative and string it along. Then, if one day I ever became brave enough to actually face her, I'd explain the whole messed up silly misunderstanding of not telling her about the fact that I was the girl who spilled coffee on her. I'd blame it on embarrassment.

She was a beautiful girl with a thoughtful soul. She'd surely understand my logic. Otherwise, why would I want to be with someone who didn't get that? Right?

Not everyone carried confidence around like a designer pocketbook. Some of us had some scratches and missing zippers and had to hold to their broken belongings a little tighter and with more protection than others.

In between rapid inhales and even quicker exhales, I imagined the picture taking. Perhaps I could hide behind some props and just reveal an overly dramatic made-up eye, complete with false eyelashes and wild, wacky, sparkly, blue eye shadow. I could dye my hair with a temporary rinse. Or maybe I could hang upside down and look fun. She'd never recognize me. I'd touchup the shit out of it.

First line of order. I'd have to buy a camera, one that could shoot miracle photos. Then, I'd probably need to invest in Photoshop because those pictures would for sure need some major overhaul.

I plopped down on my couch.

What did I just get myself into?

Chapter Nine

I didn't have a career in photography for a good reason. When I snapped a picture, I usually cut off heads, caught people in strange yawns, shot the corner of one of my fingers instead of a critical pose, or shook the camera so much while trying to be steady that the whole picture blurred out of focus and resembled a psychedelic poster straight out of the 1970s.

I went to Walmart and bought a Canon Easy Zoom. Easy zoom my ass. Even the on button screwed with my intellect. I read the instructions and fiddled with the darn thing for an hour before I could figure out how the self-timer worked. The thing had so many settings. I'd imagine if I needed to shoot the inside of a volcano, brave hurricane-force winds, or shoot a picture during a blackout, I'd probably find a setting to accommodate me and my feeble photographical skillset. I just needed the freaking thing to snap a photo of me trying to look inconspicuous. Of course, the camera didn't come packaged with that setting.

I bought a case for the camera, too, so if the picture-taking thing became a normality in my and Eva's Twitter relationship, I'd have an easier way to store it and lug it around to different locations. She'd eventually tire of the one and only feasible backdrop in my condo, my bathroom with its deep, golden accent wall behind the toilet. So, not only did I have to figure out a way to disguise three-quarters of my face, but I also needed to snap the photo in such a way that the girl wouldn't think I was taking a pee at the same time the camera clicked.

125

The lighting worked wonders with its soft, golden splash. I cleared off the extra rolls of toilet paper I had stacked on the back of the toilet and replaced the jar of pebbles and candles from the glass shelf with something less bathroom-looking – an ivy plant, a small cactus plant, and a couple of my favorite books. I stepped back and examined my props. I straightened out *The Forbidden Garden* and shifted *No Ordinary Moments* with *The Glass Castle* so they stood from tallest to shortest.

The white porcelain shined too much. Two minutes later, I covered it with a baby blue afghan my grandmother had crocheted for me years ago when I finally offered my parents the break they needed and moved out on my own. I clicked a few random shots of the scene, played around with my settings like a pro and decided I'd go with the portrait setting because it didn't highlight the dust trails on the gold wall. I would gladly turn a bathroom into a portrait studio, but wash my walls? No way.

Okay, onto myself. I pulled my hair back into an Orioles baseball cap, and lowered the lid so it sat right above my eyebrows. CarefreeJanie would be a sporty chick who liked going to see Orioles games at Camden Yards every time she could. She would play softball for a girls' league and spend hours after the games at the bar drinking beer with her teammates, who by the way, would laugh at every one of her jokes. She would also drive a Jeep Wrangler and indulge on long weekend trips to the eastern shore where she'd take a couple of her friends along with her for some beach volleyball. They'd follow up their fun in the sun with a bonfire on the beach, acoustic guitar, and maybe just for shits and giggles, she could be into weed every once in a great while.

I could turn CarefreeJanie into anyone. Eva would never meet her. Never. All the make-believe was just for fun. Eva would be the girl who introduced me to the joy of flirting. Then, one day, maybe I could venture into the real world and find me a real live Eva-type who might actually enjoy me for me. She'd be someone with whom I hadn't completely destroyed my integrity and character by lying and hiding. Girls like Eva didn't hide. I never expected her to understand the inner hauntings of a girl who needed to. No reason for tears and faded love and all that anxiety just yet, especially when I only just planned to indulge and have fun.

Without prepping too much for the actual photo, I just snapped a couple of strange angles. Each shot grew worse. My face looked bigger. My fine lines popped out along the one eye I opted to showcase. My expression looked like something you'd find on a crazy woman who took one too many drugs in her prime. The pictures went from bad to worse until, just for goofs, I held the camera above my head, looked up and snapped. That angle elongated my body, creating a cute, slender frame. The best part, my eye looked bright blue and gigantic in relation to my baseball cap and slender shoulders. I could barely recognize myself.

So, fifteen minutes into my photography session, I called it a wrap. I downloaded and reviewed it. To my horror, the pretty blue afghan had slipped off the toilet, and in plain sight, I was sitting on a toilet snapping photos of myself. Class act.

Other than that small fact, the picture was perfect.

The next day at work, desperate to claim that photo as CarefreeJanie and impress Eva with it, I did something completely out of character. I marched up to Sanjeev and asked him if I could have Photoshop installed on my laptop. "I really think Kate had some validity at our last meeting when she said my headlines weren't exactly matching the visual. I'd really like to have Photoshop so I can set up a visual when refining these headlines." He responded with a wink, a blush to his freshly shaven cheek, and an affirmative nod. "I'll get the technical team to install it this morning."

I thanked him like a polite employee, and when I walked away with an extra bounce in my step, being pretty darn proud of my assertive approach to problem solving, Katie once again mocked me with an extra sugary smile that had poison written all over it. Get too close to her men, and she turned into a territorial dog sniffing out the enemy all while shouldering a well-exercised southern bell charm.

She was not perfect. She had issues. Her husband didn't want her. She scuttled around the world lost like a dog without a home. Those facts empowered me like a little rudder hidden under a rowboat. I passed her by and lifted my mouth into the slightest smile. I, the better one, didn't shove that knowledge in her face. She could toss clever lies and cunning sneers all she wanted. None of it bothered me anymore.

She responded with a superimposed twinkle in her eye.

Not more than thirty minutes later, Jeff from IT waltzed into my cubicle and installed Photoshop on my system. Katie and her fake eyelashes and sing-song smile neared my cubicle, stretching her lanky neck and slinking it back to normal whenever I'd look over and catch her snooping.

I waited all afternoon to launch my photo. And, when I did, I shrunk it down to only twenty-five percent so that if Katie happened to walk out of her three o'clock production meeting to get a cup of coffee, I could hide it quickly. I researched how to blend and distort backgrounds, then I applied the technique. The fates of change and world wonders converged that afternoon and worked alongside me, carrying me along a nice peaceful trail where everything just slid into place for me. The result, a picture that would turn my head, too.

I was cute!

I called Larry. "I'm sending you a picture that I want to send to Eva. I want your honest opinion of it first."

A few minutes later, he texted me. "You should have worn the red bra and undies."

I exhaled. "She already thinks I'm sexy. I don't want to overexcite her with too much and leave her hanging for eternity."

"Noble gesture on your part. You're going to make a great cyber lover."

#

Larry tended to whine, but he usually reserved all-out crying for situations like insect attacks and of course when his DVR recorded over *Dr. Oz* before he could watch it. Yes, Larry adored Dr. Oz, perhaps even more than Shaun T from the *Insanity* exercise videos. Anyway, Larry sat beside me bawling with his laundry bag crumbled at his feet. I fed him tissues faster than he could swipe tears. They fell from his eyes in giant drops; I'm talking total-and-complete breakdown at a monsoon level.

"Tim is married," he managed to shovel out to me.

"Tim? Your great boyfriend Tim?"

He nodded, gulping back another round of tears. "I didn't want to tell you. I'm lousy at everything. I didn't want to be lousy at being this."

"Being the other guy?" I couldn't suppress the judgment. It flew out of me unrestrained the way air blew out of a compressor.

"I know. I'm a horrible man."

"You're not a horrible man." I handed him another tissue not sure how to comfort him when I wanted to punch him. "So what happened? Why are you crying like someone stole your Lexus?"

"He told me he was separated. So, I thought I could safely date him. But, it turns out he wasn't. We met up at lunch, and I knew as soon as I saw his strained face that something dreadful was about to come out of his mouth." He coughed and blew his nose. "He's been married to his wife for fifteen years. They have three dogs, two cats and a finch. His wife's mother lives with them and cooks all their meals, washes their clothes, and she's even on their health insurance from his work." He cried out in anguish, leaning back and covering his tear-stained face with his hands. "He's afraid to leave her."

I didn't know what to do. So, I sat on the edge of my couch, drumming my fingers on my legs and willing my best friend to get a hold of himself so I wouldn't have to do it for him. I was not qualified.

He sat up again. "He doesn't love her, but I don't believe him. How do you spend fifteen years with someone and not love her? Why would he do that?"

He stared at my empty eyes. I shrugged. "I have no idea."

"He told me he loves me, but he doesn't want to hurt her or his mother-in-law. He asked if we could see each other quietly."

To me that sounded logical and acceptable given that's how I lived my life, hidden and coiled up in the corner where not even the light of day could break in and illuminate who I really was.

At least someone in the world loved him and committed to continue loving him. I'd forfeit an arm to have someone love the real me. Couldn't he just be satisfied instead of greedy? "At least you have that."

He scoffed, and his tears suddenly dried up like the sun baked right through my ceiling. "No." He waved his finger at me. "No, you're not going to play this game. This crazy, foolish 'poor me, look at me, I have no one who loves me' game. You don't get to do that. You know why?" He hung his jaw waiting on me.

I flung my hands up in the air and landed backwards on a huff. "Oh, here we go."

"No. There's no 'here we go.' You and I both know the reason you don't have someone to love you is because you're too stubborn to put yourself out there. Everyone is not out to get you."

"You have no idea what it's like to live in my head." I stood up, rage spilling from every cell. I was an ugly person inside, and I wanted to keep the ugliness inside. I decided that, and I wouldn't let him or anyone else judge me on it. I'd already judged myself enough. "Fuck you." I tore off to my kitchen. "Fuck you and your married boyfriend, you insensitive ass." I turned on the faucet and began scrubbing my breakfast dishes, choking back tears.

"Fuck me?" He stood up and commanded the space. The room vibrated with his frustration and echoed straight to me, straight to my sponge, and straight to my heart where it strangled my selfish tantrum. He moved toward me, eyes wide open. "Fuck me? Why fuck me?" He stood two feet from me, hands on his hips with shock and hurt trailing in the fine lines around his eyes. The air whispered between us, begging us to stop the foolish nonsense and get back on the same team.

I fought with the sponge, circling it around the caked-on oatmeal from twelve hours earlier. I scrubbed it, taking out all my anger, squaring off with Larry eye-to-eye, not willing to cave on the argument. "Because." That's all I could say. I searched for a reason why and nothing compelling landed on my tongue.

131

He waited on edge, with a warning resting on his lips and angular jaw. "Because?"

"Argh." I hated admitting he was right. "Because you're right about me. Okay? Feel better now that you painted my pathetic picture a little brighter?" I didn't take my eye off him as I continued to scrub.

His jaw softened and a tiny exhale released through his lips. Fresh tears erupted. Before either one of us could stop it, we both caved and hugged each other, weeping like a couple of emotional fools hyped up on too many episodes of *Oprah*.

"What are you going to do?" I asked him.

He hugged me tighter. "I'm too deep into it. I adore him. I'm addicted to him. I can't go a day without talking to him."

I pulled away and looked at him. "He's married."

"But, he loves me."

We stared at each other, accepting one another for the weaknesses we carried on our shoulders, neither one understanding the full extent to their depths. We ended on a nod, scooped up our laundry bags, and went about our Wednesday night like we did every week.

# #

Sanjeev asked me to participate in a major company project that involved Eva Handel. "We need you to write up a public service announcement about our new initiative to bring health and fitness back into schools."

"Absolutely. I'd be honored."

He smiled like a nervous schoolboy, turning red.

In the awkward moment that followed, he scrolled down to my lips and rested for a moment too long. I pulled them in, securing them.

He looked back up at my eyes. Just as quickly as the strange moment approached, it flew away.

"Just one thing. Katie asked to be a part of it, too." He rolled his eyes. "I'd rather you take the helm on this. You always work magic on my writing, so I trust you. It's an important one." His eyes softened on me, wrapping me in an awkward embrace.

I looked away, down at a paperclip. I reached down and picked it up. "Yeah, no problem." I walked out of his office, rounded the corner, and met Katie's gaze from the collaboration room. She curled her finger, waving me toward her like a sneaky witch beckoning for her afternoon snack.

I walked in casually. "Yes?"

"What were you two lovebirds talking about?"

My face reddened. "An assignment."

"Hmm. Well, Sanjeev needs you to proof some articles. I was just about to bring them to you, but seeing as you're right here, I may as well hand them over now." She dropped them at my feet, and they flew every which way. She covered her face with her hands. "Oops. I'm sorry." She dropped her hands and offered me an apologetic nod.

"I love organizing," I said, playing her game. "So, thank you."

"Well, that's a good thing because they have no page numbers on them." She turned and walked out, pumping her hips side to side like a pendulum, like she was the sexiest, most powerful woman in the world. She turned over her shoulder. "Oh, and he needs them in two hours. That won't be a problem, will it?"

"Not at all," I said.

# #

I finally attached my Photoshopped picture into an email for Eva, and after three glasses of wine and a good firm one-on-one conversation with myself in front of the mirror, I hit the send button. I let destiny take the reins. I shuddered for a few long minutes after that, beating myself up for smoothing my skin too much with the Gaussian blur tool and setting the threshold too high on the hue and saturation. God forbid she ever saw me at the office and recognized me. She'd take one look and see the world's biggest freak for touching up to the extent I did. I would never let her meet me. I viewed my Photoshopping debut as my safety net from ever having to sweat it out one day in a face-to-face meeting.

I adored the way she adored me. Or, okay, I adored the way she adored CarefreeJanie. I knew deep in my heart that no one, especially someone as beautiful as Eva, could ever adore the real me in much the same way. The distance and mystery built an intrigue that reality would smash to smithereens if given the opportunity. I wanted the ride to last forever. Why couldn't it? If we never met, we could never get to that dull relationship stage known as comfort—that point when lovers stopped fussing over their hair, their makeup, their figure, and just plopped down next to each other and watched the sad news every night, discussing politics and bills and whether they should redo their roof or buy a new car. With the mystery, we'd always be in the discovery stage, learning new things about each other and falling in love over and over again.

I stared at my reflection in the toaster and shook my head in disgust at myself. "Why can't this ride last forever? I'll tell you why. Because women like Eva crave human interaction and aren't afraid of it, like you, you freak."

I glared at myself for the stupid person I'd let myself become over the years. Fucking Barbara. She caused all of the crap. What would my life be if she would've kept her mouth shut and ushered me off to the side of the building to ask me what the hell had gotten into me, instead of running down the hall showing everyone but the school principal what I had written about her? I also couldn't forget Rhonda. If only she hadn't been so weak. If only she could've known that inside of me was a girl just as scared and weak as she, maybe life could've taken a different twist, one less lonely and arduous.

I exhaled and locked eyes with myself. I squinted to get a good look at my ruddy complexion, at my freckles that connected into blotches now, at my pudgy lips, and at my half-moon chin. I had erased all of those features from my photo. With a computer mouse, sophisticated editing software, and a critical eye, I turned myself into a beauty queen wearing a baseball hat—into someone who would've turned heads in a crowded bar, who would've scored lots of fun friends, and who would've spent her time hanging out in gyms instead of sitting on her rump in front of the television.

I wondered how much different I would've been now had I not been pelted with rocks, burned by girls' cigarettes in the bathroom, and slapped across the face as I sat waiting for a teacher to enter the classroom?

Would've I been a best-selling novelist by now? Maybe I would've worked in New York City at one of the big publishers, sitting in a corner office with wall-to-wall windows so high, the window washers would've needed that special extender handle to reach the tip top of them. My office would be decorated with lots of planted flowers and ferns. I would most definitely be sitting at a mahogany desk complete with an ergonomic chair and head rest so I could lounge back in those moments of deep reverie and reflect upwards to a ceiling painted in swirled plaster and illuminated with accent lighting that would put the museum of fine arts to shame.

I would've been prettier for sure. I wouldn't have let myself go over the years. I wouldn't have been sitting around my condo feeling sorry for myself that girls the likes of Barbara ever existed. Maybe Rhonda and I could've turned out to be good friends. Maybe instead of wallowing in self-pity and hiding my ugly self, we would be out shopping for bathing suits for the cruise we'd be taking together with our perfect families. Or better yet, maybe Rhonda and I would've been out on dates, eating caviar with rich women, dancing the night away at lesbian hotspots, and wearing pretty dresses that flowed just above my knee and hung from my shoulders with thin, beaded neck straps. I would've pranced around in strappy sandals in summer and stylish, sexy boots in winter, sporting fine Chanel scarfs and dangling earrings. I would've treated my hair to better care so it would have sheen, bounce, and a life of its own to be admired by other pretty women and even the men on their arms. I'd wear lip glosses that were darker and more plum because my teeth would be pearl white and shiny from all the fruits, veggies, and unprocessed food I'd eaten over the years. I would've taken greater care of myself because my life would've had greater value. Why? Because people would've paid attention to the Jane I could've become. There would be purpose in getting a good night's rest, trimming my hair every four to six weeks, seeing a dermatologist about my freckles, and staying in fit condition to add quality and longevity to my valued life.

A sobering thought whacked me over the head just then. Eva was too perfect for me. She belonged with real women who didn't carry emotional baggage and hide behind computer screens. Nothing plagued that woman. I certainly didn't want to be the one to march in and untidy her pristine life. The little I knew about her already, even if I carried a hump on my back and wore pigtails, she'd offer me a warm smile and treat me with dignity. That's what perfectly nice people did.

They never let their true feelings damage others, especially those of us who were already broken.

She would pity me.

Life blew me some hard times, and hardened me to the point that I just couldn't be melted back down to the girl I used to be pre-Barbara. How could I be expected to dust off old demons of ridicule and shine a light that never fully ignited onto a world that at every chance had tried to blow out the light? Only those with big, beautiful, bright lights like Eva could keep up the shine and weather through the storms of life when people you trusted kicked you when you were most vulnerable, and kept kicking the shit out of you.

My life played out before me and I accepted it. By no means, however, did that mean a decade and a half later I couldn't dive into the shallow end of the pool and get my feet wet a little. My feet burned in the scorching sun just like everyone else's did, right? So, it only stood to reason that I would have to dip them in from time to time to heal them so they could carry me a little further down the road. CarefreeJanie operated as my shallow pool. She was my break from the blistering pain of years ago and of a future that only burned hotter, stoked by the fierce intensity of loneliness and humiliation of who the real Jane had allowed herself to become.

For that reason and that reason only, I protected that special relationship with Eva. Living in that fake world as CarefreeJanie proved safe, moldable, and easy. I didn't harm anyone that way. I could live with that, even if that meant one day Eva kept me on the side as she embarked on a real deal. I could never give that girl what she needed, for sure. I wasn't that selfish a person to ever want her to sacrifice a great life out of pity for me, someone who would never be able to be that smiling, doting girlfriend she'd be proud to show off to the world.

I was too dark for someone like her. My nightmares alone would silently freak her out for sure. I woke up too many times screaming, panting, remembering the devastation I caused myself and others. How did one hide something like that? I would never tell her or anyone else what really happened all those years ago. Opening up the past like that would be selfish, and Eva deserved better than selfish.

Life wasn't fair.

Tears stung my eyes.

I pointed at myself in the toaster, fighting back hate, anger, and frustration. "You were just as mean and cruel and evil, and you deserve this. Don't you think for one minute that you deserve to be loved or caressed. That needs to be earned, and you—" I shook my head, knocking around the insults. "—you've never earned that."

I swiped the tears from my cheek and convulsed into a fit. "Fuck my life."

Mid choke, Larry entered my condo on a whisper. I didn't hear him, smell his cologne, or sense his presence until he scared the crap out of me when he tapped my shoulder and asked me if I was all right.

"Larry." I jumped off my stool and whacked his arm. "Knock, will you?"

He cradled my upper arm, and pulled me into a hug. "What's going on?"

"We are so pathetic you and I." I cried into his shoulder and pulled at his crew neck shirt. "If you're not whining over something, I am."

He cradled me like a good friend would until I calmed down and confessed my short, painful trip down memory lane. And like he did every time I ventured down it and pulled him along, he patted my back and told me everything was going to be alright.

# #

The next morning, just as I gathered my stuff for work, someone knocked on my front door. I looked through my peephole and saw a man with a beard wearing a blue collared shirt with a nametag from Great Fitness.

"I think you have the wrong condo," I yelled through my door.

"Jane Knoll?"

I peeked again, and he swiped his forehead with a bandana, looking straight into the peephole.

"Yeah?"

"I've got a delivery for you."

The guy turned around quickly. Then, Larry came into view. "Open up Jane. He's legit."

I turned my deadbolt and opened my door to a man who looked like he stepped out of an eighties ZZ Top video. He carried a clipboard and a smile. "Just need you to sign this form and I'll go get your bike."

"My bike?" I grabbed the clipboard from him and signed.

Larry stood beside him with a huge grin. "It's going to be just the thing you need."

I handed the signed form back to ZZ Top and he skirted around Larry, down the steps and toward his colorful box truck adorned with hot bodies lifting weights. Beads of sweat glistened on their well-built biceps and quadriceps.

"You bought me a bike?"

"Exercise will invigorate you. I promise."

"I hate exercise." I folded my arms over my chest. I'd been walking and launching into a few modified pushups each day, but I was nowhere ready to wear a bikini or a pair of shorts for that matter.

He unfolded my arms and danced me around in circles. "Did you know that physically fit people enjoy sex more and they carry themselves with more confidence than their counterparts?"

I followed Larry's silly dance. "That's your solution? Buy me a bike and turn me into a sex goddess?"

"Absolutely, darling." He spun me, dipped me, and then dropped me.

I pulled myself up. "Thank you?"

He walked out my front door and turned over his shoulder. "Oh you'll be thanking me alright. I've heard the bike is good for more than just exercise." He winked and retreated to his condo on a giggle. "Read it in an article the other day."

Surely it had something to do with sex. He could be so gay at times. I flushed just as the delivery guy entered my condo with my shiny new stationary bike. "Where would you like it, ma'am?"

Ma'am? Fan-fucking-tastic. "Right alongside the couch is fine."

# #

A vulnerable cloud hung over me, and I spent the entire workday avoiding Twitter and my personal email for two reasons. Firstly, I couldn't afford to leave in the middle of a workday in a fit of tears anymore. So if Eva didn't respond to my picture or did and failed to provide at least one exclamation point, then I'd probably suffer a fit of tears and another lost workday. Secondly, I didn't want to appear too eager in waiting on her response. If she said anything flattering or used that said exclamation point I would not be able to control myself. I'd tweet her right back and appear as desperate for attention as I really was.

Self-control was a beautiful thing. I'd worked my entire life to build up enough to protect me from more ridiculous bullying episodes. I would not arm any living morsel on the Earth with the ammunition to bully me ever again. Self-control was my friend, despite the situation, and I protected it like I would protect laundry night with Larry.

When I returned home later that day, I waited until I opened my mail, paid some bills, ate some noodles, showered, brushed my teeth, and put on my red undies under my pajama bottoms—hey, a girl's got to feel sexy—before launching a full scale journey into Twitterland. Whatever the outcome, I would survive, as I always did.

I slid right over to the direct messages, and Eva's gorgeous smile greeted me with that adorable blue dot telling me she had sent me a message.

"You are GORGEOUS," she wrote.

My heart floated up above my head, to the ceiling, through the roof, and up into where the birds fly. My body spun like a charm below it, twirling round and round, enjoying the dizziness, the lightheaded effect, and the tickle of a warm breeze kissing my skin like lovely spring rain. No one in my entire lifespan had ever called me such a thing.

"You're making me blush," I wrote. I squirmed on the stool and my undies wedged just enough to calm the quivering.

I stared at the word 'gorgeous' for several minutes, enjoying how it sat prominent, in all caps. That one word massaged out all kinks, put to rest all stress, and placed me in a complete state of nirvana. Her one word caused my blood to surge as if powered by hundreds of turbines. The rush intoxicated me.

I logged onto email needing more. She didn't disappoint. Eva's response to my email sat in between my bank statement alert and a notice from Harry and David's announcing their early bird sale. I hovered above it for a few seconds trying to control my sputtering breaths, then dove in head first ready for whatever waited at the other end of it.

"I don't understand what's happening between us. But, something is. Do you feel it, too?" she asked. "I'm completely attracted to you, and this picture is just feeding that hunger to meet you even more. What are you doing to me, pretty lady?"

I exhaled and hung my head between my knees, repeating an exorbitant amount of wows. I stared down at my naked feet, and even they took on a blushed hue. I rose to the occasion and landed back on Twitter.

"You just made my day."

"I want to kiss you," she wrote.

My tummy rolled. "Seriously, the blushing is out of control now (wink)."

"Nice sweet lingering kisses."

I indulged in the ride. "I'd love to feel your soft lips on mine."

"Janie, honey, you are full of charm."

I floated again. "Mmm. You are rolling my tummy."

"I just love your tummy. It's yummy."

I placed my hand on my tummy and imagined her lips traveling around it. I closed my eyes to take in the heat. "You really know how to make me feel good."

She continued. "I bet you're very soft. I'd love to kiss your tummy. Just imagine my tongue on your navel."

My lower body twitched. "Oh my goodness. Look who has the charms here. That thought will be with me the rest of this day."

"I want it to be with you for the rest of the day and way into the night."

I hugged myself, taking in the sweet journey. "Your tongue on my navel is an incredibly provocative image. It will definitely carry into my night." My bold words spun around me in lovely pirouettes.

"And how would you like my tongue circling a little lower?"

I throbbed.

"How do you think I'd like that, hmm?"

"I think you'd love it."

My whole body trembled in delightful ripples, insanely, incredibly wondrous ripples that warmed me to the core. I was practically cyber sexing with Eva Handel. "(wink)."

"You're a sweetheart," she wrote. "I hope I didn't go too far. I can't help myself. Your new picture is teasing me with that playful eye of yours."

"I enjoyed it." I exhaled then sent her a virtual kiss.

"Hey. Control your tongue. It tickles," she wrote.

I could tickle her all night long. I didn't want it to end. I also didn't want to ruin a good thing by overstaying the welcome. My body flared, and I feared total explosion. "Take that tickle to bed with you and think of me, okay?" I flirted with attitude.

"Yeah, I'll go 'relax' now," she wrote. "Be in my arms, okay?"

"Absolutely, babe." I logged off and sat on the edge of a breath too heavy to exhale.

I highly doubted her idea of 'relax' matched my typical idea of relax. I needed to rid my body of that energy before it imploded on me. I looked to my new bike and decided to try her out. I mounted her and started pedaling away. I pedaled fast, so fast that my crotch rubbed up against the seat. The faster I pedaled, the more it rubbed, and the more it started to alter my mind in striking ways. My legs shook, and a warm tremble drizzled through me. I floated again, then I sped up, running toward the mounting island of pleasure that called out to me, beckoning me to come to it, teasing me, luring me with slippery force into its graceful, peaceful arms where the room disappeared and all that saved me from hitting the ground was that incredible rush of ecstasy unlike anything I'd ever experienced. My whole body convulsed into a fit of shakes and trembles. I hinged on the edge of the seat, dreaming of Eva and sharing that nirvana moment with her in my arms. I clung to her life force, becoming one with her, then falling like a feather against her soft skin and into her spirit where love light and peace swaddled me into the deepest relaxation I'd ever entered. I fell against the bike, hunching over it and panting like I'd just ran to New York City and back on one lungful of air.

No romance book I ever read could've prepared me for that hallucinogenic freedom, a freedom that swept away all worry, all sadness, and all guilt from myself.

Chapter Ten

I lay in bed for hours, tossing myself around like a leaf in the wind. I cradled my arms around myself, imagining Eva wrapped up in them. We tangled, rolled, kissed, hugged, and stared deeply into each other's eyes until I could no longer control my urge to get back on that bike again and release the pressure building in me, swelling that area between my legs that craved Eva's soft lips.

I rose, vibrating. I wanted to reach that sweet spot again, just stare into its illustrious light and enter headfirst. So much energy swirled inside; it seemed a shame to waste it in quick release. So, I did what any good writer would do. I embraced it, firing up my laptop and pouring it onto the screen where I could later read it again and again. I'd be able to land right back in that sugary nirvana where colors shined like prisms dancing in the sunlight, plants smelled like forests after a spring rain, and the air buzzed with the echo of a thousand tree frogs deep in song.

With fingers perched over my keyboard, I planted my eyes on a picture of a tree-lined, sunlit path that touted success was a journey and not a destination. Then, I strolled into a story about two women who met online. They wandered down that beautiful path toward each other, in search of tangible love that wasn't bound by the confinements of Internet connections and firewalls.

I closed my eyes and pictured Eva standing before me at work with her hair cascading down past her shoulders and tickling the edge of where her nipples

145

peeked through her white, silky shirt. I imagined her teasing me by twirling a piece of her hair and seductively brushing the sides of her breast with her other hand. Her eyes penetrated me, seducing me to come closer to taste her lips and tongue. I froze, too afraid to engage, to step closer, and to latch onto that moment where our worlds collided, forcing us together in an awkward moment when I, the shy girl, didn't have a clue how to even move in for a kiss.

Saving me, my mind pulled Eva away.

I stood alone in my cubicle.

I scanned the room and noticed Katie standing off near a floor plant snickering, curling up her big lips, and enjoying my defeat. Suddenly, the ground sucked me in like quicksand, pulling at my pants and yanking them down to my knees. I stood stranded above the ground in just my red undies. The entire office got a kick out of that. They started pointing and telling me my skin had turned redder than the undies. That's when I dove. I dove into the ground, and it took me in. It held me hostage under the fibrous carpeting where no one could see me, but I could see all of them. They laughed and hit their legs in obvious hysterics. Eva stared at the ground where I'd been standing. Her face turned down and her eyes glazed over. She rested her hand on her slender hip with a face that said, 'Her? My sweet CarefreeJanie is plain Jane? Are you kidding me?'

I opened my eyes and all flutters had long disappeared. A gnawing replaced them and ripped at my insides, leaving me restless, sad, and yearning for that one thing I knew at that moment I'd never have – the gift of love, of touch, of something as simple and wondrous as a first kiss.

With a melancholy tune playing on my heart, I began writing a far different story than I set out to write. The lead character, afraid to show her true self, hid under a visor and wore long sleeves to hide her scars. After years of writing back

146

and forth, she finally agreed to meet her cyber lover in person after learning her lover would marry another the very next day.

She skirted around the bend in the road and stopped when she saw her lover sitting idle in the middle of the road cross-legged, head cocked to the side, a smile prettier than any rainbow lighting up her face. The shy girl with scars running up and down her body forgot all time and place and ran to her with outstretched arms. Tears stung her eyes when she landed in front of her lover's shiny spirit. The wind picked up as she stood before the woman she loved. Her visor flew off, exposing her scars and opening up a lifetime of vulnerabilities. Her hands flew to her face and her sleeves rolled up her forearms further exposing the ugly parts of her she had carefully hidden all her life in the dark corners of her waterfront apartment.

Her lover, pushing herself up off the ground in one strong leap, stood before her like an angel shining her light from within and onto her. Love danced on her golden face and sparkled like diamonds on the spokes of her eyes. She reached out with strength and pulled her into her warm embrace, shouldering all of her hidden pain and willing for her to shed it at their feet.

Fearing nothing in the light of her girlfriend, she lowered her hands from her scars, rolled up her sleeves further, and exposed herself in new light to the girl she waited too long to embrace.

The two clung to each other under a maple tree, under a bird's song, and under the shimmering rays of a sunlight shining through them. Nature protected them from all that threatened to steal their remaining time. Their heartbeats connected, beating as one until the sun sank below the tree trunks and the crickets sang them a lullaby. At that point the girl with the scars opened her eyes and realized she stood alone, clinging to her bed pillow in the dark shadows of her lonely bedroom where the only flicker of light shone from her computer screen, alerting her to a new message.

With no time to spare, the girl hopped up from her bed and prayed her vanity hadn't caused her to be too late to embrace the one person in the world that mattered – her cyber lover who was about to get married to a man she didn't love all because the girl with deep scars failed to trust her or anyone.

I stopped typing. I reread my passage, and an emptiness so loud deafened me to all else going on around me.

I no longer felt like screwing myself on a bike.

#

"I dreamed about you last night," Eva wrote.

I couldn't type back a response just then. I needed coffee and time to absorb the loss I still carried with me since three a.m. The whole bantering thing had spun out of control. It could destroy me if I didn't play carefully. Had I avoided pain and humiliation all my adult life only to throw myself in front of it willingly? What did I think was going to happen here? I didn't know how to be that girl who could walk into a room and light it up, garnering the attention of someone real like Eva.

I had to hand it to myself, though. I did a remarkable job crafting CarefreeJanie. I showed up cute, spunky, and full of life. I much preferred being her. In fact, on Twitter I racked up the followers. People from different countries that followed Eva started following me. Eva had over two thousand followers. I neared two hundred and got pretty excited about that. Two hundred people cared what CarefreeJanie had to say?

I started to build up CarefreeJanie by retweeting Eva's quotes that she'd send out daily to me and to a good hundred or so other followers who happened to be in the film industry. She managed to grab the attention of a few actors and actresses each day. I knew that because I dove right into stalker mode soon after we hooked up online. They'd say something pleasant back to her about her quote, and she'd offer them a wink or a smile. Lately, especially that morning, her breadcrumb trail of winks started to annoy me. I wanted her winks to myself. Yet, she tossed them to pretty actresses and good-looking actors like she tossed out hard candy at a parade. They, not unlike me, probably got a little excited because they'd flirt back a reply and she'd banter along with them. One girl started to ignite my jealous twitch when she started using pet names with her like 'cutie pie' and 'sweetness.'

Instead of replying to her message right away, I decided to stalk more. I went onto her Facebook profile and read through her timeline and interactions. That same girl kept liking everything Eva posted, even if she said something silly like 'It's raining, and I forgot my umbrella in the car again.' I clicked on the girl's profile and accessed an alarming amount of information. She wanted the world to know exactly what she did with her life. I read all about her, about how she loved basketball and rollerblading on the pier and shrimp fried in beer batter. She loved Notre Dame football, live theatre, and especially her girlfriend Eva Handel, whom she'd been devoted to for the past five years.

Girlfriend.

My heart sank. My throat dried up. My blood turned thick as oil. Who was that bitch and why hadn't my Eva told me about a girlfriend?

I read more. She graduated from University of Maryland University College with a master's degree in computer engineering and moved to Boston to pursue a position at a tech firm. She loved to visit New York City, where she enjoyed meeting up with her girlfriend to watch her act in plays. She wrote a small tribute to her saying Eva was her teacher and mentor and the reason she smiled and loved life.

All feeling evaded me. I could no longer swallow. My head buzzed. My temples pulsed. Alarms in all bodily systems flared to tsunami warning levels. The ground may as well have eaten me up and swallowed me whole because I no longer wanted to be a part of that ride, that life, or that existence. I just wanted to shut my eyes and pretend I never landed on Eva's mismatched shoes, never imagined her adoring smile from afar, never tweeted to her about Old Bay seasoning, and never tangled myself up into a web that grabbed me and strangled the life from my cells like a mad tornado sucking all fixtures from a house.

I tortured myself further. I trekked into her pictures and saw several of them holding hands. I searched recent pictures and could find none of them together. I saw that gorgeous, blonde girl with hair as smooth as glass and a size two body with style, grace, and sex appeal. In her cover photo, she leaned against a red sports car wearing a set of Ray Bans. She looked like a freaking sunglasses model.

I wanted to throw up.

I retraced my steps back to Eva's profile and scanned to find more information on that chick named Sara. Nothing. I could find nothing on Eva's profile that connected the two other than Sara's incessant, compulsive need to 'like' everything Eva posted. Eva's status said single. Her pictures showed no signs.

I reread her message to me. Was that the norm? Flirt online where your lover won't catch you? Were they lovers? Was she taking me on a fake ride to see how far she could get me to go?

Was she just a big fake like me? Did we cancel each other's fakeness out and that made it okay for us to mingle and flirt? I savored my secrets, she savored hers. Two wrongs making a right?

I needed to understand that in full detail.

I would bait her. I logged into Messenger. "What did you dream about?"

"You and I were acting in a short film together. One that you wrote. I stood before you as a professor and you sat as my pretty, flirty student."

And just like rainwater, her words and charm washed away my envy, lifting me up to higher ground where I no longer wanted to punch something. The girl could've just had a crush on my Eva. Who wouldn't? Eva didn't commit a crime here. "Maybe one day I'll surprise you and write something for you."

"I love surprises."

"I bet there's a lot you love," I wrote. "I want to know more about you."

"Like?"

"Like how did you get involved in acting?"

"I played the Good Witch of the North in *The Wizard of Oz* when I was in second grade. That's when I got the itch."

"You must've been adorable."

We continued to message back and forth for two hours. I fed her question after question and enjoyed learning all about Eva Handel's passions and silly fears. She would volley me a question, and I pointed her away with the skill of an Aikido master, focusing her right back to herself. Eventually, she stopped me and begged that I tell her something personal about myself.

"I hate talking about myself."

"It's weird because most people like it."

"I'd rather let my story unfold naturally."

"Well at least talk to me about your writing. Have you written me another sweet story yet?"

"I wrote one last night. It's not sweet, though. It's sort of sad." I hung my vulnerability on the line like I would a set of wet towels. Progress?

"Good writing needs to be honest. Sadness is part of life. I want to read it."

"I'll send it to you." I wanted the attention off me and back on her. "So tell me more about other good things happening in your life." I hoped she'd take the bait and offer something up about that girl.

"Well, my company just offered me an incredible opportunity. I'm going to be the spokesperson for them. I'll be the face of Martin Sporting Goods in a series of public service announcements."

"Wow," I wrote, sounding markedly surprised. "That sounds fantastic."

"I'll be filmed right here in a film studio. I get a wardrobe allowance. I get national coverage in commercials."

"I'm so happy for you."

"My aunt and uncle are thrilled. I'm finally going to be able to pay them off for when they bailed me out of a bad house deal."

"Oh? What did you do? Buy when the market climbed too high?"

"Sort of. I went through an ugly divorce when I was nineteen. We had to sell low and we still owed money. My aunt and uncle bailed us out so we could sell it and make a clean break."

Girlfriend? Divorce? What next? Fuck the mysterious and discovery phase. My heart couldn't take anymore. "You were married?"

"Just for a very short time. I married my high school boyfriend. It ended ugly. We never should've gotten married. I realize now that I only did because he was a way out. Thankfully, it's behind both of us now."

I wanted to know her story. Was Handel even her real last name? Why was it ugly? How could anything with her be ugly? "Can I ask you something personal?"

"Of course, honey."

"Are you dating anyone? And, if you are, you don't have to hide it."

"Are you?" she asked.

I chuckled on that one. If she only knew. "No."

"I've had this on-again, off-again, relationship with this girl for several years. Right now, we're off."

"What's her name?"

"Her name is Sara. She's just really jealous and possessive."

"How so?"

"She doesn't want me to act because she doesn't want anyone else near me."

"That's not fair."

"No, honey. It's not. I don't want to hurt her, but this is my dream."

"I'd never do that to you."

"I adore you," she wrote.

"I think I adore you more."

#

The next night after work I couldn't resist. I combed through her Facebook profile again, searching for some clues about an ex-husband. That girl appeared again, liking everything Eva posted. Eva still had yet to like any of hers.

Good girl.

By ten o'clock, I caved and just asked her. "I want to hear about your ugly divorce. Did he treat you badly?"

"No. I wish I could say yes. I was sort of a bad person."

I defined a bad person as a mass murderer, an animal torturer, a child abuser, or an elderly exploiter. So, I exhaled on the faith that she was none of those. "Spill it."

"You have to answer at least one personal question for me first because my story is going to get deep."

I blew out hot air. "What's your question?"

"What is your typical day like?"

"I wake up, I work out, I sip coffee, I stalk you on Twitter—hehe totally kidding—and I sometimes fantasize about winning the Pulitzer Prize."

"Why are you so afraid to talk about yourself?"

"I don't understand. I just did."

"That could've been anyone's life. I wanted something personal to you. It's like you're hiding behind that baseball cap brim."

The inevitable started. "Give me time. I unpeel very slowly."

"Okay. That was super sexy and hot."

A warm ripple surged through me. "Mmm. Well, that's because you have a way of bringing that out in me."

"Well, I wish I could bring out more in you."

"Here's one more piece of my puzzle and it's back to you. I love John Denver."

"Whoa. Way too much information."

"I thought so. Now spill your story."

"Here goes. I cheated on him and got pregnant. I passed it off as his until I discovered it was a molar pregnancy."

I already typed in molar pregnancy to my search field before she sent her next message.

"He blamed himself for the molar pregnancy, so he scheduled a vasectomy because he didn't want me to ever suffer again."

I read the medical site. It described that a molar pregnancy was when tissue that normally became a fetus instead became an abnormal growth. The pregnancy was thought to be caused by a genetic issue of the egg or sperm. The growth needed to be removed immediately or hemorrhaging could occur. Sometimes the disease kept growing after the molar pregnancy was removed and turned into cancer. My chest sunk. I imagined her crying, sadness seeping into every morsel of her life at that moment, planning one minute to be a mommy, the next to end up a cancer patient.

"I confessed that I had gotten pregnant when he had been out of town for a month. He assumed I was two months pregnant when in fact I was three. That's how I knew the other guy had gotten me pregnant."

I kept reading the medical article and learned that a woman had to be blood tested for the following six to twelve months to ensure no more of the diseased tissue remained. If it appeared, it could turn into cancer.

"Was it cancer?"

"You're researching this right now, aren't you?"

"Well, tell me."

"I cheated on my husband. Did you read that part?"

"You were nineteen. I get it. Was it cancer or not?"

"It was not cancer. The guy I slept with served in the war. Some soldiers at the time had issues producing healthy babies."

"Thank God." I always wanted her healthy and glowing, hair flowing, eyes sparkling, and lips pouty and full of color.

"So, penises, huh?" I asked.

"I went through a phase."

"Isn't it usually the other way around?"

"I've never been one to abide by the norm."

"Good news for me (wink)."

"Those winks get me every time, honey."

My libido hung on the line with my vulnerability waiting on the breeze for its dance. I wanted to play. "I'm glad." As long as both of us were probably still hiding a couple of things, why not? I didn't plan on a real relationship with her anyway. CarefreeJanie craved more euphoria, more stoking, more fire. "Did I tell you that you woke me up caressing me with your yummy lips?"

"Ah, Janie. What are you doing to me?"

I moaned at her cuteness. I needed more. "I like your lips."

"I like yours too. Both sets (wink)."

My body rose to her song. "And I'd like to feel your lips on both of them. Mmm, I just know you'd send me over the edge." Yup, I reeled out of control and loved it.

"Your lips are wet and tasty."

"If you keep tempting me like this, then I'm going to be forced to go 'relax.'" There, I said it, and the magic stirred in me like a well-mixed drink, smooth and tasty.

"Let's both go and 'relax' and think of each other."

I could've orgasmed on the spot thinking of her fingers getting naughty. I reached down into my undies and felt my wetness. Warm, slippery, and swollen, it pulsed under my touch. "Already started," I managed to type with my left hand.

"Oh, you are too much, Janie. I'm joining you."

I pictured her, feet up on her coffee table, sprawled spread eagle with her lovely swollen clit wide and smelling earthy and wild. Her fingers, dripping wet and flicking against her pink folds, would bring out her moans. Her gentle strokes would fire up a hailstorm of pleasure that would cause her hips to grind, her mouth to open in a small seductive slit, and her eyes to rest at half mast, until finally, her whole body would scream out for me. I swam to nirvana again. My spirit merged with hers as I scaled the waves and rode them out to the open sea where I bobbed up and down and climbed the walls of great water until I came upon the highest one. On top of it, Eva floated, holding out her hand and urging me to grab hers. When I did, she pulled me up, and I flew to her lovely warm embrace, landing safely in her arms where I caved onto her in a heap of pleasure too great to confine. My legs trembled, my body buzzed, and my lungs screamed out for breath to enter. "That was incredible."

"You sent me over the edge, Janie."

"Wow," I wrote. "Wow. That's all I've got." I panted, heaving in and out, hugging myself, and wishing it were Eva.

# #

I sat across from Larry eating a salad splashed with oil and vinegar, something of an oddity for me. I typically smothered my rabbit food in thick, yummy ranch dressing, indulging and not caring one iota about the hundreds of extra calories I consumed. That all changed in a matter of one moment, one exciting, climaxing moment. I could no longer afford to consume useless calories, because I could no longer stand to grow my fat for reserve any longer. I would get fit. I would lose the extra twenty pounds I'd carried around since high school. I would fit into a size six one day soon. Maybe I might even expose myself to her one day. For that, I needed to prepare.

I forked another mouthful of tangy lettuce into my mouth and munched down on it as if chomping on a piece of delicious, juicy steak hot off the grill.

"You're freaking me out. Why are you making love to Romaine lettuce?" Larry asked, cutting into his chicken parmesan drizzled in decadent marina sauce.

"Eva and I shared an orgasm last night."

His eyes flew open. Before he could swallow, he spoke. "And, you're telling me this in a crowded restaurant, why?"

"So you don't go making a big deal out of it." I squared off with him, squinting to match his squint, then remembered my new skin care regimen I started right after I pleased myself that morning. I could afford no more wrinkles. No more squinting. Sunblock every moment in the sun. When I laughed, I'd do so carefully so as not to cause my eyes to crease. I straightened and opened my eyes wide. I was a woman in love, and I wanted to keep it that way.

He leaned in, planting a silly grin on his face. "Did you zoom off to some other world?"

I leaned in and grabbed a hold of his hands. "I did."

We erupted into a fit of giddy giggles.

"I could tell," he said. "You're glowing. You're eyes are shiny. You even styled your hair." He ran his fingers through my smooth ends. "You're also not eating the bread." He pointed his eyes to the basket of parmesan crusted Italian sweetness sitting next to the ketchup bottle. Looking back at me, he dropped his fork and knife and latched onto my hands. "Are you totally in love?"

"I don't know what this is. I just know I love it."

"Now you know what I'm going through." He thinned his lips and tilted his head. A thin layer of pain stretched across the plain of his face. "We went out

158

again last night. While standing under the moon in Centennial Park, he cradled my face in his hands and whispered to me that he loved me."

A mixture of envy and pride swelled in me. "Did you say it back?"

"I almost did until a group of runners sped by, scaring the crap out of us and ruining the moment."

"Maybe just as well? I mean he's married. How will it ever work, Larry?" I sat back now, crossing my arms over my chest ready to have an honest conversation with my friend now that I was all experienced in that thing called love. "Are you prepared to be that third wheel?"

He picked up his knife and fork again and cut into his chicken. He tore at it, dissecting layers of it as if operating and searching for a sign he could cut out and avoid. "I never intended to get in the middle of a marriage. That's the last thing I want to do. Karma. What comes around goes around. It's not his fault he fell in love with a man and is married to a woman. Is it?" His face blotched. Sadness trailed his eyes. He stabbed some more at his chicken, then involved his green beans in the massacre. "I'm in trouble, aren't I?"

"You are." I dropped my arms from my chest and continued back into my laborious salad journey. I'd never tasted anything more flat and lifeless. "My problems are worse."

"How so?"

"She loves CarefreeJanie, not plain Jane. I'm two people. I'm nothing like CarefreeJanie."

He puffed his cheeks up and exhaled. "Tell her now while you still see the world in color. Otherwise, you're going to get hurt and I'll have to go in and save your sad little ass from misery. I just don't have that in me because I'm dealing with my own tragedy right now." He bore into my eyes with a warning. "Seriously, tell her now before it gets too much more out of hand."

His words landed inside me, but slipped right out as quickly as they entered. The thrill ride would not end just yet. "You're probably right."

We sat eating our lunches in silence, he sipping his iced tea, I downing my boring water with a slice of lemon that tasted too tangy. The restaurant cleared out aside from a group of three boys goofing off over heaping plates of burgers. They laughed and called each other assholes and dickheads, slapping one another upside the head for macho effect I could only guess. Larry rolled his eyes a few too many times over them, and I just tried to ignore their rants. Finally, as we paid our check, the boys paid theirs and left us to a few moments of peace before we had to circle out and get back to our jobs.

We walked out together, Larry cradling my shoulder and urging me one last time to confess myself to the girl or find someone more available who would care and love me the way I deserved. I assured him I would think on it, nodding on point, inflecting my words so convincingly I could've even fooled myself. As we passed the general store, he realized he had forgotten his notepad on the table. So, I waited, leaning against the storefront wall as he retraced back for it.

Meanwhile, the trio of boys sat on their bicycles blocking another boy from walking past them. The boy, timid and scared and clinging to his scrawny self, looked up at me with a plea in his eye. I froze, remembering how that felt to have to get past the bullies who laughed and toyed. I wanted to reach out, take the boy's hand, and assure him that one day he'd look back at that moment and not let it define him.

I sucked at lying. It would define him. It would stick to him like thorns poking him in the middle of the night, startling him whenever he ran into three or more people staring at him. He would look at himself in the mirror and question why he had to be born scrawny, born weaker to others' strength, and born with a sign above his head that said 'go ahead, toy with me. Everyone else already does. It's my purpose to be your personal punching bag.'

Stuck a moment too long into my trek down memory lane, Larry had run past me and powered his way up to the group, saving the young boy from the misery I had already sentenced and locked him up into. The boy wept as Larry led him back to us. The boys on bicycles laughed and snickered calling him a faggot. I winced. The boy cried more. Larry turned to the group and chucked them the bird.

I stood frozen not even able to embrace the poor boy who looked like he'd been through three warzones and back. I saw Rhonda's face, tear-stained and blubbering, looking to me for mercy. Just as I had failed her, I failed that boy, too, in a moment that really mattered.

# #

On the drive back, I stared out the window in silence, embarrassed and sad because of my weakness.

"Are you okay? You haven't said a word and it's freaking me out."

I wished I could release the chaos that clamored me shut, but not even Larry could handle what I refused to confess. "I could use some cheesecake." My chin started to quiver, and the tears rolled. Larry reached out and held my hand, braving onward.

"I'll drop by the bakery on the way home and pick one up."

"Isn't tonight date night for you?"

"It is. He'll just have to wait."

I picked up his hand and kissed the back of it. "Thank God for you."

161

I managed to get through the rest of the day without wallowing too much. I saved that for Larry. He knew what to do with bad feelings. He knew how to pile them up in one neat corner, organize them until they formed logic, and then tuck them away in a safe place far from my mind.

Doreen saved an extra blueberry muffin for me. "You look like you could use this."

I went to toss it into my mouth, but then my conscious mind appeared, waving a finger at me to remind me how many hundreds of calories sat laden in that muffin. "You know, I'm still full from lunch."

I handed back her muffin, and she cocked her head. "Did that wench say something catty to you?" She balled her hand up into a fist and grunted. "Do I need to go punch her little beady face?"

I laughed out loud on that one. "I actually haven't seen the wench at all today."

Doreen backed down. "Then, what's wrong?"

"Nothing." I turned my back to her and pretended to get to work. "I'm just irritable because I'm getting my period any day."

"Okay, sweetie." She patted my shoulder and walked away, leaving me alone with my memory of the young boy with the panicked face looking to me for help, as I just stood there wallowing in my own self-pity and selfishness.

#

When Larry arrived with cheesecake in hand, I wasted no time. I dove into it, knowing he had better things to do with his night than sit and help me figure out how to feel good about something that stunk of everything wrong.

I shoveled in a few bites and took stock in the situation. "I should've done something for that poor boy, but didn't."

"I knew it." Larry sat back, kicked his feet up on the coffee table, and folded his hands in his lap.

That's when I saw his new ring, a black opal surrounded in platinum.

I grabbed his hand. "When did you get this?"

"Two hours ago."

The ring, polished to perfection, fit his ring finger perfectly. "From him?"

He nodded sheepishly. "I know. It's wrong. It's all I've got right now, so leave it alone."

"It's gorgeous." I dropped his hand and shoveled a piece of cheesecake into my mouth. "So does this mean you're committed to each other in a non-ceremonious way?"

"This cheesecake session isn't about me right now." He arched his eye and bit into his slice. "What were you going to do? Jump in between the boys?"

"Most people would've."

"I would never expect you to do something foolish like that. The boys could've hurt you, too."

"That's sexist." I pointed my fork at him and squinted, then remembered the wrinkles I needed to avoid now.

"You're not exactly martial arts material. I'm a black belt, remember?"

"He pleaded with me to help him, and I just looked away." I couldn't even look Larry in the eye with that confession.

"So because you didn't step in, you're just as guilty?"

"Without a doubt. Growing up, teachers and other people I relied on turned their backs on me getting punched, stepped on, kicked, and pelted. They witnessed the torturing and turned to talk to a fellow teacher, ignoring my pleading eyes for them to step in and help. I hate those teachers to this day. If I saw them, I'd probably walk up to them, kick them, and ask how they liked the pain sizzling through their veins. If that boy walked up to me now and kicked me, I'd understand and take on the punishment. I would deserve it. I am against bullying, yet I allowed it to happen right in front of me. I'm no different than a bully."

"You're being too hard on yourself. I only interfered because I have training. I deal with these types of kids at the center and at my church. I know their limits. I know mine."

"Compassion doesn't require training, Larry." I spooned another piece into my mouth. "I'm really useless."

He pondered that over another bite. He nodded his head, deep in thought. I could see the wheels cranking in his brain. Like a kid waiting on the carnival game that spit out toys, I waited for Larry to spit out his advice. "Being physical isn't the only way to stand up to bullies."

"Go on." I moved in closer, waiting for the magic to spur from his mouth.

"What are you great at?"

"Don't force me to play this self-confidence game. Not tonight."

"Okay, well besides your newest talent of flirting with cuties on Twitter of course."

I laughed. "Comic relief. Fantastic." I punched his arm. "Okay, well dare I say writing?"

"Bingo. Get cracking. I challenge you to write an article for my LGBT group about bullying."

"And say what?"

"Tell a story," he said, slowly and sternly.

"But, what—"

He stood up. "—just tell a story." He patted my head and walked out of my condo, leaving me with countless permutations of stories I could tell.

Chapter Eleven

A blank screen is as scary and intimidating to a writer as an expansive desert with no sign of life or water is to a thirsty, lost traveler. It sucked any productive, lucid thought from the mind and rendered the person useless, the edges of her creativity tattered, shriveled, curled up, and unable to produce much of anything but crap.

Crap. Yup, that pretty much summed up my writing so far that night. I typed a sentence with no meat to it. I erased said sentence only to falter at the sight of the blank screen again. So, I typed a few more words that pretty much sat there tormenting me, like a bully sticking out her tongue at me and mocking me for my useless attempt to create something uplifting and positive out of my faulty personality.

Writer's block sucked. Did all writers suffer? How did those bestselling novelists who shot off a book every three months do it? Were they just born with lucky writers' brains that overflowed with brilliant ideas? Could they could tap into them at any given time? Did they sit at their computers and instantly fill the blank screen with words that people would want to read? Did the ideas spill out of their brains like a waterfall, deliberate, focused, and purposeful?

I stuck out my tongue to the blank screen, angry at it for tormenting me so. I had no story to tell. Why would a bunch of bullied teenagers want to read my words, my thoughts, or my advice to them on how to live their best life while someone pounded on their hearts with hurtful, vicious attack?

The longer I stared, the whiter the screen glowed. So, I did what any writer probably did when faced with such devilish torment. I turned to the Internet for distraction.

I ventured onto Twitter and read Eva's newest message to me.

"Missing me or not, honey?"

My heart swelled and formed a light, breezy melody that frolicked around, tickling me, kissing me, and warming the coldest regions that up until that moment had never allowed in the sunshine. I loved that girl.

I wanted her to see me in my best light, always. I wanted to stand before her and watch her face grow into a smile that streamed light and love from her pure heart. I wanted her eyes to drip with admiration for me, the girl I really was, the girl she loved back. I wanted to have a moment with her where the two of us stood facing one another on a mountain top surrounded by blue skies and puffy white clouds with birds flying ahead singing their song. I wanted her to caress me with her loving eyes. I wanted to be that girl she believed me to be—strong, intelligent, insightful, full of promise and intrigue, and romance.

I wanted to be that girl who could stir a person's soul with her words, touching people with viewpoints that changed the world. I wanted to be that girl who inspired, encouraged, and enriched lives through careful reasoning, bringing up questions others were too afraid to ask and ponder. I wanted to dissect social injustice and lay it out on the line for people to see the real deal. I yearned to expose the raw emotions that erupted when idiots threw their fists into the faces of innocent people just trying to get by in the world, just trying to blend in and be a part of society like every other person had a right to do. I wanted to take the bullied by the hand and show them they didn't have to stand for the abuse. They could rise up above the chaos and shed their light onto the world, instead of snuffing it out in the dark corners of their abused minds. They didn't have to hide in the shadows of people who didn't have a clue about compassion, people who would rather trip a girl than lend a hand in helping her back to her feet, or people who would rather laugh at the unfortunate humiliation of another instead of standing up for that person and laughing with her instead. I wanted to give voice to those bullied victims who sank down with their heads buried in the sand, choking on grit and burning up under the scorching firestorms. Victims should not have to suffer the consequences of a first lashing, first scarring, or a first public humiliation that turned them from a potential bright star into fizzled-out stardust at the hands of the most incapable, most destructive, most lethal form of human beings on the planet—bullies.

Bullies were just fearful individuals, too, full of poison fed to them by bullies before them. I knew that to be true. I had been one. I shelled out the hurt and caused permanent damage to not only the victims, but their families, their would-be lovers, would-be friends, would-be constituents, and would-be colleagues.

My anger superseded any fear I had of white space at the moment. I started typing out a four beat rhythm with my fingertips, slashing the consequences of fear with my words and building up a safe place and refuge for the injured. That safe place contained greenery that filtered the toxins from their lungs, reenergized their skin cells, and restored them to their precious state of pre-bully days. That oasis for the victims shined with sunlight twenty-four seven and sprinkled mist to soften and replenish their spirits, leaving rainbows to remind those people that hope lived and flourished. That oasis would offer them the promise of coming out of the hell storm alive, unscathed, and a productive member of society. The answer to dealing with bullies was not bowing down to their attacks and allowing them to steal their souls, their light source, or that special thing that raised them up on their unique pedestal. No, the answer was not to fight back. That only antagonized. The answer was to dig deep, find power from within, find their special gifts, and shine that sucker on their bullies so brightly that all not willing to see its beauty would simply be stilled by it.

The process of realization needed to take place long before the rocks pelted, before the feet tripped, or before the laughter escaped the bully's mouth. Every person had a life source, and along the way, that life source was either kicked to the furthest recesses of her mind and covered up in the shroud of doubts, despair, and fear, or it sprang forth and powered the person to move forth in the world proudly, acknowledging her gift and sharing it with the world. Someone would cherish the gift. And even if one person cherished it, wasn't that enough?

I kept typing. The words just flew out of my brain and onto the keyboard. I imagined Eva reading it, her lips curling up into a smile at the honesty and integrity behind the words. She'd be my proud cheerleader, hoping one day I'd create something just as beautiful for her. I wanted her to admire me for the gift that was all mine and not CarefreeJanie's. She — my muse, my saving grace — sat front row to my words.

I continued typing feverishly, my soul unloading itself onto the computer screen. Tears ran down my cheeks. I landed in a zone. I thought of that young boy being bullied and wondered about his life source. Maybe he was an artist who painted meaning onto a canvas, and one day that painting would touch someone so profoundly. The ripple effect would touch the lives of many, maybe even save a life or two or more. Or what if he was fantastic at pitching a baseball and could be that boy who brought a group of twenty kids to the playoffs, giving hope to not only the team, but to the parents, siblings, and community? Or maybe that kid was really good at seeing the best in others and would one day counsel someone on the verge of a nervous breakdown, saving that person through his brilliant ability to pull out of him his magical healing gift.

We need solutions, I wrote.

Bullies will always exist. A society cannot spray bullies down and wipe out their inclinations to torment like we can do to cockroaches. They might move out of one life, but assuredly, they'll find a way to move into another life before long. They will always exist. So, where are we, as a society, to better face our focus? If we can't eradicate the behavior, what then?

If we can't change them, who do we change? I asked.

If we can't control their actions, whose do we control?

We can't control others, but we can control the way we react to others.

So, that boy, getting laughed at and passed around like a hot potato, couldn't control the others, but he could've controlled how he reacted to them. Fear and insecurity no doubt swelled in his chest as his heart pounded, his flesh clammed up, and his scared mind envisioned his fatal demise right there on the sidewalk at the hands of derelicts who controlled his world at that moment in time. What was a kid to do under such dire circumstances? Put up his fists and fight off four others who stood taller and had the comfort and security of numbers on their side? Certainly the boy grew up playing video games and not practicing martial arts, so to fight back would be irresponsible advice.

I sat back, stumped, with no clue where to go from there. How could've that scrawny kid turned the situation around? Best reaction? Duck, roll, and run? Feasible? Hardly when cornered by that swarm of idiots. Toss out a comedic phrase, and hope they latch on and laugh like the kid's the funniest thing since

Robin Williams? Hardly. The kid could barely breathe let alone conjure up witty words to escape his mouth.

What fueled a bully? What fueled a fire? Kindling. Fear disguised itself as just another form of kindling. Toss fear into an escalating situation and it exploded into something grander than it had to be. Its flames would shoot up to the tops of trees if stoked enough. Extinguish the fear, extinguish the flame, and end the torture, the burning, and the smoldering. What was left? Ash. The brilliant thing about ash was that it could be swept away by a gentle breeze. All the fear that once created the flames that produced the ash weren't so heavy and powerful anymore when a gentle breeze could come and blow it away into nonexistence.

Squash the fear, end the victimization.

Everyone came equipped with different resources. My way of squashing fear would be far different than Eva's way, Larry's way, or that boy's way. We owed it to ourselves to dig deep and find out what tools we had in our disposal to crush the shit out of our fears so we could get on living our best days. Those who helped guide others to find and lend their tools would reap rewards far too powerful for any bully to come in and swipe away. The leverage in digging deeper and serving others, offered power. When a person came outside of that shell to protect another, he helped erase fear and replaced it with a light so powerful no one could extinguish it.

I ended on a question. *Is this the secret? Find the good even in your enemy and bring it out?*

I sat back and smirked at the screen filled with words. I couldn't wait to share it with Eva.

\# \#

I edited the story a few dozen times, then sent it off to Eva. Within fifteen minutes, she responded back with twenty exclamation points. Yup – twenty.

My heart soared.

I then forwarded my essay to Larry on a Monday after refining it a couple dozen more times. He barged into my condo moments later in tears, hugging me, and telling me he'd never read anything as touching and beautiful. Something strange occurred as he congratulated me.

Instead of balking at his praise as just another fluffy, friendly thing he did, I allowed it in, absorbed it, and cherished it.

I deserved the praise. The piece shined.

Larry promised to publish it in the newsletter that Wednesday.

In between bouts of elation, where I skipped and frolicked in the wonderful paradise of a serious writer's high, Eva and I flirted like crazy with each other. She would say things to me like, "I'd love to be with you, just the two of us hanging out in a grassy field, wind gently blowing, enjoying you in my arms." And, I would respond with a reserved, "Ah. So beautiful."

Her sweet, loving words sent me reeling and took my mind off waiting for Wednesday's newsletter release. On Thursday afternoon while at work, after reading my essay in the newsletter ten times, Eva and I hooked up online.

"Come, let's have lunch, honey," she wrote.

"I'm eating right now," I said, offering a smile.

"I want you to eat lunch with me."

"Yum, I'd like that. If only I had a private jet to get me there quickly enough. What would you feed me?"

"Well, I'm standing in the main headquarters branch right now and they're serving up some yummy Indian food," she wrote. "I just piled my plate with daal, roti, butter milk, salad, papad, and veggies cooked in different gravies called sabji." She continued. "Oh, and apparently it's mango season, so we also have ripe mangoes. Yum."

I stuck my fork in my mango. My blood pressure spiked. My temples throbbed. Even my earlobes beat with vigor. I dropped my roti onto my daal and scrunched down low in my seat. A bead of sweat sprang onto my forehead. My skin pricked. The little hairs on the back of my neck stood up at attention. I could hear her laughing along with Sanjeev and Katie. "Doreen," I whispered over my cubicle. She didn't answer. I bent low and snuck around to her cube. She wasn't there. Then, I heard her cackle coming toward me, and Eva asked her if she preferred white rice to brown. I glanced around, planning an escape. Then they rounded the corner to our aisle. There I stood, crouched down like a cat ready to pounce over the cubicle walls. My face lit up. I knelt down and pretended to be fixing my sandal. Katie followed right behind them.

"Hey, Jane, there's still some more food in the collaboration room," Doreen rang out.

I didn't look up. Instead, I rose and pretended to be plucking lint from my shirt, hiding my beads of sweat and flushed face. "Thanks," I whispered and scooted into my cubicle.

Eva's eyes followed me. I wanted to die.

My Twitter profile filled my screen. I ran in front of the screen to block it and turn it off. Any more shocks, and I would've surely passed out.

"Jane, is it?" Eva asked.

I swallowed hard, wiped my forehead with my bare forearm, and turned to meet her smiling eyes and extended hand.

"We meet again," she said.

I tripped over my insecurity. "Yes."

"I heard you're going to be writing that piece for the public service announcement."

Katie coughed.

I couldn't look directly at Eva, so I landed on Doreen who stood guard against Katie only inches away. I escaped to her concerned eyes. "Yes, isn't that right Doreen?" I nodded at her, begging her with frantic eyes to save me.

"She's the best."

"So I hear." Eva looked down at my sandals. "At least you know how to match your shoes." She crawled her eyes back up to meet mine and winked. My heart exploded. My flush reignited.

My eyes darted every which way afraid to set too long on hers. If she recognized them, my life would unravel faster than I could save it.

I reached behind me and gathered my plate overflowing with Indian food. "Please excuse me." I brushed by her. She even smelled sexy. "I'm going to get a little more."

She chuckled, staring at my plate. "It's good stuff. I don't blame you."

I rushed up the aisle, rounded the corner, tossed my plate in the trash, and took off to the bathroom where I prayed I'd find some solitude.

Standing in the stall, I messaged her back. "Wait, so you're in Maryland again and didn't tell me?"

A few seconds later, she messaged me back. "They called me last night, and I'm leaving right away back to New York this afternoon to lead an event."

"Oh, what a bummer." I played the part well. "So, you said something about mangoes? I love mangoes. I also love roti."

"Ah that's why I like you so much."

"Mmm. I can say the same about you." How best could I end it? "Enjoy your lunch, Eva. Think of me as you're spooning some mangoes between those yummy lips of yours (wink)." I ended the messaging with a big virtual hug, kiss, and promise to reconnect later when we both returned home.

Five minutes later, safely back in my cubicle and Eva tucked away into the boardroom, Larry called me.

"Your story was a hit. The analytics on that page are showing six hundred and thirty-three hits since yesterday. We typically get fifty or so per page."

A huge smile sprang to life. I squealed. "Am I getting a raise?"

"I'll see to it that you get a company car, too."

"I love you, my friend."

"I love you more," Larry said. "Oh, and be sure to check your email. You may get some responses because I included your email address at the end of your article."

I memorized my short story enough to have already known that.

"Will do," I said. "Oh, Larry. Thank you for asking me to write it. What a rush."

"Good because we need more."

"I'll get started on more right away." I hung up on a smile.

"Hey, Doreen?" I asked.

She popped up. "Glad to see you're back to your normal color."

"Was it that obvious?"

"You were purple at one point." She scrunched her face. "You looked adorable. You have such a crush on her, don't you?"

I groaned. "Stop." I raised up my hand. "Can you tell Sanjeev I'm working the rest of the day from home?"

"Are you feeling alright?"

"Yes. But you're going to tell him no." I pointed my finger at her. "Right?"

"Right." She winked and disappeared back over to her side.

# #

For two days, I received numerous emails thanking me for writing the story. Some sailed in from grandparents, from parents, from teachers, from school administrators, and one even came in from a former bully. "I knew I hurt people, but I didn't realize just how deep I cut until I read this. I am a few years past those horrible days when I used to bully a classmate of mine, but not a day goes by that I don't regret what I did. Reading this story hurt for obvious reasons, and I needed to hurt. Sometimes in life we need these painful reminders to keep us pointed in the right direction. Thank you for sharing and for opening up a pathway to greater change."

I sat in my cubicle at work with a knot in my throat, pushing back the tears, when I clicked into the next message from a boy named Travis.

Ms. Knoll, I just wanted to let you know how much your story has meant to me. Just three days ago, I sat in my bedroom with a revolver in my mouth ready to pull the trigger. I contemplated my troubles and spent several hours with my finger on the trigger trying to decide if shooting myself would be better or if I should just swallow a bottle of pills. I couldn't decide. So, I stuck to my original idea and left that gun in my mouth, ready to shoot when bravery kicked in. It never did kick in that day.

I eventually removed the gun, but kept it ready and loaded in my hand, staring at it, raising questions in my mind as to my purpose on this Earth and why God would've made me gay, scrawny, and the only black kid in a school full of white rich snobs. These kids are mean to me. They torture me with their stares, snickers, and rolling eyes. If just one of them could stand up and respect me, I'd be able to live out my high school days in peace. Instead, they all clamor together, one big pack of weak people who together run an army too strong to defeat with my tormented soul. There's only so much a kid can handle.

I sat on my bed staring at my dad's revolver, thinking how much easier it would be to just shoot myself. I would no longer have to hide in the bathroom stalls at gym time, eat lunch in the nurse's office at the chair reserved for sick kids who had real issues, sneak around school buses to avoid being seen walking home, stress about standing in front of a class and public speaking to a group of kids who made faces at me the entire time, or to ignore the fact that all my teachers, principal included, turned the other way when kids attempted to trip me and pull at my shirt.

Public humiliation hurts as you can imagine, but not nearly as much as the scars left behind. Scars cover my arms and legs, these left behind from vicious attacks on my walk home. For no reason kids jump out of bushes and launch full scale attacks on me saying they don't need any gays at their school. It hurts. I'm a good person and I know this. I'm scared, which is why I wanted to kill myself. I eventually placed the gun on the desk and went on to the LGBT website of my community center and found your story. God sent me an angel that day. He wrapped me in His arms, nudged me forward, and placed me in the softness and light of your beautiful words. I felt comforted, united, and understood. I just wanted you to know that you saved my life, and I will forever be indebted to you, Ms. Knoll. Your words touched me, and I don't know if that means a lot or not, but it sure meant the world to me. Thank you is all I want to say. Thank you for helping me to see through the hurt by reminding me that I've got my own spotlight to shine and light my path. With that, I've got strength and am hopeful I will be just fine. Yours truly, Travis.

I stood up, straightened my wrinkled shirt and pants, and marched my butt toward the bathroom, keeping it together even as I passed Katie's double cubicle and her fake smile. I carried myself to the last stall, closed myself into it, and then unable to hold it back, lost it.

Chapter Twelve

I attributed my newfound success in writing completely to Eva. In between flirty, sexy messages, she would encourage me to write her something that would stir her soul. So each night, after saying goodnight, I would pound away at the keyboard writing short stories like they were emails. They just flowed and poured out of me. I'd share them, and she'd go nuts, begging for more. At her insistence, I sent the stories to magazines and waited out responses without much regard. Eva kept me focused on producing more. Within a month, I banked up several dozen short stories and quite the ego.

At Eva's prompt, I started a blog and shared my short stories on it. It seemed CarefreeJanie had quite a bit to say and the world wanted to hear it. I started to gain more of a following on Twitter. People commented on my stories using descriptive words like 'talented,' 'touching,' and 'powerful,' and that further stroked my ego. But, nothing stroked my ego more than the way Eva responded to all the attention CarefreeJanie earned.

"You're a celebrity these days."

I'd blush at that and end up writing another story to release the energy. Eva was my muse in more ways than one. She infused energy and charge into my life. She revved me up, my secret fuel, and sent me speeding with ease down an open runway where possibilities grew like wildflowers. My mind expanded through her loving support.

I loved our messages to each other. I couldn't get enough of them. I craved her words like a drug addict craved a hit. Eva helped me to see new colors, new sunsets, and new beauty. I saw past the barriers that once blocked creative thought. I saw past the ridicule that once imprisoned me. I saw blue skies and puffy clouds and enjoyed the tickle of grass blades on my ankles as I strolled through the breezy fields of change, purpose, and full-out life. I embraced each day with hope, with a smile, with a lightness that lifted me like a plume into the wind, carrying me through the day with love in my heart.

Eva brought out the best in me. I loved the new me, the new CarefreeJanie, the cool, talented, enlightened girl behind the screen. I soon tossed aside the girl who wept, who pitied herself, and who shied away from walking with a bounce in her step at the mall for fear someone would laugh or trip her. I tossed the old Jane aside and allowed the new carefree Jane to take over. No one could penetrate the new me with hurt. My sweet and precious Eva, my muse, protected me with something so powerful, so giving, so loving, and so full of life.

Our relationship blossomed. I connected to her. I was in love with Eva Handel, and I was pretty sure she loved me, too.

"What are you doing right now?" she asked me one morning.

"I'm writing. I'd much rather be sipping a cool drink with you by my side. What are you doing?"

"If you were here, I would take you out for a long drive on my motorcycle."

I could just picture the beauty of her chocolate hair blowing around her face, wild and free. "You know how much I want to be tucked up against you on that open road, don't you?"

"I want you right there beside me, holding me tight as the wind whips around us."

"The rush would drive me wild." I fanned myself.

"Gosh, I really want to feel your lips against mine."

"I'm all warm and tingly now," I wrote. "I might have to go 'relax' (wink)."

"Aw. I wish I were there to 'relax' you."

"You always are."

The messages just kept getting hotter to the point I could no longer stop their ultimate progression and aim.

I cooled them down by asking her more questions about life. I learned that she loved adventure because it challenged her. She confessed that while growing up, she didn't allow failure into her life. Her parents failed miserably at things like paying bills on time, putting a safe roof over her head, and getting her to school on time. She mothered them, leading them to choices that would help get them onto the path of a better life. Where they failed to take action, she followed behind, scooping up the broken pieces and salvaging their survival. She didn't hate them for stealing away her childhood. She thanked them for turning her into someone who fought hard for her success. Through her tough times, she learned to survive, to rebuild, and to not take crap from anyone.

The more I learned about her, the more I loved her.

"No one has ever cared so much about me like you do," she wrote. "You make me feel so good, like you really care about me as a person."

"No one's ever made you feel like that before?"

"No. No one's ever listened to me like this before."

She attempted to get me to talk, too, and I just clammed up, not wanting to build up more lies than I could already handle. She would ask me where I worked. I lied and told her I worked as a freelance writer. She asked me if I played sports growing up. I lied and told her I played softball, basketball, and even ran road races as a teenager. When the questions poked at a more personal level, like asking about my family, my best friends, my fears, and my passions, I shut down, pretending I had to shove off to finish an assignment.

I hid well, and she respected that for a while. Then, one day while I was at work, she asked me what I was doing. "I'm eating lunch."

"Hmm. So are you eating alone?"

"Yup. I'm sitting in front of my computer alone."

"Can you jump on Skype?"

My heart stopped. I spit out my sandwich. A picture, I could doctor. A live stream, well, not so much.

"I don't have Skype."

"Then come on video chat."

"I don't have a webcam."

"We have to do something about that."

"I'm terrible on camera."

"You're gorgeous. And I want to see you live, talk to you in real time, and get to know the real you."

Her words struck at my shock center, firing off all sorts of alarm bells. "One day."

"What's your mailing address? I want to send you a webcam."

I wheeled away from my desk, searching my brain for an answer on how I could keep the ride going. The inevitable time had come when the adventure would end. Just like reading the last word of a novel, I couldn't take the thousands of words I'd just read and erase them from my memory. They were logged and earned their rightful spot in the recesses of my mind. Eva asked the question, and I could not go back in time and pretend she didn't ask it.

If I just got the inevitable over with by facing the heat and revealing my true identity, maybe I could put to rest all the anxieties and just get on with my life. How much longer could I keep up the charade? After a couple of months of dodging her pointed questions about my life, and her begging me to tell her more about me, I could finally rest the guilt of not being honest. I could stop stressing and just move onto the next chapter in my life. Otherwise, what would I do? Spend the next fifty years flirting with her behind my computer screen in the hopes that would be enough to sustain her love and affection for a girl like me?

But, I couldn't end it. I needed her. I could buy more time.

"My editor's calling. I've got to run," I wrote.

After I logged off, I called Larry.

#

Larry knocked on my door with cheesecake in hand. "I ran to the store just in case."

I let him in and resigned with a sigh. "I've got a serious problem."

He handed me a plastic fork. "Dig in."

I did. I dug my fork and swallowed a hefty piece. "I might need the entire cheesecake for this one."

"Talk to me." Larry dug in, too.

I told him everything that happened up to that point. I didn't leave one crumb on the plastic plate. I told him about how things intensified between me and Eva, about how we shared intimate moments online, and about how she wanted more. I confessed about how I would rather die than suffer her disbelief when she discovered the real me, the girl who lied and hid in her cubicle, running away from all opportunities to come clean.

"Wow," he said out loud. "What are you going to do?"

185

I massaged my full belly and waited for some miracle. "Not send her my mailing address."

"And when she asks you again?"

"I hoped you could tell me."

"Just tell her who you are." He labored those words, as if yanking them from deep in the ground and hauling them over hundreds of miles in the hot desert.

"I can't now. It's too out of control. I can't even look her in the eye. How am I supposed to be sexy and desirable with that handicap?"

"Let her be the judge."

"It's perfect as it is. I don't want to mess with it."

"You're having sex with a bike seat. This isn't perfect."

As if on cue, we both looked over at my bike seat. It sat lonely waiting for me. We landed back on each other's eyes and fell into hysterics, punching, slapping, and kicking the pillows, even howling at one point.

Later after Larry returned to his condo, I logged back into Twitter to get my fix.

"I miss you," I wrote.

"Oh come here, my sweet girl. Let me give you a kiss."

We bantered back and forth for an hour, ending somewhere in nirvana and blanketing each other in virtual kisses and hugs. I couldn't give it up.

#

Running became a sort of therapy session for me. As I charged forward, my brain uncluttered, my heart opened, and my senses came alive. By the halfway point around the loop at work, I opened up my stride and enjoyed the fresh smell of honeysuckle and the sparkling sunshine dancing on the leaves.

Since meeting Eva I had lost a total of fifteen pounds and all my clothes hung too loose on me. Larry bought me three outfits out of the blue one day. He left them sprawled out on my bed as a surprise. When I saw the size twelve, I laughed. I hadn't fit into a size twelve since high school. To my surprise, they fit perfectly. I danced around my condo thrilled to be wearing a size less than the average American woman.

Even after losing some weight, my bulge still hung out like an unwelcomed visitor. I panicked whenever I jiggled. I would never hop on a webcam because of it.

I went for a run at lunchtime that day. I had panted and grunted my way up the inclines surrounding the Martin Sporting Goods campus and returned a sopping mess. After showering and changing, I returned to my cubicle and Larry had called. "Travis wants to meet you."

"Me?"

"You saved his life. He held a gun between his teeth and your wisdom prevented him from pulling the trigger."

"What can I say to him that I haven't already said?"

"I'll be picking you up Saturday at ten. Wear jeans and a long sleeved shirt. And sneakers."

"But—"

He hung up.

#

On Saturday morning, dressed to order, I waited for Larry to knock on my door. When he finally did, I opened it. A scrawny, tall black kid with big owl eyes stared down at me. His face lit up the moment I smiled.

"Ma'am." He extended his hand like a politician.

I shook his firm hand and stopped the ma'am calling immediately. I might've been twenty-nine-years-old and a virgin to kisses, but I didn't need to add ma'am to that category, too. Next thing I'd be walking around the mall in curlers, setting my unruly hair for the week, and wearing flowery dresses that hung like potato sacks to my ankles. "Please call me Jane."

"So, where are you taking me?" I asked Larry as we climbed down our condo steps.

"You'll see."

On the drive, we didn't talk about my article or about the gun. Instead, I sat up in the front seat and he sat in the back. Larry just turned up the volume of his radio. We drove in silence. Larry filled the voids with overdramatic singing. The entire drive I wanted to connect with the kid and tell him how I understood what plagued him. I wanted to hug him and tell him everything would be okay one day. But, maybe it wouldn't. Maybe he'd live a fate similar to mine, always worried that one day the love of his life would discover the real him and not love him back for it. Maybe, like me, he'd want to change into someone different and hide behind a computer screen so no one would ever discover the real deal under the façade.

At one point, I turned around and smiled at him. He returned it with a weak smile and hesitant shrug before retreating back to the window and safety of the trees. I couldn't blame him. What teenager would want to listen to a strange woman trying to bond over misfired lives?

I fidgeted. Bouncing my leg up and down, I tried to come up with something I could say to the boy that would alleviate the awkward breaks in between Larry's atrocious singing. I tried things out in my mind like 'Hey, so what do you do when you're not hanging with Larry?' and 'So, I hear you hang out at the community center a lot.' I bored myself with those tired and useless fillers and just surrendered to the silence.

Larry pulled into the parking lot of Savage Mills and parked in front of the Terrapin ZipLine and Adventure Park. "I would never do that," I said.

"Never say never." Larry climbed out of the car with a smile too broad to mean anything good.

"I'm not zip lining," I said, climbing out and meeting his grin.

Travis climbed out and stared up at the nets and lines. "Oh, this is going to be fun." Joy sprang from his eyes, lighting up his face and erasing the look of a teenager who just tried to kill himself and more like one who spent summers at camp laughing with all his friends.

The sun peeked through the cover of trees, and screams, and laughter filled the air. My heart bucked. "Do you really want to do this?" I asked him.

Travis looked down at me. His eyes filled with sparkles and hope. "More than anything." He pulled in his bottom lip. "Do it. Don't be afraid."

Our eyes locked in a moment of shared delight. "I'm going to throw up."

"It'll be okay. What's the worst that could happen?"

"We die."

He shrugged and a smile crept on his face. "Exactly. So, big deal, right? We're going to die eventually. Let's enjoy some fun while we're on the way to it."

His smile erupted into a chuckle, and before long the two of us started cracking up. Larry joined in, then the three of us, arm-in-arm, bounded toward the building to sign our release forms and to get busy living.

We left our troubles and insecurities behind and embraced the air blowing through us. We whizzed down the zip line laughing, hooting and giggling like little kids at the playground.

A funny thing happens when people fly through the air. Their insecurities and fears vanish. Another funny thing happens. Like with alcohol, people tend to loosen up after sharing such a rush and they start to act like those people they swore they'd never act like. For me, after we landed and welcomed our new adventurous vibes to set in, I turned to Travis and told him I had once tried to commit suicide when I was just about his age. Mine ended in an epic failure because I didn't know how to properly secure a knot in the noose I built.

He nodded without judgment.

A few minutes later, we sat together, laughing and sipping strawberry smoothies with tapioca pearls. We watched as Larry continued zooming down the zip line, cutting in front of others to get his rush.

"Why didn't you just take some pills after the rope thing didn't work?" He asked.

I squared off at him. "Because when I fell to the ground I realized I enjoyed the new air filtering into my lungs."

"Were you happy after that?"

"Not at all."

"What kept you going?"

"Every night, I'd lay in my bed rubbing a rock I found in my father's garden and dream of the life I eventually wanted to live. This kept me going."

"Are you living that life?"

I reflected on his question, careful not to burst the bubble I so carefully inflated for his sake. "Partially."

"The day before I almost blew my head off with a gun, I had been released from Howard County General Hospital. I still had deep purple bruises over my entire body, including my face. My eye was just about opening up again at that point. The doctors had told my parents when I first arrived in the ambulance that I might suffer brain damage. Apparently the kicks to my head were so severe the damage could've affected my speech and possibly even my higher level brain function. I improved. My cousin, Jacques, hasn't. He's still in a coma. They just transferred him to a hospital closer to his hometown about two hundred miles from here. He was visiting for a family reunion and came with me when the group attacked. I caused this, even though the therapist tells me I didn't mean for this to happen, so therefore I am vindicated from carrying the burden with me for the rest of my life."

The air closed in around me. My chest ached. The pain etched on his face tore at me. It ripped me open and exposed a pain so raw, so buried, that I cried out in a wince. He comforted me with a gentle smile. "I'm okay. I am."

"Why would you blame yourself for something others did?" Even as I asked that I understood the culpability of the ego and its evil manner of absorbing all shockwaves and suffering through the concussions of ill fate brought on by no means of our own. Yet, people like me and Travis soaked it up and took it on anyway, blaming ourselves for things completely outside of our control and hiding from the things that were within our control.

"I take full blame. I dragged him to a place I never should've ventured. I needed a ride. I knew he wouldn't judge. So, I asked him to take me to meet someone. We planned that he would wait in the car while I met him by the lakeside. But when he saw four of them jump on top of me and start beating me, he jumped in to rescue. Someone set me up. Apparently, according to the police, this kind of thing is happening more."

"So you never met the person you were going to meet?"

"I answered an ad that seemed to talk straight to me. The person sought a black male who enjoyed English literature and Mozart. They targeted me."

"Do you know who did this?"

"I have my suspicions and offered them to the police. No evidence though." He slurped his smoothie.

"You can't carry this guilt with you."

"I don't know how to get rid of it."

And, I didn't know what to tell him. I could only shrug and swallow the sadness along with the tapioca.

#

I went home and messaged with Eva about Travis. I spoke about his pain, about his guilt, and about his desire to want to help others facing similar circumstances. Eva latched onto that, counseling me through my sadness for him, and helping me to sort through something that ran deeper than our flirts and that silly CarefreeJanie game I played with her.

"He'll come out ahead," she wrote. "Bullied kids who survive attacks are the strongest."

She opened the window. I could fly right through it with my truth. I could swoop in and be rescued by her beautiful embrace, her soft smile, and her generous care. But I didn't want her pity. I wanted her love. "I didn't know what to say to him. He asked me how to get rid of the guilt. I just shrugged and sipped on my smoothie."

"Oh, honey, don't beat yourself up over that. How would you know how to deal with this kind of pressure?"

The air circulated in the window of opportunity, welcoming me to fly through and admit my troubles. I could spill my sorry story at last, allowing her to get to know the real me, the weak me, the vulnerable me, and the me who couldn't stand up for herself and allowed others to kick her, pelt her, and destroy her.

Fuck no. I wanted her to see me as strong, vibrant, and a pillar of gentility and character. "He's such a sweet soul and wants to do something positive."

"He should take all that negative energy and do something positive with it, something purposeful."

"Like what?"

"Imagine the power he would gain if he could do something to save others and bring awareness?"

"That would be incredible."

"My heart is soaring right now. I've got a flood of ideas swimming around my mind. I see it all being played out in front of me."

"Share please," I wrote. My heart pumped new life.

"Let's do a short film. You write it. I act in it along with some of my actor friends. I'll produce it, edit it, add the background and dubbing, and then we can have Travis showcase it."

My heart beat wildly. "So, a documentary-type thing?"

"It needs to be heartfelt. It needs to tug. It needs to expose raw feelings. It needs to anger people and will them to take a stand against bullying."

Ideas swam in my mind. I saw bullies, victims, and champions. I saw defeat and mercy. I saw bittersweet trials and victorious wins. I saw reality meshing with drama and forming a memorable scene that would have parents talking to their kids and teachers protecting their students. The film would produce one voice, one stand, and one community working together to bring awareness and peace to those who might otherwise travel down the lonely despairing road of tragedy and fear. "Where will he showcase it?"

"We could orchestrate a regional or even national anti-bullying conference and have him present this short film along with his story to countless people who will then circulate beyond our wildest dreams."

I'd have to meet her. I couldn't turn back. I couldn't act on my selfishness any longer, not with something as important as that resting in the balance. It was about a boy named Travis and hundreds of thousands of other kids just like him. "Your enthusiasm is coming through my computer screen."

"We have to do this," she wrote.

"We will."

"Go get writing honey."

My heart zoomed out of control.

#

My fingers couldn't keep up with my mind. The story unrolled ahead of me, unfurling in a straight line with no wrinkles or bumps, just plush and fantastical as could be. The grandest audience could bear witness and never imagine for one moment that an ordinary girl with a wall decorated in rejection letters could tell such a perfect story. The ideas popped into my mind and flowed. I only had to picture Eva reading it with her eyes wide open, a smile hinged on her face, and a crisp nod of approval at the brilliance of the words to open the spigot and release everything my heart and soul had been gripping to for the past decade and a half of my life. Everything I ever wanted to say to those fools who bullied me, everything Travis wanted to say to those idiots who placed a gun in his mouth and almost forced him to pull a trigger, everything every bully in every school across the world ever said to a scared child, released into the story that bore witness to the unnerving problem the country faced because of scared, spineless bullies. Those words needed to spike their way into the bloodstream of every person and cause them to jump to their feet. The words needed to stare straight into the eyes of the residual ferocity of insults, rock pelting, kicking, beating, and vicious attack on the countless mental states of innocent people just trying to stand on their feet and create a life worth living. We needed to give victims a voice, a chance at a normalcy, the opportunity to bring out the best in themselves and others, and the ability to leave a legacy of friendship, truth, justice, and love behind.

My main character took me on a journey, weaving me into his brain and allowing me to see through his eyes. He taught me, in those four hours it took me to write the short story, that being strong required standing up for what he believed in and not for stomping out what he didn't. Heroes came in many shapes and forms, but the underlying string of serving others in time of need tied them all together. His name would be Sean, and he would rise to the occasion despite risking his reputation, his beautiful face, and his place in the world of Hope High School. Sean would befriend the victim. He would share a lunch table with him and offer him a safe walk to class. He would help him find his value so he could showcase it and earn the support of many. Before long, using the tactic of ignore and avoid by means of shifting focus to other more positive actions, the victim becomes the next hero who would be willing to help defend the honor of those who came after him and needed a gentle nudge toward their greatness. A movement would start—a heroes' movement, and every good soul would want to take part. By taking someone under his wing who needed it, standing up for those in need and offering help, lending his guidance, confidence, and strong support, he forged a lasting impact in someone's life.

I spent another two hours refining the story before going to bed. When I rose three hours later, I read it again with fresh eyes. My heart soared. The sense of empowerment tickled my core. I couldn't wait to share it with Eva.

When I did, she responded with a forest of exclamation points. "You outdid yourself."

"You really think so?"

"I can't wait to work on this. We need to meet up and discuss. What is your mailing address, by the way?"

I soldiered past that question. "I'll get it to you. Hey, have I told you lately how much I adore you?"

"I adore you more."

Several weeks later, she showed me how much she adored me when she sent me a link to a YouTube video. I sat in my cubicle and bawled. She played the school principal who rose to the occasion and helped turn bullies and victims into young men and women who walked with purpose and conducted themselves with respect. They stood up and honored their unique talents and abilities, by serving each other, and by bringing out the best in each other so they could bring out the best in themselves. Doreen, my confidant, cried along with me. I had told her everything, about my alter ego and about my growing love for Eva. We dabbed at our eyes and sniffled as we watched the rolling credits, including my pen name Janie. Eva captured my story and brought it to three-dimensional life in a twenty-eight minute short film.

Eva got started right away on planning the anti-bullying event. She would hold it in Washington D.C. and open it up to five hundred guests. The proceeds of the twenty dollar ticket would go to fund a new Heroes Program, and the program would start at Travis's school, with Travis leading the group.

I adored her.

Chapter Thirteen

I continued to write short, romantic stories for Eva, and those stories pulled us closer together. "I've never met you, yet I can't imagine life without you," she wrote one day. "I feel so connected."

I understood the reason had more to do with her connecting to my words than me.

Our flirts intensified by the day. I pushed up the danger level. I couldn't help myself. I'd say things like, "Imagine the sweetness in our first kiss?"

"You'll stop my heart. I know you will," she'd say back.

"You know what I'd love to do?" I toyed. "I'd love to run my fingers through your hair. I can just imagine how soft it would feel."

"Ah. I would love the touch of your fingers."

"I'd love to touch them to your lips," I dared braver.

"I'd love to kiss them," she said.

"Oh I would love the feel of your lips on my fingers."

"Come hang out with me under this bright blue sky. We'll snuggle up under a tree and take a nap together. Mmm, how nice would that be?" she asked.

"I'd love to kiss you."

"I want to kiss you for real," she wrote. "When are we going to meet?"

I stood out on the ledge and wavered, then wrote, "Tell me what you'd do to me if I were really right there in front of you. Come on, make me tingle (wink)."

"I would take you in my arms and hug you, then kiss you softly. I might even nibble on your lips before I play with your tongue." She continued. "Then, I'd kiss your neck and slowly travel down to explore more of you."

Oh she knew how to make me tingle. "Go on."

"I'd travel all around you, discovering your sweetness. Then, I'd caress you at that moment when I send you over the edge of ecstasy."

I sat in my cubicle drenched. "I wouldn't even know what word to type to express what your tease just did to me."

"I need to meet you."

"I know, babe."

"When?"

"Soon."

"That's not good enough. I need a date."

Could I do it? Could I prep for such a thing? I could arrange a hair and makeup session, clothes shopping, and a manicure and pedicure. I could workout endlessly until she arrived. I could mentally and emotionally prepare to reveal myself. It had to happen eventually. I had played the CarefreeJanie game too well. "When are you coming to town again?"

"I'll be there in another two weeks."

My heart skyrocketed.

# #

Travis and I met up for regular talks. I confessed my love for Eva during one of them. I told him about my fears of revealing my true self to her. With the maturity of a fifty-year-old man, he counseled me, advising that I needed to have faith in myself and to love myself and all the faults and scars that came along with being me, Jane.

200

He understood my fear. I trusted him.

"When you're ready, you'll know," he said on more than one occasion.

Well, the time had arrived, ready or not.

I prepped for Eva's visit with excruciating detail, determined to come out to her as the real deal.

Larry set me up with an appointment with his stylist, a transgendered girl named Eloise who stunned all in her stiletto heels and fitted summer dress. Her impeccable makeup mystified me with its perfect lines. She smelled like a field of wildflowers. She sat me in her chair, examined me, and set out on what I could only guess would be the hardest job of her life. She slathered color goop on my roots and weaved colored foils throughout. As I sat with the goop on my hair, she asked her assistant to manicure my nails and paint them red. When it came time to rinse my hair, her assistant massaged my head with shampoo that smelled of mint and tingled like menthol. When I finally landed back in Eloise's chair, she wore a sneaky grin. "I can't wait to shape your hair. You do own a Chi iron, I hope?"

I just shrugged and sat like a helpless fool. She assured me she'd set me up with all the right stuff and then started chopping, texturizing, and slicing into my hair like an artist chiseling. Thirty minutes later, smelling like I just escaped from a perfume factory, I bounced out of the hair studio looking like a superstar. Eva would arrive later in the week, and I prayed I could replicate the look.

When Larry picked me up at the salon, his jaw dropped. "Hello, CarefreeJanie!"

"Do you think it's too much? Maybe I should've had her do fewer highlights?"

"Darling, you could show up with gray roots at this point and I think she'll still want to toss you up against a wall and take you on a ride."

"My tummy just rolled." I swallowed the knot in my throat.

# #

Larry dropped me back at the office. He pulled up to the building and wished me well. I climbed out of the car, straightened my skirt, and then looked up when I heard a motorcycle zoom down the row. "Oh my God, it's her." I jumped back in the car.

She slowed down and parked her bright blue motorcycle in the front spot near Sanjeev's BMW. She looked every bit like the star in a sexy action flick. My heart pounded. My face flushed. "She's a week too early."

"You can do this," he said.

I looked to my friend and to his stoic eyes that warned of the dire actions he'd take if I screwed up that moment. "No. No I can't."

From Larry's front seat I stared at her. Her hair flowed out from underneath her helmet. Her long, sleek legs, adorned in a pair of black dress pants, dangled like beautiful vines, free and stretching. She removed her helmet and tossed her hair around, easing it free with her fingers. She stood tall and dismounted, looked around with a smile on her face.

"She's gorgeous," he said.

I searched my brain for CarefreeJanie. I needed her confidence, wit, and intellect now more than ever. "What will she ever see in me?"

"Darling" he said. "You've been virtually sexting each other for long enough. Stop acting like this is some sort of arranged marriage meeting. If you don't like her, you walk away."

"If *I* don't like *her*?"

"Just get out of the car."

My skin itched. She walked toward the building, light and bouncy as if a soft jazz ensemble gathered in her head. A flirty gaze rested peacefully on her face. "I'm not ready for this."

"Get out of the car and stop acting like a fool with a goofy crush."

My legs trembled. My fingers fidgeted with the car door lock. "But I am."

He pushed me. "Seriously, out."

I fell out of the car and onto my wobbly feet as my best friend shoved me into the wild with little more than my new highlights and a burning desire to bolt to the tree line. As I managed an unstable smile, my cynical brain said things to me like 'stupid move to bait her about Old Bay seasoning' and 'you never should've mounted that bike' and 'you couldn't have called yourself PlainJ instead?'

I treaded water too deep to swim in, too rough to be brave, and too awe-inspiring to call natural.

She trekked forward, her smile growing, hips swaying, hair flapping around her like a model posing in front of a fan. What if she took one look at me and regretted the months of flirting? Would I know? Would she be too polite to be honest and just go along with me anyway for the sake of being a good cyber lover?

I checked my skirt and lipstick. Then, I smoothed my hair to ensure it was behaving. Finally, I cleared my throat.

By the time she walked halfway over to me, I wanted to faint. My breathing chopped. My eyes squinted. My nose itched. My head fogged. I searched the far recesses of my mind for protection against the inevitable panic attack that would soon wrap itself around all sense of reason and choke me. I couldn't do it. I couldn't face the humiliation of her not liking me, of me disappointing her, or of jumping into my first kiss with someone as beautiful and experienced as Eva. I couldn't do it.

Just as I reached down and grabbed for the car door handle, Larry backed out of the spot and sped off with a wave. Eva closed in on me now with more determined steps. Her hair flittered around her, wild and messy. I stood with my arms hanging down by my side like useless branches on a dying tree. My chest bellowed in and out.

She landed in front of me smiling, her face all aglow, and a sparkle in the center of her large pupils. "We meet once again," she said in a playful whisper. She brushed her wild hair away from her face, tossing it over her shoulders.

I nodded. She stood before me with an easy smile. I searched for my voice deep down under the rubble of my fearful years. I could only manage to bite my lower lip and hold my erratic breaths from spurting out and ruining a most perfect romantic moment.

She moved in close, so close I could see the shimmer of her blush and eye shadow. I could smell her minty breath. I could hear her light breaths tickling the air between us. She placed her hand on my forearm and cradled it. Her light, caring touch sent shockwaves through me. They raced through every nook and cranny of my being; speeding up as they weaved down my arms to my fingertips, up to my heart, down to my belly button and to the tips of my toes. Warm and comforting, I stood in her grace, admiring her beauty and relaxing under her embrace. "Are you okay? You look like you're about to faint."

"I'm not feeling well." I searched out Larry. He had stopped at the entrance, waiting on nothing. No cars traveled by. He just waited. All the confidence I needed faded into the milky air and left me alone to fend for myself.

"Let me see if I can track your friend down." She waved her hands to Larry and headed toward him. Her hair bounced around the middle of her back, happy and jovial.

Larry's brake lights flashed, and he backed up, circling around and opening his window for Eva. I panicked, praying Larry would not say anything stupid. I just wanted to run from the awful mess that pinpointed a time in my life where I knew a year, two years, twenty years from then I'd look back on and regret.

I couldn't manage to look her in the eye. How would I ever manage to stand tall with a warm smile and insert myself into the lady's life as plain Jane? She needed the arms of a confident woman with a history that sparkled with accomplishments, awards, friends, travels, adventures, and interesting quirks, not ones that would smother her good heart.

Larry drove toward me. Eva trailed behind giving us space. Before hopping into his front seat, I looked up at her. She waved. I waved.

I drew the curtain. The dreadful tug of a teary goodbye to a life I wanted had climbed up from the horizon and made its landfall on my heart. I had just ruined my chance at a life worth living. I would spend the rest of my life hashing out that moment, the moment when I closed the door on any possibility of a life with Eva Handel that included more than a laptop computer and emoticons.

Chapter Fourteen

Without delay, I wrote my email to Eva. I told her I couldn't meet up with her the following week because something had come up, something that would take over my life. "I'm so sorry. But, I'm going to be unavailable for a while. I'll miss you, babe."

"But I'm here now."

"I'm sorry. Things have come up, and I'm not available." I sent the reply, and my heart broke in half.

When she responded with questions I had no answers for, I simply pretended to rush off to a project that robbed me of time to message, time to chat, and time to carry on with our 'relationship.'

# #

My world turned blacker than black in the days that followed. As if someone dropped a brick down my throat and tossed me into the Patapsco River, I sank to the lowest point. Barely able to lift my head high enough to acknowledge the threat, I balled over, challenged not to throw up, and eager to vacate from that most despicable part of my life. I spent the better part of my days sobbing into my couch pillows like someone had removed my heart, stomped on it, and tried to put it back together again to no avail.

Larry broke through my door on really bad days and comforted me. We ate lots of cheesecake in the weeks that followed my oath of silence, so much so that

I grew back into my above average sized clothes. On his recent cheesecake visit, after I couldn't button my pants, I took one look at his offered cake, reached up and smashed it to the ground. Then I stomped on it, splattering cheesecake all over the place, on the cuff of my pants, my sandals, my carpet, my leather couch, even my stationary bike that started the addictive behavior. I grabbed onto the handles and yelled. "Take this bike out of here. I don't want to see it." I pushed it toward the door, and it got stuck on my carpet. I pulled back for leverage, then fell backwards, clobbering poor Larry in the mouth. He bent over in a scream.

The scene ended badly with Larry bleeding and pressing several ice cubes in a white towel to his lips and me scrubbing cheesecake into my carpet as I tried to clean it up, sobbing, heaving, and punching the ground. My knuckles bled and swelled up within minutes. I spent the rest of the evening balled up, staring at my empty Twitter messages, crying into my pillow, and wishing I were dead.

# #

I sipped black coffee and scrolled through our past emails, reminiscing over the most precious times in my life when I meant more to Eva than just the girl who dumped her without a warning over some 'busy stuff.'

I wanted to reconnect and go back in time to the fun.

Travis kept me in the loop on the progress for the anti-bullying event. He assured me over and over again that he kept my identity a secret from Eva and that he understood my fears even though he didn't agree with them. Travis and I had gotten close, and we confided in each other about our nightmares, our fears, and our insecurities. Travis always ended on a high note, reminding me to take the high road whenever possible and be gentle with myself.

I'd feel stronger after our conversations and realize that I had lived the past twenty-nine years alone, so I could survive the next fifty the same way. Avoid the lure, and wipe out the addiction. Ignore the bully, and wipe out the problem. Same strategy could work for both.

I learned from those gloomy bullying days that the best way to prevent walking through that dark tunnel was to head in the opposite direction. Facing demons head on never resulted in anything good. Things blew up with that idiotic tactic, just like with my cheesecake fiasco with Larry.

I struggled terribly in the first month. Eva had sent me several 'good morning' messages, and I ignored them. They stopped coming altogether now. Their absence sucked the air out of my lungs.

On more than one occasion, I hovered over sending her a smiley face that asked her how she was. Then, after abiding by my ten-minute rule of walking away and returning to the unsent message, I'd always delete it. The walk to and from the toaster or fridge always strengthened me. I could do it, I would say as I hit the delete key. Time would erase the dreadful pain. I willed time to bless me.

Then, one morning, two months into my lonely struggle, she messaged me. "I can't take it. Why are you ignoring me?"

I couldn't ignore the question. So, after several seconds of deliberating, I messaged back, "I'm sorry. I just think you're better off forgetting about me."

Grit scratched at the back of my throat as I sent that hurtful, but necessary, message. Better to destroy the bridge than to risk being lured back over it and getting burned even more later on when the fire burned that much hotter.

In the weeks that followed, my core hollowed out a little more each day to the point nothing could fill it. I tried walking and blubbered the entire time. I tried writing and stared at a white screen. I tried watching funny videos and spent the time chucking the bird at the computer screen. I tried ten different flavors of cheesecake, only to throw up after indulging. I tried focusing in on an investment class and ended up failing miserably. I tried smoking a cigarette and puked off my balcony. Ultimately, I surrendered to the loneliness. Why fight it?

On my darkest days, I'd venture into Eva's Twitter and Facebook and really torture myself. Her happy voice had returned. Her exclamation points now celebrated other people's joy. The decent girl in me should've been happy for her, but instead it angered me. How dare she move on so quickly? Was CarefreeJanie not that special to her?

One night I got drunk on several Seabreeze drinks and almost chimed into her tweets. Vodka had a way of erasing inhibitions. Instead, I strolled way too far into her Twitter feeds and mentions and embarked on some flirty tweets between her and Sara, her on-again, off-again possessive girlfriend. They exchanged several winks and playful short remarks about fun, the city, and wanting to dance. My chest constricted. I clicked into the chick's recent images, and her romantic eyes, pouty lips, olive skin and thin frame saddened me.

The dread crawled up my spine like a snake in grass. I caused it. I opened her up to that fun. I made my life. I chose to live alone.

All the past choices piled up one after the other causing a jam at the base where logic used to form. I chose to not kiss that boy back when I had a chance. I chose to cower at the sight of a group of people. I chose to be miserable all those years. No one put a gun to my head and said to live like a reclusive hermit afraid of my own shadow. No one forbade me to walk out my front door and embrace life. No one but me. I chose that life.

It didn't choose me.

That predicated the notion that I could still choose my life. It didn't have to choose me. Like I could dictate my storylines, I could dictate my life. I guzzled more Seabreeze.

I stood and paced my living room, fueled by anger, impassioned by Seabreeze. At any one moment in time, I could take back control, push crap I didn't want to deal with to the backseat, and continue the drive as I saw fit. If I wanted to hug the curbstone, then I'd hug it. If I wanted to drive like a maniac, then I'd push the pedal down further. If I wanted to take a lovely Sunday drive, do the speed limit, and aggravate the shit out of everyone behind me, then that would be my prerogative. I chose. No one could choose for me.

I felt like Mel Gibson in Braveheart suddenly, fist in the air, screaming out to the enemies and the haters who struck at me with their pointy spears. I could be the better person here. I didn't need to be wallowing in tears over a lost love. If I wanted to love someone, I could. I gained power and control.

I tripped over the edge of the coffee table and spilled some of my drink. I could let Eva know that I fully supported her relationship with that gorgeous girl on Twitter, and she would maybe once again view me as someone worthy of her past love, of her past torture, and overlook the fact that I acted like a complete bitch.

Drunk on empowerment, I messaged her. "I hope all is going great for you. You seem happy."

There. Easy. Done. I swiped my hands, proud of my trek out onto the edge of the cliff. A blur later, she responded. "I am happy."

"Travis tells me the event is coming along great."

"It is."

Her short words cut through me. "So what's new?"

"What's new? Lots."

She hated me. "Are you going to make me dig?"

"Do you really want to know?"

211

"Of course. Tell me."

"I'm seeing Sara again."

My heart dropped. Gravity, mean and powerful, cut off my parachute and dropped me to the ground like a rock. The large tears poured onto my lap, soaking and drowning me. My head pounded. My throat dried up. All moisture evaporated, leaving me caked with grit and regret for what I'd let happen.

Her heart belonged to someone else now. That easily. All those tummy rolls, heart leaps, and urges would be filled in by someone other than me. She didn't need me anymore. She would read my tweets and brush over them like the other hundred or so she got every day. I would be that girl she once had a thing with. That girl she no longer needed. That girl one day, a few years from now, she'd remember and chuckle. A small smile might creep on her face as she skipped along a steamy memory we shared, and then it would disappear as quickly when her lover wrapped her arms around her golden shoulders, kissed her soft skin, and told her how much she loved her.

The pain tore through me, ravishing everything I had built up in me to protect myself against such harsh elements. I no longer could fend off the abrasive torches, the pounding rocks, and the cuts of knives that sliced through my surface. I stood exposed, vulnerable again, unprotected from things that could kill my spirit.

I couldn't bear to face the rest of the night with knowing she doted after someone else, sprinkling her spirit with her warm heart.

"Wow, good for you," I wrote as tears spilled down my cheeks. So honorable of me. So mature of me.

I drank more waiting for her response. Oh how I wished I had a superpower that would allow me into her head so I could tinker with it and never let her fall in love with anyone but me.

I did this. I drove her away. I told her to go. I opened up the door to my heart and pushed her through it. I sealed it off from her. She could never enter again with the fortress I built. She had no choice but to march forward without looking back on me. I never tossed her a good reason to look back on me.

I'd get over it just like got over everyone else who disappointed me. She deserved to be happy. She deserved to be with someone who could stand up to her ghosts from the past and push them aside. She needed someone who didn't huddle behind a laptop and plagued by scars. She certainly should love someone not easily destroyed by the hands of others. I would go on with my life just like I had before I fell into her Twitter feed. Before that, I could spend countless hours on the couch watching *House*, eating popcorn, and taking long baths listening to Baroque. I never once felt sideswiped, steamrolled, or terribly sad.

Everything she admired about me no longer mattered. So what if I published short stories in magazines? So what if I touched countless LGBT youth with my stories? So what if I wrote a beautiful tribute for her to showcase at an event that would gift her with massive attention? So what about any of that anymore? She had a better love to track now, a lover to admire, and a lover to rediscover and explore.

Oh, that hurt. My stomach twisted and my heart mangled from the trampling. My broken heart with all its chards flew around like shrapnel, jabbing me, stabbing me, and cutting me open. The pain rolled over me, flattening everything.

How else could I respond? With envy? Then she'd challenge me. If she challenged me, I'd have to challenge back, and we'd be right back where we were before, struggling to find a footing that made sense. I'd never be that girl for her, the balanced girl, the unscarred girl, or the brave girl not afraid of being bullied into submission.

Fuck myself and everything I'd become. I hated myself. Why couldn't I be normal? Why couldn't I face the world with one confident foot in front of the other like everyone else?

I balled up on my bed, clinging to my bed sheets, and cried.

A few hours later, I rose and faced my computer with a determined fierce intensity to be the kind of girl Eva loved. The kind of girl I created in CarefreeJanie. The kind of girl I wished existed in the real me. I wrote her a message and said, "I'm happy for you, babe. I think she's very lucky."

The rest of the afternoon, I busied myself with organizing my canned goods according to type, then size. I also tore down my curtains and washed them all, then hung them back up to de-wrinkle. I vacuumed and shampooed my carpets. And then I began construction on my bedroom closet, hanging shelving I'd bought long before Eva entered my life. By midnight, I decided enough time had buffered between my last heroic tweet message and I could face her response.

I logged in.

Nothing.

I fell to the ground and wept some more, reopening all the pain gates, the vacuum seal on my air, and the wounds that hadn't quite healed over enough to protect my insides from being torn out again.

# #

The next morning at work, I logged on to Messenger and Eva popped online. My heart clenched. "Hey you," I wrote as casually as my fingers could manage.

"Hey."

"Did you get my message?"

"Yes," she wrote.

"Okay. Good." Her choppy answers rattled me. "So what's going on?"

"The event. The event is. Are you going to be there to help or are you too busy?"

I had already destroyed my chance with her. She hated me. "I won't be able to be there."

"You make no sense. One day you're making love to me online, the next you're telling me how happy you are that I'm back together with my girlfriend."

"I am. I want you to be happy."

"What is going on with you? Did I say something to offend you?"

"No, of course not."

"Then why?"

"I'm going through some things," I wrote. "It's just too complicated to get into right now."

"You're always hiding yourself. You've never once told me something deep or real. I don't understand."

"I've got some dark things that you wouldn't understand."

"Well you could've tried me."

"It's better this way. I really think it's better if I don't go."

"You are so selfish." Despair lingered in her typed words.

I couldn't handle the slap of her insult. I signed off on a tremble.

A few minutes later, I went into my email and Eva had written to me. *I always dug to learn the real you, but you never let me in. You hid behind a flirt or a virtual kiss. And now you're hiding behind a fear that has you gripped so tightly you're willing to turn your back on someone who really needs you now. Shame on you. Where is that girl I fell in love with? Hmm? Where are you, CarefreeJanie? This event isn't about us. Life is more than who you are, more than who I am. It's about being there when it matters.*

Regret crawled up the back of my throat and traveled into my brain. It sat like a heavy fog, drowning out the sun light and all the good I'd managed to do along the way.

Chapter Fifteen

I walked into work the next morning and poured myself a cup of coffee to the vibes of Kelly Clarkson singing "Miss Independent."

I spotted Katie in her cubicle. She bent over, and her underwear showed. I could've taken that to a winning level where I claimed the one-up position for the day. Instead, I sat idle at the coffee stand chewing on a coffee stirrer and contemplating the mess I created every time I indulged in messing with her.

I threatened her somehow. I threatened her equilibrium. I attracted her husband, her boss, even the friend she could've had in Doreen. I stole the limelight of credit on that big project, garnered a raise when the company had buckled their belts tighter and no one else got one, won the affection of our boss, and received those things that Katie desired most—recognition, raises, great parking spots, high-profile projects, a seat in focus groups, pretty much everything she wanted. She deserved the right and pleasure to hate me.

I didn't hate her. I should've hated her for being too pretty, too shapely, too athletic, too focused, too determined, and too intelligent. Yes, the envy ripped through me and forced me into discomfort, but not enough to hate her.

She annoyed the shit out of me. She laughed too loudly, played too roughly, and tried too hard to be chummy with higher-ups. She put two-and-two together with Sanjeev offering me special privileges, and her husband checking me out, and Doreen shunning her for me, and squirmed in her high heels.

I toyed with her because I could. I knew she could handle it. And, it felt good because in those temporary moments, I craved a mighty and powerful control over the present, helping to shadow the past. But in the moments that followed, I hit the ground hard, empty, and cowardly.

I sipped more terrible-tasting coffee, hoping it would block the sadness crushing my heart. How I wanted to go back to that day when the sweet wink in Eva's tweet and the sultry smile in her picture melted through my troubles and fears. I wanted to be CarefreeJanie again, the girl who lived a good life, the girl who never bullied another girl out of fear of losing ground with her friends, the girl who never exposed her weak heart to a best friend who would destroy her life moments after the discovery, the girl who never uprooted her family and sent them off to a prison sentence where they sought unsuccessfully to recapture the light that once shined on their great lives, or the girl who Eva Handel first fell in love with.

Now, another person had captured her heart. That new person surely didn't come riddled in the sticky sap of a dying tree. She most likely could declare her innocence and beauty without fear of being uncovered as sinful. She'd never have to fear that look of disgust in Eva's eyes, the sudden detachment of her love, or the hollow gap after she ran from the ugliness of lies.

I tossed the coffee down the drain, watching it spiral away from me. Then, I turned on the faucet and washed out my mess. I would not heave my ugly past into her life and drag her down into my tunnel of darkness. She deserved the bright light of purity, not the shadows of sin. I would work that day and focus on what I could control. I would proofread Sanjeev's annual report and make it shine. I could control that. I would eat lunch with Doreen and listen to her stories of her grandchildren and genuinely smile and nod at her inflections.

I walked out of the collaboration room, determined to stay in control. I walked past Katie. She shoveled pictures into a box. None of her usual paperwork cluttered her desktop. She looked up at me and her eyes leaked tears. Her face flushed.

"What are you doing?" I asked.

"Congratulations. You win." She dumped a can of pens into a box.

"What do you mean?"

She pulled in her upper lip and bit down hard, but the pain won out and her face strained under the pressure. The tears fell in giant drops onto her naked desk. "I was fired a few minutes ago."

A sight of her sitting in an unemployment office begging for work flashed in my mind. Ravaged from months of no paycheck, her eyes swelled, her face puffed, and her lips cracked from all of the biting. She'd be skinnier with sallow skin due to the cruel shedding of nutrition from her life. Her eyes would be sunk, lacking that creative, competitive spark all because I messed with her, causing her to mess with me, and with one ugly insult after the other, our lives were inextricably pulled out from under us both. The fun stripped away, we would spend our lives trying to get back to that place we filled before the silly games began. "How?"

"I took things too far." She tossed a couple picture frames into the box. "I hacked into your system, stole your idea for the new public service announcement, and handed it in as my own."

She exhaled a shaky breath and looked around her empty cube. The tears rained down hard. "My envy got out of hand."

I shook off the stunning blow. "I feel like I've just been punched in the face."

"I'm sorry," she said, staring at me with hollowed eyes too similar to Rhonda's. "Like I said. You win. I'm out of your hair for good."

I walked away still numb to the news. I sat down at my seat and opened to the daily e-newsletter. I scrolled through it and counted two comments from Katie. My heart sat heavy, and I labored for air. Another sadness joined the one already in me, and that one coated me in an emptiness of unease. Losing Katie didn't feel good.

My lips numbed, my fingers buzzed, and my head pounded. I couldn't take that burden on, too.

I stood up and walked back over to Katie. She was blowing her nose. "Why do we do this to each other?"

We stared blankly at each other like two defeated and tired boxers without gloves. Blood dripped from our foreheads, cheeks, and mouths as we steadied to throw in the towel.

"You just rattle me to the point I can't think straight," she said. "I can't compete with you on regular terms. You've got all the balls in your court, and I'm left with these flat ones that don't bounce. I had to level the playing field somehow. I figure, you stole my credit last time. I could steal yours this time around, and we'd be even."

"How did they find out?"

"Sanjeev knows your writing. He took me out for a coffee this morning and asked me if I had stolen it from you. I couldn't lie to him."

"You thought that I wouldn't have challenged you on taking my idea?"

"I didn't care. I figured I'd just tell him you were lying and jealous."

Our tangled mess of tactics bunched up between us. We were both equally as guilty of destructing each other and at playing that warped game. I thought back on my article and the question I posed in it. *Was this the secret? Find the good even in your enemy and bring it out?*

"We can fix this."

She looked at me and a flicker of hope danced on her wet eyelids. I saw a child reaching out to me from the dark, murky depths of a cold, harsh lake, begging for me to save her from the unknown below her. She stared at me with the same beg as Rhonda did so many times before. I definitely couldn't carry another burden.

"I don't think so," she said.

"Sure we can."

"I don't know."

I felt sad for her. I was the one left holding the prize of a job that I didn't even want. "I'm about to do something really stupid."

"Well, don't let me stop you." She smiled weakly, tossing out one last hurrah.

I smiled sweetly at her for the first time since before her husband groped me on the side of the bar. Then, I tore off to Sanjeev's office.

# #

He was typing away when I entered.

"Can we talk?"

He stopped typing. "Sure."

"Don't fire her."

"I already did." He turned red and folded his hands.

That gave me power to continue. "Unfire her. Please?"

He sat back. "I don't understand. You two don't exactly strike me as friends."

"She's good at what she does. I wouldn't be nearly as successful without her."

221

"She stole your work."

"I handed it to her. She embellished it. We worked on it together."

"But she didn't give you credit."

"She was getting even with me for the time I did the same to her."

He sat up and raised his hands. "I don't want to know any more."

"We mess with each other constantly. It's what we do. Things got out of hand. I wiped out all of her files on her computer and she freaked. So, she retaliated with the PSA project, claiming it as her own. She was just teaching me a lesson. And, when she found out that I actually saved all her data to a flash drive, she confessed to me about handing in the PSA project under her credit. We're both guilty, and were just toying with each other."

He buried his head in his hands. "You two are killing me here."

"Please don't fire her. We're actually good together. We play off each other's talents."

His face blotched. He searched my eyes for direction.

"Please?"

"I don't think she would've come to your rescue like this."

"Of course she would. She's actually a nice person when you take away the insecurities. No one is perfect, and we're all just as scared by this revelation as the person next to us."

He stared at me, dazed and confused by my philosophical introspective moment.

"Are we okay here?" I asked.

He nodded. "Just ask Katie to come into my office on your way past her?"

"Sure thing." I walked away feeling lighter. Then, I walked right up to Katie. She was bent over her file cabinet and looked up on a sigh.

"Boss wants to see you."

Panic popped on her face. I just winked, giving myself one last hurrah.

# #

I felt more alive in the days following Katie's revival back to the land of Martin Sporting Goods. We stopped messing with each other and actually made great headway on some looming projects.

Then, Eva came to town for a meeting. She didn't stop and say hello to me, Doreen, or Katie. All business, she simply slipped into the conference room for her meeting and ducked out afterwards.

I checked her Twitter feed during the rest of the day, and she hadn't posted anything.

I felt so disconnected and hollow all over again.

I took to visiting her Twitter feed regularly in the weeks that followed, and that just stirred up more anxiety. I dove into a funk again.

Travis called me several times over the course of my funk. I dodged his calls and would later return with a text message apologizing for missing his call. I'd tell him I was super busy those days with work projects and that soon we'd catch up on life. I'd wish him well and end those inappropriately long text messages with a smiley face.

Larry was not pleased. He knew me well enough to understand work would never steal my time. He didn't bother to knock the night he barged in on me while I was knee deep in another one of my crying tirades. "Would you just get off your pride horse and go call the woman?"

"I can't." I blew my nose. "It's too late."

"You look terrible." He shook his head, disgusted with my current state.

"Well, we can't all have the perfect fairytale love story like you and Tim. Man meets man; they fall in love, and live happily ever after sneaking around behind the wife."

He stretched his eyes in horror, scoffed, and waved me off before shoving back through my front door.

I hated the world and everyone in it. I picked up my glass of water and slammed it against my living room wall. Water and glass sprayed every which way. It felt remarkable. So, I picked up my coffee mug from the morning and tossed that, too. Again, ceramic and coffee rained back in delight. Incredible release. Off to the kitchen. I reached for glass after glass and flung them toward my living room. Some hit walls, some hit end tables, some hit the bike that Larry placed back in my condo after my initial freak out, and some hit the carpet and bounced, unaffected by my game. I needed them affected. So, I stormed into the living room, picked up the glasses, and pitched them to the ceiling where they sprinkled down on me. I wanted to get hurt. I wanted to bleed. I wanted to feel something other than the dread.

By the time Larry arrived back in my condo and scooped me off of the pile of glass, blood trickled beneath my bare feet. He cried with me as he carried me out of my hell and into his clean, fresh, crisp condo. He brought me to his bathtub and ran water over my bleeding feet yelling at me, cursing me out, telling me what a fool I'd become. All the while, tears sprang from his eyes and his mouth downturned into a deep frown. The water stung my feet where the glass still remained planted in my skin. At one point, the sting overcame me, and I fainted. The next thing I remembered was waking up in Larry's bedroom with gauze wrapped tightly around my throbbing feet and Larry's concerned eyes bearing down on me. "Why?"

I could only shrug. Not even Larry would understand the pain of perpetual loneliness.

"There's someone here to see you." He turned toward his living room and waved.

Travis walked into his bedroom with a hesitant step, staring with horror at my gauzed feet.

"What's wrong," I asked him. "You act like you've never seen someone try to hurt herself before." I laughed at my wit.

He didn't.

Neither did Larry.

Larry stood. "I'll let you two chat while I make us some dinner."

"I'm not hungry," I said to him.

"I don't care." His face steamrolled into a blank abyss. He really didn't.

Travis walked up to the bedside and stared at the edge of the bed.

I patted it. "Have a seat."

He nodded as if bracing to climb into a tank of spiders, and then he sat next to me. He fidgeted with his fingers, failing to look up at me.

"I know what you're thinking," I said to him. "You think I was trying to end it all. But, I wasn't."

"I know that," he said, staring at the headboard instead of me. "Otherwise you'd be dead, and I'd be kneeling beside your coffin instead."

That should not have been a thought that shocked me. But, I shook like someone had just submerged me in a tub full of ice.

Travis grabbed the blanket on the edge of Larry's bed. He covered me up. "The pain feels good. I know. It feels better than the emotional pain. That just sucks the lifeblood right out of a person."

I looked up and met eyes with the most mature seventeen-year-old kid I'd ever met. His eyes didn't mock or strain under the pressure of seeing someone so foolish. No. His eyes sat soft, welcoming, waiting for me to open up and trust that I was safe and free to spill my secrets. "When I was slamming the glass against the wall, I felt free. And when it cut my feet, all the sadness left me. Well, at least for a little while."

"You're better than this. You know that, right?" He pointed his mature eyes at me, poking and urging me to accept that notion as truth.

Fresh tears burned the back of my eyes instead. "Whatever you say, kid." I stared up at the ceiling fan wishing it were whirling so I'd have something dynamic to look at other than the caked-on dust on the edge of the blades.

"What happened?" He asked with such sincerity that the tears just spilled. Before long, the truth followed.

"I'm just tired," I said to him. "Tired of constantly bowing and running away from life."

"Why are you then?"

I told him everything about how I screwed up a good thing, about how even as an adult I let fear bully me into a life I didn't want to live, about how my past caught up to me, and about how I punished myself for something terrible I left behind.

"Then go back, get it, and set it right." He shrugged. "It's as simple as that."

"It's too late for that," I said with a stretch to my voice.

He frowned. "I'm worried about you."

"Look, I'm fine." I sat up to show my strength. "I really am. It was a stupid thing I did tossing glasses every which way. I get that. I'm fine."

"If you're truly fine, then, maybe I can still convince you to come with me next weekend to speak at the event. I really want you there. We're going to show the short film, but before we do, I really want you to speak to the audience about your experiences. This could be your chance to set things right with your past, face your demons, and show these kids they're not alone. I think it might really be cathartic to talk it out and share with others facing similar paths."

"I can't, Travis." I sighed.

He stared at me without anger, hate, or remorse. "Do you know how valuable you are to me?"

I mocked that display of gratitude with a scoff. "Stop being so mushy. It's so not what I'm about."

"You don't get it do you? You don't get how valued you are."

"The world would still rotate if I left it this very second. How much value do any of us really hold?"

"You pulled me from suicide. The fact that you still don't think you're valuable just shows how you view me, as having no value, too." He stood up and walked to the door. He turned before walking through it. "It's not always about you. Until you realize that, you're going to continue tossing glasses against walls and have people come to your rescue. Why would you want that for yourself? Why don't you want to be the rescuer instead?"

"How?" I yelled at him.

"Start by taking action." He slammed the door.

# #

My words, originally crafted for others, came back to me and knocked sense into me. *We owed it to ourselves to dig deep and find out what tools we had in our disposal to crush the shit out of our fears so we could get on living our best days. Those who helped guide others to find and lend their tools would reap rewards far too powerful for any bully to come in and swipe away. The leverage in digging deeper and serving others, offered power. When a person came outside of that shell to protect another, he helped erase fear and replaced it with a light so powerful no one could extinguish it.*

"Larry," I called.

He appeared in two seconds. "Yes, darling?"

"I need you to find me something appropriate to wear next weekend to this event."

He broke out into a smile. "That a girl."

"And, I might need a ride." I looked to my battered, wrapped feet and sighed.

"I'll pick you up and haul you over my shoulders if I need to."

Chapter Sixteen

Sometimes in life, people had to learn to swallow fears and walk past the shadows that lurked. I approached one of those times. It wasn't about me anymore. It was about so much more than me.

We entered the ballroom at the Hilton. Hundreds of chairs lined up in rows and covered the marble carpeting. Hundreds of people chatted, stood idle, or ate carrots and hummus while soft jazz filled the space. Chairs filled up quickly as people climbed over stranger's legs in search of the perfect seat. We stood back behind a wall of hotel workers who wore black aprons and carried sterling silver water pitchers. A sense of pride for Eva's efforts and talents coursed through me. She had arranged all of that.

I sipped on some lemonade, alongside of Larry and his boyfriend, Tim, who were feasting on strawberry parfaits. A slideshow played on all the big screens showing statistics about bullying and showing kids holding up signs with phrases like, "your words stay with me forever" and "I cry myself to sleep every night" and "I'm afraid to go to school."

Travis walked by us without notice, followed by Eva who was reading a document and straightening her dress as she walked up the main aisle. They walked up the stage's side steps. Travis turned to say something, and Eva stretched her gaze out toward us. I ducked, pretending to fix my shoe. I suddenly felt foolish just showing up like that, as if doing them a favor. They handled everything just fine on their own without my help and interference. I'd been such a coward and such a waste of space in their lives recently. I imagined they thought, 'Who was she to just waltz back in unannounced and think we'd open up our arms wide, inviting her back in without question, without struggle, without proving she was worthy of being part of something so critical and important?'

"What's the plan? Do you go help now or wait?" Larry asked me, plopping a chunk of strawberry in his mouth.

I remained glued to the ground, fixing my unbroken shoe. "I don't want to be in their way."

He reached down and pulled me up, then stared straight into my frightened eyes. "Darling, it's time you stop this charade and be strong."

I froze under his order, not ready to be that person. I wasn't equipped to be that person. "I'm just here to show my support. I can do that afterwards."

They looked well-positioned and congruent in their maneuvers around the stage, unaffected by my lack of presence on their important day. I curled in on myself, feeling very much like a third wheel on a mountain bike, useless, unnecessary, and in the way. "I don't belong here," I said.

Eva smiled at something Travis said, and he laughed, flipping his head backwards and holding his stomach. The scene was perfect. The lights were perfect. The food was perfect. The audience was perfect. They were perfect in their suit and dress.

I wanted to run.

Then, the perfect scene unraveled slightly. Travis and Eva spoke over paperwork. The sound check guys ran up the stage stairs and looked flustered. One of them spoke into the microphone with no success. The other flagged someone in the back of the room. They ran around the stage to the speakers, adjusting wires and arguing. Travis and Eva fidgeted with the laptop on the desk near the podium, shaking their heads and wiping their foreheads.

"I think I should go help," Larry said.

"Don't leave me." I grabbed his hand. "Let's just go find seats."

Larry shook his head at me. His lips straightened into a line. "I can embarrass you and get this ordeal over with sooner rather than later so you might be able to enjoy the event."

I stopped walking and pointed my finger at him. "Keep it up, and I will talk of spiders and screams to your boyfriend."

He pushed me forward. "Find us a seat then."

All the seats in the back were filled. So, I had no choice but to choose aisle seats in the fourth row from the front. I scrunched down in my chair and watched Travis and Eva work as a team. Then, Larry tapped my shoulder. "Why are Doreen and Katie here?"

The two women scanned the room as they settled in two seats on the opposite side a few rows behind us. When they spotted me, they waved.

I waved back with a question on my face. "How did you know?"

Doreen shrugged and giggled. Katie winked.

Larry rose.

"Where are you going?" I asked, getting up and climbing over Tim's legs just as quickly as he did.

"To get some water."

I followed him as he trekked like a track star across the floor toward the water. Then, once we landed at the refreshments table, I looked over at the girls. I needed to say hello.

"I'll be back," I said. I headed in their direction. When I arrived at their seats, they greeted me with smiles. Katie's was much slyer than Doreen's.

"Who told you about this?"

Doreen pointed to Katie. "It's all her doing."

Katie arched her eye at me. "You can't expect me to stop tormenting you cold turkey now, can you?"

I hinged on panic. "What are you up to?"

"Just here for moral support." She shrugged. "And, of course a little fun watching you get worked up."

"I can't take this right now," I said.

She placed her hand on my wrist. "Relax. I said fun, not evil." She cleared her throat. "I've got a little confession."

"Spill it." The panic rose.

"Okay, CarefreeJanie."

All blood rushed from my face. "How did you know?"

"You can't leave your computer unlocked and expect me not to snoop. You made it too easy."

The lights dimmed and the jazz music vanished. A man crept up to me and asked me to take my seat.

"You're still a crazy wench," I said with a wink.

Doreen slung her arm around Katie's shoulder. "She sure is. But, a nice wench at least."

Katie smiled under the submission. I'd never seen her look more relaxed and at peace.

"Ma'am, please take your seat now," the usher whispered.

I walked toward the back of the room and stopped at the refreshment table where Larry still stood. "I'm not in the mood to sit. I'll just stand here, too," I said.

"Then, we'll stand together." He sipped some water. "You look stunning."

"Thanks, my friend." I wished I felt like that girl he saw in me. "I'm glad you came with me."

"That's what best friends do. We support each other even when it's uncomfortable to do so."

"Do you think Tim will ever leave his wife?"

"I don't know." He stared straight ahead looking doubtful. "I never meant to fall in love with him."

"Bullshit."

He sighed. "He had me the moment he flashed that smile."

"Same with me."

We stared ahead toward the stage, two screwed up friends accepting each other.

"Come on," I said. "Let's go back to our seats so Tim isn't sitting alone."

Larry followed me. I walked slowly, bowing my head to avoid Eva's eyes.

The presentation of the hero awards started with the President of a local organization. He spoke about their upcoming community awareness projects. Eva and Travis sat on stage next to each other. Travis bowed his head and looked scared. Eva cradled his arm, comforting him. When the presenter finished his speech, he introduced Eva. She rose, and that's when I noticed her shoes. One black, one blue.

I stared at her shoes and a big smile erupted on my face.

Eva rose with confidence, mismatched shoes and all, and strode to the podium. She began by thanking everyone for coming, then she read some alarming statistics before getting to the heart of her speech.

"I think the real issue lies in the helplessness that kids experience when they are being bullied. They feel alone, isolated, like no one would ever understand how badly it hurts to be shunned, made fun of, and beat up. Helplessness destroys people and renders them incapable of doing great things out of fears and insecurities that over time build up to the likes of concrete walls. They view everyone and everything as a threat to the protected status they've worked so hard to build. Even when these people love and adore them."

She paused and continued. "When I was younger I lived with my aunt and uncle because my parents decided they wanted to move to the UK and felt I might get in the way as they settled down. So, the day after Christmas, my parents hugged me, then hopped on an airplane to London. It would be five years before I saw them again. I'd get cards and a few tokens gifts like a bracelet or a license plate for my bicycle, but never a visit or a ticket to visit them. They planned to open a boutique and sell lingerie. After five years, they returned empty-handed and ventured straight to the unemployment office in New York City to see about how much they could collect. When they were turned down, they pulled me along to the social services office, dressing me in worn and tattered clothing with streaks of mud on my face to show how much in need we were. They handed us a book of food stamps and a promise to get us on the list for Section Eight housing. As we walked home that afternoon, and I listened to them bicker on and on about how my father wanted to buy cigarettes and my mother needed to buy roll-on antiperspirant instead, I promised myself right then and there that I would never beg for a handout for as long as I lived."

Tears rolled down my cheeks.

She adjusted the microphone. "That very afternoon, I began knocking on front doors handing each neighbor a carefully thought out flyer designed using a ballpoint pen and crayons detailing the benefits of hiring me to clean their house, iron their clothes, and babysit their kids. This started the formation of my self-reliance—a thing most bullies enjoy taking away from their victims."

She leaned forward. "Many people will assume they have control over your life and your destiny and that one wrong move on their part has the power to double you over and ruin your life. I am here to say to you that that is not true. At least not for those who have been taught from a very early age that as long as you wait for someone to hand you something, you will always wait for someone to hand you something. The moment you make the clean break to go out there and fish for yourself, you will have more fish than you'll ever know what to do with and automatically be in a position to give instead of seek. Once a person realizes this, she is free."

The audience hummed up and down like a wave.

She continued. "One person or one event should never have the ability to ruin your life. Great trials may be suffered, challenges may arise, but with self-reliance comes a freedom to start over and stand tall once again. I challenge all of you kids to not be that person who sits around waiting for someone to hand you a fish to eat. I challenge you to never sit there with open hands begging for nourishment from anyone. Learn to make your own breaks and you will learn the valuable lesson that as long as there are other bodies of water out there, you'll never go hungry. You'll never be pushed down so far you can't get back up. You'll never be a victim to the hand of someone else. Instead of seeking nourishment, be the one to give it."

The audience applauded. She bowed her head and nodded as the cheers rose and fell, then rose again. "Thank you." She ushered them to quiet down with a few hand waves. "I appreciate that. Now, I'd like to introduce you all to a brave young man who has single-handedly changed my outlook on life. He has taught me that the power in perseverance doesn't come naturally. It's something we have to consciously set our minds to and work at each day, and when we do, the result is far-reaching and impactful in ways I'm still trying to grasp. Ladies and gentlemen, I'd like to introduce you to Travis Stafford."

Travis rose and shook Eva's hand. We all climbed to our feet and applauded him. He stood in front of the podium, proud and smiling. Then, in one defining moment, he scanned the room, landed on me, and nodded.

He began by explaining the short film he would soon present, and spoke about how the idea stemmed from the horrible incident in his life. As he spoke, he wiped his cheeks over and over. "Someone special once told me never to give up on myself. She advised I should rise above." He sniffed. "I'd like to read something from an essay she wrote that really stuck: *Every person has a life source, and along the way, that life source was either kicked to the furthest recesses of her mind and covered up in the shroud of doubts, despair, and fear, or it sprang forth and powered the person to move forth in the world proudly, acknowledging her gift and sharing it with the world. Someone would cherish the gift. And even if one person cherished it, wasn't that enough?*

He looked right at me. "She gave me the best advice when she said that I should release whatever's on my mind so I can get on with my life. I would challenge her to do the same; to stand before others and tell her story so she can move forward in life and be the positive influence she doesn't even know she's capable of being."

He paused and waited for me to act.

Larry placed his hand on my leg. I cradled it, soaking up his friendship, support, and nourishment. Then, I stood up. "I'm about to do something really crazy, Larry."

My heart galloped. Now or never. As Travis once said to me, what's the worst that could happen? I die? I inhaled deeper than I'd ever inhaled and marched confidently up the aisle. The audience chatted loudly. Eva narrowed her eyes. Recognition spilled on her face as I climbed the creaky stairs. Her familiar smile comforted me. I approached and stood before her, vulnerable. She stood and greeted me with a hug.

"I'm CarefreeJanie," I whispered, trembling in her arms, tears spilling out of me.

She hugged me tighter. "So nice to finally meet you."

I pulled back, braving all and stared straight into her eyes, revealing myself, my true self, my carefree self. "Nice shoes."

Her smile set me free.

I winked and chuckled, then looked away at Travis who stood waiting for a hug, too.

I went to him and rubbed the tears from his cheeks with the back of my hand. "I've got a story to tell, and I'm ready now."

They both backed away and sat down.

I began my story with the first time I felt special to someone. The first time Barbara invited me to her sleepover.

"My best friend Barbara took me under her wings and flew me up higher than I'd ever soared, up to a place I'd only dreamed of after reading storybooks about best friends sharing bracelets and giggles over teacups. When Barbara introduced

237

me as her best friend, she completed me—about as complete as any eight-year-old freckled-faced kid could feel."

"That feeling," I explained, "was one I have been trying to get back ever since the day she shattered this ideal vision and rendered me someone incapable of believing that I held any value in life other than to take up space in a cubicle at Martin Sporting Goods."

I inhaled, steadying my shaky voice. "There's something else that I've never told anyone that I wish to confess now." The audience sat still. Soft, forgiving eyes swaddled and empowered me to release the shackles of guilt. "Back before bullies bullied me, I bullied others." I paused, summoning up the courage to release the burden and come out of hiding, just dropping it all on the stage and letting someone sweep it far away from me. I looked out to Larry. He cupped his chin with his hand. His energy gave me hope and power, and helped me rise to face my guilt. I felt safe to finally confess my awful sins and hope someone might learn from them and do good things as a result.

"There was a girl named Rhonda. She was a pretty girl with strawberry blonde hair and a fun laugh. I dove in and bullied her without much regard for what I thought about her. I just wanted to fit in and be accepted, so I launched my insults. One mock turned into many." I paused, clinging to the podium. "Then, I remember this one day. She was sitting on the front steps of the school. Blood dripped down her knee. She wiped it with a sock. I wanted to help her. I looked around first to make sure no one was watching, then, I walked up to her. I was about to hand her my package of tissues when she looked up at me through the pain and fright. "Oh God, please no more. I can't take any more from you," she whispered.

She dashed off, limping, whimpering, and dripping blood. That afternoon she committed suicide and left a note that said she was tired and needed a good long nap."

I paused, caved into a series of shivers, and then braced for more honest unleashing.

"I will spend the rest of my days haunted by Rhonda's eyes that day. Bullies are just scared individuals. Some are full of poison that's been fed to them by the bullies before them. I was a bully once, and for that I'm terribly sorry. I hurt people and ruined lives. I don't know who Rhonda would've grown up to be had I not pelted her, laughed at her, humiliated her, and scared her every school day. I will never know and this is what has kept me hiding from life. But hiding isn't helping the greater cause. I know this now thanks to Travis and Eva."

I paused, taking up refuge in the silence that cradled my broken spirit and blew soft, forgiving kisses at me. Larry cupped his hands around his mouth, taking on my pain. I drew a deep breath and saddled onto the back of a new freedom that steered me away from my old, cluttered path and onto a new one where the sun danced on the leaves of healthy, vibrant plants, lighting up the horizon like shimmering jewels. My breaths lightened. My mind cleared. My soul opened up, and I continued to talk for a good twenty minutes, spilling the remnants of my life. I disclosed the burden of my scars, the frights that encased me, the nails of injustice that I caused and I suffered, nails that pierced through me and held me hostage to a life that lacked wholeness, unity, and freedom to soar to those heights everyone should get to enjoy.

I would never be free until I unstrapped those tired cuffs and trusted that the key I held could open them.

I held the key all my life and never knew it. I spent that time hiding behind a smokescreen so deep and stoked that the key appeared to be nothing more than another obstacle in my way. The time to shed that old tired life and start fresh presented itself to me.

I could've chosen to stay hidden and create a silence so stark no one would hear it or I could've chosen to free my story for others to learn and pass on. I chose freedom. And when I did, the smoke cleared.

"The day I wrote this film I stepped outside of myself and into the heart of someone else who, despite having been through hell and back, still allowed his light to shine on me and others. My hope is that kids like Travis will be moved by it and realize that if they can love abundantly without expectation, they will harness all the power from within to change the world and eradicate bullying."

I backed away from the podium, numb and shaking, dizzy from emptying the most personal parts of my soul to a room full of strangers. I descended the stairs, then walked in wide strides back down the aisle not sure what to do with all of that lightness. I knew at that moment, regardless of what came my way, I would be okay now. I flew freely and safely.

I landed outside in front of the building. The warm air circled me and swaddled me in comfort. I knew without a doubt that everything would work out now. I walked to the edge of the trees and took in their beauty. I breathed in their freshness.

"Jane," Eva called out to me. I turned, and she ran over to me, her hair flapping in the gentle breeze. When she got to me, she scrolled her eyes around my face, taking me all in, and making me feel like a princess. "You are so beautiful."

I gulped back tears.

Her eyes softened on me. "I am so sorry for all that you had to go through. I get it now. I get why you hid. I get why you ran away from us. I get it, honey."

Fear melted. Elation rose. Tingles returned. And, the hungry need to reach out and touch her beckoned me to act. So, I did. I placed my hand on her cheek and brushed her skin with my thumb, soaking up her softness, her sweet breath, and the love that sprang from her eyes. Under the budding sunrays, circled in a golden hue of light and love, I leaned in closer and enjoyed the tug of arousal, the euphoric rush, the sweet flavor of her joyful smile, and the comfort that it provided, ready at last for my first kiss.

She smiled wider and cooed, leaning in and speaking to me through her eyes, reassuring me, and urging me to come closer. I released my anxiety and settled into the beautiful moment that we'd waited an eternity to enjoy. I circled my gaze down to her lips, her wet, moist fleshy lips, and desperately craved to taste them. I braved all and traveled my finger up to them, tracing them and melting at their warmth. Caught up and cocooned in the moment, I moved in and kissed them with my own trembling lips. They felt so right, so tender, and so perfect against mine. She cradled my face in her hands and pulled me tighter to her. She breathed out and I breathed her in.

"I'm glad it was you," she whispered into my mouth.

"Really?"

"Those eyes." She gazed at me. "They attracted me that first day in the bathroom."

I kissed her again. Then, I asked the burning question. "What about your girlfriend?"

"I ended it. She is just no Jane Knoll."

I sealed in that admission by closing my eyes. She ran her soft touch along my cheek. "I really adore you, CarefreeJanie," she whispered.

Warm ripples wrapped around me. I pressed into her hungry for more. I pushed past her lips and flirted with her tongue, enjoying the dance, forgetting we were two women standing in a parking lot, making out. We continued kissing, seeking warmth in each other's breaths. Then, she stared at me the way one would stare at a beautiful girl. I pressed against her and kissed her like she was my life source, my nutrition, and my entire world.

#

She held out a helmet for me. "You're going to look adorable in this," she said, handing it to me with her lips slightly parted.

I took it from her slender hands and stared at it. "Put it on for me?" I handed it back to her.

She moved in close. Her warm breath brushed my face. Up close like that, her face looked delicious, natural, and held the perfect combination of smooth and soft. She didn't take her eyes from mine as she placed the helmet on my head and secured it under my chin. When fastened, she continued to tease me with her smiling gaze. "You're safe now, honey."

"Really?" I asked with a raspy edge to my voice I'd never heard. "I feel slightly reckless right now."

She ran her fingers through the edges of my hair. "I have to admit that the entire time we were finishing up in the event, I could think of nothing else than you holding me tight around my waist, hugging me."

That image of me pressed up against her, feeling my chest beat against the arch in her back drove me wild. "Let's go," I whispered.

She placed a helmet on her head and mounted her bike. "Hop on, beautiful. Your chariot awaits."

I slid onto the bike's black seat and slipped naturally into the cradle of her butt. I pulled up on my skirt so it covered the top of my legs. My crotch rested smack up against her ass. If she were naked, she'd feel I wore lacy undies. She reached for my hands and circled them around her small waist. She caressed my hands, and I leaned into her, indulging in her sexy, clean scent. I rested against her, sealing into the moment when I cradled a woman in my arms. I desperately wanted her to turn around so I could kiss her again. I wanted to feel her soft tongue in my mouth, twirling with mine in a seductive dance of chase where we took turns flipping, rolling, and tumbling around each other's breaths.

She cranked the engine, and the seat vibrated between my legs, revving high then low, then high again, percolating beneath me, sending wonderful flutters through me. "Hold on, okay?"

I pressed my cheek against her shoulder blade and squeezed her tighter. She backed out of the spot slowly, checking behind us several times. My heart raced for what was to come. Never had I indulged in such danger or exhilaration before. Just an open road ahead of us, we tore off down the parking lot like a couple of wild girls heading out for spring break with just the clothes on our back and a pocket full of lust to sprinkle.

At our first traffic light she yelled out to me. "What do you think of heading out to western Maryland to see some of the farm scenery? I don't get to see farmland in New York City."

I yelled above the engine. "Whatever you'd like, babe. I'm all yours."

She revved the engine with that.

We headed out on the back roads toward Frederick. We passed through grassy towns where cows hung out in fields. Gentle, rolling green hills sloped around us. We owned the road. We stopped at one point to check out some horses that grazed close to a wooden fence. She cut the engine. I dismounted on her cue. I released my hair from the helmet and tossed it around, sure the frizz flew with the wind.

She dismounted, shook her hair, too, and placed her helmet on the handle. I placed mine on the seat. We stood facing each other. "I just want to hold you," she said.

I opened my arms to her and she fell into them. We embraced, rubbing each other's backs and resting our cheeks on each other's shoulders. I sought out her lips that time, and she responded with a lovely moan. I couldn't imagine how the scene could've gotten more romantic. But, then she backed away, took my hand in hers, and began running toward the fence. When we reached it, she tore off her shoes. I tore off mine. We giggled, latched onto each other's hands again, and climbed through the wooden fence. We started running through the open field of overgrown greenery and wild flowers. Larry would've died thinking of all the insects crawling on the blades. Exhilarated, I squeezed Eva's hand. We galloped together like a couple of wild horses, laughing, panting, and jumping over tall cattails and wild hyacinths. We ran past a silo, past an old beat-up farmhouse with a broken door and holes in its sides, and past an abandoned, rusted old car that resembled something straight out of the nineteen twenties. The sky smelled as fresh as spring dew. We ran in a heaven of our own, side by side. We ran like that for several minutes not bothering to notice the dark clouds rolling in from the west until they started to drop large pellets of rain on top of us. We stopped, looked up, and bent over in hysterical giggles before clinging to each other and spinning around in circles. The rain pelted us and urged us closer. "The rain loves us," she said.

"I can't blame it."

She cupped her hands around my jaw and lifted my mouth to hers, kissing me passionately. "I want to make love to you. Right here. Right now."

I melted in her arms, weak to her touch, surrendering to her love. I thought of the old barn we had just passed. I reached for her hand and ran with her in that direction, that time taking the lead. We ran fast, so fast that we tripped at one point and landed in a heap on top of each other, matted to the grassy field as if one with the Earth's beauty. We rolled around in the mud, kissing each other passionately and hungry for more. Then, the thunder clapped, and she bolted to her feet, pulling me up with her. "Ah, hurry," she said, pulling me toward the old barn.

We giggled and tore through the rain, dodging raindrops the size of dimes until we reached the broken door. We pushed through it, and entered the old building. The ceiling looked about ready to collapse under the weight of the giant raindrops.

"Do you think it's safe?" she asked, looking up at the holes in the ceiling. Her hair clung to her golden, wet skin, beckoning me to twirl it between my fingers.

I reeled her in close and twirled it, loving the cool, messy feel of it on my skin. Her breaths quickened and bathed me in warmth. We stood staring into each other's eyes, dripping, muddy and high on love. She pressed into me and nudged me against the wooden plank wall. She pushed against the wall behind me and caressed me in a deep, lingering kiss. Heat passed through her to me, turning my body to mush, melting me like sweet butter.

"You're trembling," she said.

I kissed her bottom lip, nibbling on it lightly. She moaned and that caused me to nibble a bit harder.

She pulled me away from the wall, and I yanked her back. She pressed harder against me. She wedged her leg provocatively between my legs and I rocked against it, feeling the familiar rush of moisture. "You don't mind the mess in this barn, do you?" she asked, lifting her lips from mine in thoughtful gesture.

I grabbed hold of her hair and ran my fingers through it. "I don't care about the rusty walls or floors. All I'm focused on is you. Everything is a blur, except you."

She pushed me harder against the wall, and kissed me with a new hunger. "You're intoxicating. I just look at you and melt." She lifted the edge of my skirt and nudged it up one exhilarating inch at a time, until it rose up around my waist and brushed against her leg that wedged between my wet inner thighs. She caressed me with her fingers, and I swelled against her touch. I clung to her, resting my head on her shoulders cooing, panting, and caving into that most intoxicating ride. My eyes closed, my lips sought out her neck, shoulders, and breasts.

"I can't get enough of you," I whispered.

She lifted my head. A tease rested on the spokes of her eyes. She kissed me gently, then lowered me to the ground, gently placing my head against the matted hay. She spread my legs, and then landed between them. Her warm breath swirled around my now sensitive, hungry wetness. Her soft lips felt like honey, soft, warm, and gentle. My head spun in wonderful circles, dipping, twirling, and pirouetting on beat to her perfectly executed love.

"You're sending me over the edge," I said. She sent me reeling and flying through the air on nothing more than euphoric dust, gifting me with the most relaxed feeling ever. I moaned and screamed out in pleasure as she rocked me gently, slowly, lovingly, coming to rest on my long exhale.

She rose to her knees, straddling me and sprinkling me in gentle kisses from my forehead, to my eyelids, to my cheeks, and to my chin. I never felt so loved, so protected, so safe as I did in that moment. "I love you so much," she whispered when she landed her wet lips on mine.

"I love you more," I said, holding nothing back. I sat up, and she sat down next to me. She took me in her arms and held me tightly. I rested my head against her beating chest. "I'm so weak now. I can barely catch my breath."

She kissed the top of my head and caressed me tighter. "I loved pleasing you." She ran her fingers through my hair, doting on me like a princess. We held each other for several minutes, then I propped up on my knees and guided her to the ground and began to explore her beautiful curves, her golden skin, her navel, her hips, and finally her sweet wetness. She tasted salty, earthy, and beautifully natural. My lips and tongue sought her out with a natural know-how, like I'd been doing that all my life. All fear evaporated. A hunger replaced it, a hunger of wanting nothing more than to please her by feeding her my love. She responded as I did, with lovely moans, trembles, earth-shattering jolts that told me she traveled to that place of ecstasy where grass grew a million times greener, where rain smelled a gazillion times fresher, and where the body disappeared and tingles overtook it.

We spent the next hour clinging to each other, professing our love, and promising more journeys just like that for as long as humanly possible.

# #

The next day Larry called me and told me Tim had a talk with his wife and confessed his affair. His wife confessed an affair she'd been having the ten-and-a-half years they'd been married. He would move Tim in that night.

"And what about you? Have you talked to Eva?"

I turned to Eva and smiled. "You could say that." I kissed the tip of her nose.

"And?"

"That's going to require some cheesecake."

"Oh no. Are you okay?"

I twirled Eva's hair and gazed into her eyes. "We're going to need to rethink our cheesecake outings. We need to keep traditional New York Style for those typical 'cheesecake nights,' but we also are going to need a blueberry or strawberry cheesecake for happier ones."

"Strawberry it is."

"Well hold on. Jumping a little soon to conclusions, aren't you?"

"This new ring to your tone of voice suits you so much better, darling. Maybe we'll just really change things up and turn our strawberry cheesecakes into double dates."

"Let's make it at least a week from now. I think we both need some time to enjoy being New York Style-free for a while."

"Indulge." He hung up on one of the gayest giggles I'd ever heard escape his mouth.

# #

Within a month, Sanjeev signed off on the paperwork that would allow Eva to work out of the main branch in Maryland. Doreen, Katie and I worked for days emptying out a small meeting room and dressing it up with pretty plants, new furniture, and plenty of office supplies.

The Saturday before she was scheduled to start in the Maryland office, she pulled up on her motorcycle in front of my condo. She climbed off, removed her helmet, and shook her beautiful head of hair all while staring up at me as I stood on the deck admiring her. We shared a smile before she leaped forward and bounded up the stairs to her new home.

We spent the entire weekend wrapped up in each other's arms, dreaming up where we'd go from there. We both agreed that the first order of business was to sign me up for motorcycle lessons. From there, we'd just let life take us on a ride and surprise us.

Several months later

We entered Tim's friends' backyard. The weather forecast called for severe thunderstorms all day, and yet not a cloud brewed in the sky. Eva and I sat in the last row, center aisle. I snapped a picture of the flowered archway and posted to Twitter with the comment: All we need are the grooms. Katie responded immediately with "Larry's probably still manicuring his nails!" I showed Eva, and she jumped on and said: "He's going for hot pink today. He's going to be a lovely groom."

Travis walked out the backdoor to Ellis and Matthew's house wearing a black tux, looking so handsome. He wore a proud smile, embarking on surely one of the biggest honors of his lifetime. Tim's ex-wife walked out next. She wore a beautiful, fitted black dress and dazzled. She walked by us, up the aisle, and stood opposite Travis. Next Tim walked out. His blonde hair blew in the breeze, and his eyes danced wildly with joy as he passed us by and walked up the aisle. He stood tall next to Travis. Then, finally the door opened and out waltzed Larry wearing a white tuxedo with a hot pink bowtie. He passed me by with a wink, looking more relaxed than ever. Eva cradled my back as we watched him walk up the aisle toward the man he loved. Tim looked at Larry with adoration. Two men free to love, free to start a life together, and free to bring out the very best in one another. My dear friend was marrying the man of his dreams, the most perfect man.

They stated their vows before us all, professing their love and honor and commitment for a lifetime. His ex-wife looked on with love in her eyes, wiping her tears through a smile, and appearing honored to be a part of her best friend's special day.

Later at the cocktail hour at The Boat House, Larry stood up and said to his family and friends, "I realized I loved him when he first pulled up in a 10-year-old car with a broken door lock, and he smiled and said he drove it because his dad gave it to him." Everyone laughed, raised their glasses, and cheered them on. Tim mirrored with, "I knew I first loved Larry the moment he offered me a slice of strawberry cheesecake. I knew I had met the man of my dreams." He leaned over, and they kissed.

Everyone cheered again.

My heart swelled in joy at the open display of affection. Smiles spread on everyone's faces. As we sat down to enjoy our meal, Travis leaned over and raised his glass to us. "Here's to exciting times ahead with the launch of our movie."

"Here. Here," Eva said. The three of us clanked glasses.

I soaked up the scene. Gone were the days of standing idle. There were way too many people who needed a voice. They needed someone to stand up for them and give them that voice. Through the movie deal we received, Eva, Travis and I would be able to rise together and make a real difference in the lives of would-be bullies and victims. We had a long way to go, but together we were stronger; the community was stronger; Eva and I were stronger.

Eva turned to me and kissed me openly. I stared into her eyes and soared with her, past the champagne, past the smiles, past the chatter and laughter, past the clanking glasses, past it all, as two gals free to fly as high as the wind wanted to take us. She continued to gaze back at me, Jane Knoll, her girlfriend, her partner, her breath. She winked.

"I love your winks," I said. "Mwah."

"I love mwahs."

"Just any mwahs? Not mine?" I teased.

She cupped her hands around my face. "Only yours, honey."

We danced the night away under a blanket of stars and good vibes. We wept alongside Larry and Tim as we watched their love unfold in a slideshow played to the music of Brandi Carlile and Rascall Flatts. We sang "Piano Man" with them on the dance floor as we spun each other in wide circles. We giggled as they smashed cake in each other's faces and Larry squealed. And we fell in love even more that night, as we walked away from the most beautiful wedding we'd ever been to. As we strolled to our car in the dim-lit parking lot, we huddled against each other enjoying the sea breeze, the faint mist of an upcoming thunder storm, and the flashes of lightning in the distant sky. I savored every second of that walk, reflecting on how far I'd come since meeting that beautiful woman, my muse— in writing, in life, and in love.

NOTE FROM THE AUTHOR

As with all of my books, I enjoy giving a portion of proceeds back to the community by donating to the NOH8 Campaign www.noh8campaign.com and Hearts United for Animals: www.hua.org. Thank you for being a part of this special contribution.

A SPECIAL REQUEST

If you enjoyed reading this story, I'd be so grateful for your honest review of it on your favorite book retail site. Just a sentence or two saying what you liked about *The Muse* will help others discover it and help me to serve you better with future books!

www.ingramcontent.com/pod-product-compliance
Lightning Source LLC
Chambersburg PA
CBHW050028180626
46810CB00002B/617